Dear Reader,

Welcome to my newest series and the newest family that has captured my heart. The Cavanaughs are everything we would love families to be: supportive, loyal, noble in a human way, teasingly loving and, as an added bonus, each better looking than the last.

Patrick Cavanaugh is an offshoot of the main branch, a Cavanaugh cousin who has benefited from his association with the family patriarch and former police chief, Andrew. Patrick has his dark secrets, but his past has never gotten in the way of his being an honest cop. However, even the most honorable of people can be held suspect when it's guilt by association, and Patrick's former partner was found to have dirty hands. It's up to Maggi McKenna, posing as his new partner, to prove Patrick guilty or innocent, not an easy task when the subject is a loner who is basically noncommunicative. The task gets even more difficult when Maggi finds herself becoming more and more attracted to him.

I hope you find these two as interesting as I did and that you'll come back for a prolonged visit with each of the Cavanaughs as they tell their own story. As always, thank you for reading, and I wish you love.

Marie Ferrarella

INTERNAL AFFAIR

Marie Ferrarella

Silhouette Books

Published by Silhouette Books
America's Publisher of Contemporary Romance

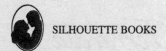

SILHOUETTE BOOKS

ISBN 0-373-21836-2

INTERNAL AFFAIR

Copyright © 2003 by Marie Rydzynski-Ferrarella

Visit Silhouette at www.eHarlequin.com

Printed in U.S.A.

MARIE FERRARELLA

This RITA® Award-winning author has written over one hundred books for Silhouette, some under the name Marie Nicole. Her romances are beloved by fans worldwide.

To the brave men and women
who put their lives on the line for us every day.
Thank you.

Chapter 1

"No!"

Every fiber of his muscular body tense and alert, Patrick Cavanaugh bolted upright in his bed, ready to fight, to protect. As adrenaline coursed through his veins, it took several moments before he realized he'd been dreaming. And it was *the* dream that plagued him. The one that he'd been having night after night for the past month. Ever since Ramirez had been shot right before his eyes. And killed.

Ramirez had been one step away from him.

One step away from being saved by him.

Awake now, Patrick shivered. His bedroom was cold. December in Aurora, California, tended to be bitterly cold at times. Because the dream had been so vivid, because he'd relived every second of it, his upper torso was covered with sweat, cooling him even more.

Getting back to sleep was impossible. Not now. Habit had him reaching for the pack of cigarettes on his nightstand. The pack of cigarettes that was no longer there. Not wanting anything to have a hold over him, he'd quit smoking the week after they had put Eduardo Ramirez into the ground. Twenty-two days and counting.

He sat for a moment, dragging his hand through his hair, trying to focus on the day before him. Dark thoughts hovered around him like the ghosts of years past, searching for a chink, a break in the armor he kept tightly wrapped around himself. Waiting to get to him.

Every man had his demons, he told himself. His were no bigger, no smaller than most.

It didn't help.

Patrick swallowed a halfhearted curse. He wondered what it felt like to wake up with a smile on his face, the way he knew his sister Patience did.

No use in going there, he thought. It wasn't anything he was about to find out. He'd always been the somber one in the family. Not without cause. Patience was the mystery, he'd decided long ago. Happy despite everything. Despite the home life they'd had growing up.

Any happiness that existed in their lives had come by way of his uncles Andrew and Brian and their families. It certainly hadn't come via his own, at least, not from his parents, Mike and Diane.

Patience was another story. She was the reason he'd plumbed the depths of his soul and discovered that he was a protector and capable of feeling an emotion other than anger. He had to, for Patience's sake.

Patrick narrowed his eyes, looking at the blue digital numbers. Six-thirty.

Time to get up, anyway, he thought. Time to get ready to serve and protect.

As he rose from his rumpled double bed, the sheet

tangled around his leg and then fell to the floor. He didn't bother picking it up. His whole bed looked like the scene of a battle.

And had been. Because last night, as he had almost every night since his partner's death, he'd fought the good fight. He'd led Ramirez and the other detectives and patrolmen into the crack house. Except that somehow, Ramirez had gotten in front of him just as shots were fired and all hell broke loose.

And he'd been too late to save Ramirez.

Again.

Don't go there, Patrick ordered himself coldly. He muttered another curse as he walked into the tiny adjacent bathroom, naked as the day he was born. He couldn't afford to think about Ramirez, couldn't afford to allow himself to dwell in the land of "what ifs." The guilt was still too raw, weighed too much. Dwelling on the pain left him winded and bleeding inside.

It was the beginning of a new week and he needed to be sharp. To survive the way others before him hadn't survived. He owed it to the department, but mostly to Patience. They had uncles and cousins, but he was the only immediate family she had. If he let this consume him, likely as not, he'd get himself killed. Leaving her alone.

Wasn't gonna happen. Yet.

Blowing out a deep breath, Patrick wrapped his anger around himself and stepped into the shower.

The shower handle was poised on cold. He pulled it and let the water hit him full blast. Jolting him into Monday.

"New assignment, Mag?"

Depositing the frying pan into the dishwasher, she

picked up the breakfast she'd prepared and placed it in front of her father. She'd been too preoccupied to hear his question. "What?"

Matthew McKenna pushed forward his coffee cup. An independent man, he lived alone now and liked his space. He liked it even more when his only daughter, his only child, dropped by before beginning her mornings. It wasn't something he took for granted. "Today, don't you start your new assignment?"

"Yes. Right."

The words came out like staccato gunfire. Mary Margaret McKenna—Maggi to those she considered part of her inner circle, or 3M to those who enjoyed honing in on her no-nonsense nature—poured coffee into her father's cup. She was bracing herself for the morning and the change of venue she was about to face.

She supposed that was why she'd stopped by this morning to make breakfast for her father. To touch base with what she considered to be her true self. Before she left that behind. Belatedly, she offered her father a smile along with cream for his coffee.

She was what she was because of her father. And because of him, in an indirect way, she had chosen the less-traveled path within her career. Patrolman Matthew McKenna had been one of Aurora's finest until a bullet had ended his career less than six months ago. The bullet had come from one of his own men. One of those awful things that happened in the heat of battle when shots went wild. The other policeman was found dead, a victim of one of the so-called suspects' deadly aim, or dumb luck, take your pick. But it was the service revolver in his hand that had fired the bullet which had found its way into Matthew's hip and left him with a slight limp. And a new appreciation for life.

She had been living in San Francisco when she'd gotten the call about her father. Without any hesitation, Maggi had handed in her resignation and come home to Aurora, to stand vigil over her father in the hospital and then nurse him back to health. When she was satisfied that he was on the mend, she put in for a job on the Aurora police force. It took little to work her way up. And when a position in Internal Affairs opened up, she applied for it.

The thought of spying on her fellow police officers bothered her. The thought of rogue police officers, giving the force a bad name, bothered her more. She took the position, signing on to work undercover. She still grappled with her own decision. It was a dirty job, she'd tell herself. But someone had to do it. For now, that someone was her.

Matthew sighed, looking at her over the rim of his cup. "You know, Mag, this isn't the kind of life your mother and I envisioned for you, dodging bullets and bad guys."

She finished her breakfast in three bites—toast, consumed mostly on her feet. Impatience danced through her, as it always did at the start of a new assignment. She thought of it as stage fright. A little always made you perform better.

"We all make our own way in the world, remember?" Maggie dusted off her fingers over the sink. "That was what you taught me."

Matthew shook his head. "I also taught you that there was no shame in taking the easy way, as long as it wasn't against the law."

Maggie laughed, partially to set him at ease. He worried too much. Just as much as she had when he had been the one to walk out the door wearing a badge. ''Where's the fun in that?''

His expression was serious. ''You think it's fun, my sitting here, wondering if you're going to walk in through that door again?''

Maggie refused to be drawn into a serious discussion. Not this morning. The seriousness of her work was bad enough. She needed an outlet, a haven where she could laugh, where she could put down her sword and shield and just be herself.

So instead, she winked at him. ''I could move back up to San Francisco, take that burden away from you.'' Her grin widened as unspoken love entered her eyes. ''You're old enough to live on your own now.''

She'd moved back home to take care of him. And once he was on his feet, with the aid of a quad cane he hated, Maggi knew it was time for her to leave. But one thing after another seemed to get in the way and she remained, telling herself that she'd look for an apartment over the weekend. She'd finally moved out less than three weeks ago. But this still felt like home. She had a feeling it always would.

The somber expression refused to be teased away. ''You know what I mean, Mary Margaret.''

''Oh-uh, two names. Serious stuff.'' Inwardly she gritted her teeth together. She'd always hated her full name. Hearing it reminded her of eight years of dour-faced nuns looking down at her disapprovingly because she hadn't lived up to their expectations. All except for Sister Michael. Sister Michael had tried to encourage her to let her ''better side out.'' She suspected that Sister Michael had probably been as much of a hellion in her day as she was accused of being in hers.

She'd turned to Sister Michael when her mother had

died and she felt she couldn't cry in front of her father. Couldn't cry because she was all that was keeping him together.

She crossed to him now and placed her arm around his shoulders. "Dad, you know damn well that you're my hero and I was honor-bound to grow up just like you."

The sigh was liberally laced with guilt. "I should have married Edna," he lamented. "She would have found a way to shave those rough edges off you."

"No, Edna would have turned out to be the reason I ran away from home."

Edna Grady was the woman his father had dated when she was fifteen. The widow had her cap set on marriage and would have stopped at nothing to arrive at that destination. She had a host of ideas about what their life was going to be like after the ceremony. It hadn't included having a stepdaughter under her roof. That was when her father had balked, terminating their relationship. Maggi had been eternally grateful when he had.

Maggi paused to kiss the top of her father's snow-white head, her heart swelling with love. He really was her rock, her pillar. "You did just fine raising me, Dad. You gave me all the right values. I'm just making sure they're in play, that's all. And that everyone else shares them."

While he applauded the principle, he didn't like the thought of his daughter risking her life every day. He vividly realized what his wife must have gone through all those years they were married and he was on the force.

He looked at her, disgruntled. "If I hadn't been shot, you would have been married by now."

"Divorced," she corrected, "I would have been divorced by now."

She firmly believed that. Maggi thought of Taylor Ramsford, the up-and-coming lawyer she'd met while working on the vice squad. He'd dazzled her with his wit, his charm, and they'd gotten engaged. But Taylor, it turned out, was not nearly the man she'd thought he was. Beneath the appealing exterior, there was nothing but a man who wanted to get ahead. A man centered on his own goals and nothing more. Marrying her had just been another goal. When she'd told him she was going home for an indefinite period of time to care for her father, he wouldn't stand for it.

"Your place is with me," he'd told her.

She'd known then that her place was anywhere *but* with him.

She gave her father a quick hug. "You know you're the only man for me."

He patted her hand affectionately. The day she was born, his partner had expressed his regret that his wife hadn't given birth to a son. Maggi was worth a hundred sons to him, and he told her so.

"Not that I'm not flattered, Mag, but I'm not going to live forever."

"Sure you are." She walked over to pick up her service revolver and holster from the bookcase in the family room where she'd left it. "And I don't need a man to survive. No woman this day and age does." She spared him a tolerant glance. "Catch up to the times, Dad."

He thought of his late wife. Maggi looked just like Annie had at her age. She'd had a way of making him feel that the sun rose and set around him without sacrificing a shred of her own independence. She'd been a rare woman. As was his daughter. He hoped to God that she'd find a man worthy of her someday.

"'Fraid it's too late. No new tricks for me. I'm the old-fashioned type, no changing that."

"Don't change a hair for me," she teased. Glancing at her watch, she knew she had to hit the road or risk getting stuck in ungodly traffic. She strapped on her holster, taking care to position the revolver to minimize the bulge it created. It was wreaking havoc on the linings of her jackets. "I've gotta go, Dad. Have a good day."

He nodded. It was time he got to work as well. To pass the time while he'd been convalescing, he'd taken to writing down some of his more interesting cases. Now he was at it in earnest, looking to crack the publishing world with a fictionalized novel.

Matthew rose from the table, walking Maggi to the front door. "Would I be threatening some chain of command if I told you to have the same?"

Have a good day. That wasn't possible, she thought. Her new assignment was taking her back undercover. Not to any seedy streets where the enemy was clearly defined the way her old job had been, but into the bowels of the homicide and burglary division of the Aurora force. She felt this was more dangerous. Because there were reputations at stake, and desperate people with a great deal to lose did desperate things when their backs were up against the wall.

Was Detective Patrick Cavanaugh a desperate man? Was that what had led him to betray the oath he'd taken the day he'd been sworn into the department? Had it been desperation or greed that had made him turn his back on his promise to serve and protect and made him serve only himself, protect only his own back?

Not your concern, Mag, she told herself. She wasn't judge and jury, she was only the investigator. Her job was to gather all the information she could and let someone else make the proper determination.

If that meant putting herself in front of a charging bull, well, she'd known this wasn't going to be a picnic when she'd signed on to help rid the force of dirty cops.

She frowned, thinking of what her superior had told her about Cavanaugh. The detective had a list of honors a mile long and he was braver than the day was long, but he was as hard as titanium to crack. And as friendly as a shark coming off a month-long hunger strike. The dark-haired, scowling detective went through partners the way most people went through paper towels. The only one who had managed to survive had been Eduardo Ramirez. Until the day he was shot. Ramirez had managed to last two years with Cavanaugh. According to what she'd read in his file, that was quite a record.

Detective First Class Patrick Cavanaugh was the product of a long blue line. His late father had been a cop, one of his uncles had been the chief of police and he was the nephew of the current chief of detectives. Not to mention that he had over half a dozen cousins on the force at the present time. Possibly covering his back. In any case, she knew extreme caution was going to have to be exercised. There could be a lot of toes involved.

She was Daniel, entering the lion's den, and all the lions were related.

But then, she'd always loved a challenge.

Maggi flashed a smile at her father, meant to put him at ease. "I'll see you tonight."

He watched as she slipped on her jacket, watched the

weapon disappear beneath the navy blue fabric. "I'll hold you to that."

She winked and kissed his cheek before leaving. "Count on it."

He did.

The call had reached him before he ever made it to the precinct. An overly curious jogger had seen something glistening in the river, catching the first rays of the dull morning sun. It turned out to be the sunroof of a sports car. An all but submerged sports car. He'd called in his find immediately.

A BMW sports car had gone over the railing and found its final resting place in the dark waters below. Patrick told dispatch he was on it and changed his direction, driving toward the river.

Even before he'd closed his cell phone, he'd been struck by the similarity of the case. Fifteen years ago, his aunt Rose's car was discovered nose down in the very same river. All the Cavanaughs had gathered at Uncle Andrew's house, trying to comfort his uncle and the others—Shaw, Callie, the twins—Clay and Teri— and Rayne. It was the only time he had seen his uncle come close to breaking down. Aunt Rose's body wasn't inside the car when it was fished out. Or in the river when they dragged it. Uncle Andrew refused to believe that she was dead, even when his father told him to move on with his life.

Patrick had been in the room when his father had said that to Andrew. They didn't realize he was there at first, but he was, just shy of the doorway. There was something there between the two men, something he hadn't seen before or since, something they never allowed to come out, except for that one time. His uncle came close to striking his father, then held himself in check at the last minute.

But then, his father had a way of getting under people's skins and rubbing them raw. It was what held him back. And turned him into a bitter drunk in his off hours. He never showed up for work under the influence, but the minute he was off duty, he went straight for a bottle. It was as if he was trying to drown something inside him that refused to die.

The tension between his father and his uncle that day had been so thick they might have come to blows if Uncle Andrew hadn't seen him standing there just then. The next minute, Uncle Andrew left, saying he wanted to go to the river to see what he could do to help find her. Uncle Brian went with him.

Eventually, everyone stopped believing that she was still alive, but he knew that Uncle Andrew never gave up hope. His uncle still believed his wife was alive, even to this day.

Hope was a strange thing, Patrick mused as he turned down the winding highway that fed on to the road by the river. It kept some people going, against all odds. He thought of his mother. Hope tortured others needlessly. His mother had stayed with his father until the day he died, hoping he would change. His father never had.

Patrick blocked the thoughts from his mind. This wasn't getting him anywhere. It was time for him to be a detective.

When he arrived at the site, there were ten or so curious passersby milling around the area, craning their necks for a view. They were held back by three patrolman who had been summoned to the scene. A bright

yellow tape stretched across the area close to the re-
trieved vehicle, proclaiming it a crime scene.

He was really getting to hate the color yellow.

Exiting his car, Patrick nodded absently at the patrolmen and strode toward the recently fished out sports
car. Except for a smashed left front light, the car
seemed none the worse for wear. The driver's side door
was hanging open, allowing him a view of the young
woman inside. She was stretched out across her seat,
her body tilted toward the passenger side. She was
twenty, maybe twenty-one and had been very pretty
before the water had stolen her last breath and filled
her lungs, sealing the look of panic on her face.

He judged the woman in the trim navy suit bending
over her to be a little older, though he wasn't sure by
just how much. He didn't recognize her. Someone new
in the coroner's office, he imagined. She looked a little
young to be a doctor.

Or maybe he was just feeling old.

Patrick took a step back, partially turning toward the
nearest patrolman. "Who's that?"

The officer glanced over his shoulder. "Detective
McKenna. Says she's with you."

Irritation was close to the surface this morning.
Okay, who the hell was playing games and why? "Nobody's with me," Patrick retorted tersely.

He thought he heard the patrolman mutter, "You
said it, I didn't," but his attention was focused on the
blonde kneeling beside the vehicle.

Crossing to her quickly, he wasted no time with pre-
ambles and niceties. He didn't like having his crime
scene interfered with. "I thought I was assigned to this
case."

Maggi raised her eyes from what she was doing. The

male voice was stern, definitely territorial. From what she'd been told, she'd expected nothing less. From her vantage point, six-three looked even taller than it ordinarily might have.

Patrick Cavanaugh.

Show time.

He was more formidable looking than his photograph, she thought. Also better looking. But that was neither here nor there. She was interested in beauty of the soul, not face or body. If she was, Maggi noted absently, someone might have said she'd hit the jackpot.

They'd said that Lucifer had been the most beautiful of the archangels.

"You are," Maggi replied mildly.

Because she didn't like the psychological advantage her position gave him, she rose to her feet, patently ignoring the extended hand he offered her. Ground rules had to be established immediately. She was her own person.

"Then what are you doing here?" Patrick demanded.

With the ease of someone slipping on a glove, she slid into the role she'd been assigned. Once upon a time, before the lure of the badge had gotten her, she'd entertained the idea of becoming an actress. Working undercover allowed her to combine both her loves.

"I guess they didn't tell you."

He had a crime scene to take charge of, he didn't have time for guessing games initiated by fluffy blondes compromising his crime scene. "Tell me what?"

"That I'm your new partner."

Chapter 2

"The hell you are."

Patrick glared at this woman who looked as if she would be more at home on some runway in Paris, modeling the latest in impractical lingerie than standing beside a waterlogged corpse, pretending to look for clues.

"Yes," Maggi replied with a smile. "The hell I am."

No one had notified him. He hated having things sprung on him without warning. In his experience, most surprises turned out bad.

"Since when?"

"Since this morning. Last night, actually," she corrected, "but it was too late to get started then."

He couldn't believe that someone actually believed that he and this woman could work together. He found working with another man difficult enough; working with a woman with all her accompanying quirks and baggage was out of the question.

"By whose authority?" he demanded.

"Captain Reynolds." She gave him the name of his direct superior, although the pairing had not originated with Reynolds. The order had come from John Halliday, the man in charge of Internal Affairs. A fair, honest man, if not the easiest to work with, Halliday had found a subtle way of getting her in so that not even Reynolds knew the true purpose behind her becoming Cavanaugh's new partner. "He said you wouldn't be thrilled."

Patrick's frown deepened. He knew why Reynolds hadn't said anything. It was because the captain didn't care for confrontations from within. Well, he couldn't just slide this blonde under his door and expect things to go well from there.

"Captain Reynolds has a gift for understatement." His voice was brittle. "I haven't seen you around."

His icy blue eyes seemed to go right through her. She could see why others might find him intimidating. "I've been there. Around," she clarified when he continued to stare at her. She shrugged casually. "I can't help it if you haven't noticed me."

Oh, he would have noticed her, Patrick thought. A woman who looked the way she did was hard to miss. She was the kind that made heads turn and married men stop to rethink their choice in a life partner. He wasn't given to socializing, but he would have noticed her.

Something didn't feel right, though. "How long have you been a detective?" Patrick asked.

"Three months."

Three months. A novice. What the hell was the captain thinking? Even a man as photo-op oriented as Reynolds had to know this was a bad idea. This woman needed training, aging, and that just wasn't his line.

Patrick waved her away. "Tell Captain Reynolds I don't do baby-sitting."

"I don't think that'll matter to him," she told him crisply. "He doesn't have any school-aged children." She indicated the vehicle next to her. "Now, why don't we just make the best of this and get back to work?"

Patrick looked at her sharply, about to make his rejection plainer since she seemed to have trouble assimilating it, when her words echoed in his brain. "We?"

"We," she repeated. There was more than ten inches difference between them in height. Maggi drew herself up as far as she could, refusing to appear cowed. "You've got to know that working with you isn't exactly my idea of being on a picnic."

His eyes were flat as he regarded her. "Then why do it?"

Halliday had told her to blend in, to stay quiet and gather as much information as possible about Cavanaugh and his dealings. The less attention drawn to herself, the better. But from what she'd managed to piece together about him, a man like Cavanaugh didn't respect sheep. He sheared them and went on. What he respected was someone who'd stand up to him, who'd go toe-to-toe without flinching. That kind of a person stood a chance of finding out something useful. Someone who blended in didn't.

Maggi had her battle plan laid out. "Because I go where they send me and I always follow orders."

His eyes pinned her to the spot. "Always?"

She met his stare head-on, his blue eyes against her own green. "Always."

Well, knowing Reynolds, that didn't exactly surprise him. He wondered if she was someone's daughter, someone's niece. Someone Reynolds owed a favor to.

You never knew when you had to call a favor in, especially when you had your eye on the political arena, the way Reynolds did.

"Terrific." He looked at her without attempting to hide his disgust. "A by-the-book, wet-behind-the-ears rookie."

She was far from a rookie, but this wasn't the time to get into that. For now, she left him with his assumptions. "Guess that's just your cross to bear," she quipped, turning her attention back to the victim.

He was accustomed to people withdrawing from him, to avoiding him whenever possible. This was something a little different. He wondered if stupidity guided her, or if she had some kind of different agenda. "You've got a smart mouth."

"Goes with my smart brain." Deciding that the corpse wasn't going anywhere, Maggi looked at the man whose soul she was going to have to crawl into. "I graduated top of my class from the academy."

If that was meant to impress him, she'd fallen short of her mark, he thought. He couldn't stomach newly minted detectives, spouting rhetoric and theories they'd picked up out of the safe pages of some textbook. "There's a whole world of difference between a classroom and what you find outside of it."

"I know." It was going to be slow going, finding his good side. From what she'd gleaned, he might not even have one. But she felt he'd be less antagonistic if he felt she had some sort of experience. "I was in Vice in San Francisco."

His eyes slid over her, taking full measure, seeing beneath the jacket and matching trousers. It took more than fabric to disguise her shape. She'd probably made one hell of a decoy. "Stopping it or starting it?"

Her grin was quick, lethal. "Now who's got the smart mouth?"

He looked away. "Difference being, I don't shoot mine off."

The wind kept insisting on playing with her hair. She pushed it away from her face, only to have it revisit less than a beat later. "I'll remember that. See? Learning already."

Annoyed, Patrick knew there was nothing he could do about the situation right now. If he ordered her away, he had a feeling she wouldn't retreat. He didn't want to go into a power struggle in front of the patrolmen. No one had to tell him that behind the sexy, engaging smile was a woman who'd gotten her way most of her life. You only had to look at her to know that.

He could wait. All that mattered was the end result. He didn't want a partner. He wanted to work alone. It required less effort, less coordination. And less would go wrong that way.

Patrick sighed. "Well, I need to learn something about you."

His eyes were intense, a light shade of blue that seemed almost liquid. She wondered if they could be warm on occasion, or if they always looked as if they were dissecting you. "Fire away."

"Your name. What is it?"

She realized that she'd skipped that small detail. She put her hand out now. "Margaret McKenna. My friends call me Maggi."

He made no effort to take her hand and she dropped it at her side. "What do people who aren't your friends call you?"

"The repeatable ones are McKenna, or 3M."

Despite himself, he was drawn in. "3M? Like the tape?"

Her gaze was unwavering. "No, because my full name is Mary Margaret McKenna."

He could see that the revelation pained her. She didn't like her name. That was fair enough—it didn't suit her. She didn't look like a Mary Margaret. Mary Margarets were subdued, given to shy smiles. Unless he missed his guess, the last time this woman had been subdued had probably been shortly before birth.

He laughed, his expression remaining unaffected. "Sounds like you should be starring in an off-Broadway revival of *Finian's Rainbow*."

Surprise nudged at her. She wouldn't have thought he'd know something like that. "You like musicals?"

"My sister does." Patrick stopped abruptly, realizing he'd broken his own rule about getting personal with strangers. And he meant for this woman to be a stranger. He didn't intend for her to remain in his company any longer than it took to get back to the station and confront Reynolds about his misguided, worse-than-usual choice of partners for him. "I work alone."

"So I was told." She'd also been told other things. Like the fact that he was a highly decorated cop who'd never been a team player. Now they were beginning to think that was because he was guarding secrets, secrets that had to do with lining his pockets. Rumors had been raised. Where there was smoke, there was usually fire and it was her job to put it out. "I won't get in your way."

"For that to be true, you'd have to leave."

From any other man, that might have been the beginning of a come-on, or at the very least, a slight flirtation. From Cavanaugh, she knew it meant that he regarded her as a pest. "All right, I won't get in your way much," she underscored.

He sincerely doubted that. But for the moment, he was stuck with this fledgling detective, and he didn't have any more time to waste on her.

Patrick took out a pair of rubber gloves from his jacket pocket and pulled them on. He nodded toward the vehicle that had been fished out. "What have you learned so far?"

"The victim seems to be in her early twenties, on her way to or from a party."

"How do you know?" The question came at her like a gunshot.

"Look at what she's wearing. A slinky, short black dress."

His glance was quick, concise, all-inclusive before reverting to Maggi. "Professional?"

Maggi paused. The panic on the victim's face made it difficult to see anything else. "A hooker? Maybe, but not cheap. A call girl maybe. The dress is subtle, subdued yet stylish."

He looked further into the vehicle. "Any ID?"

Maggi shook her head. "No purse. Might have been washed away, although I doubt it."

He looked at her sharply. Even a broken clock was right twice a day. "Why?"

She'd already been over the interior of the car and found nothing. "Because there's no registration inside the glove compartment. The glove compartment was completely empty. Not even a manual. Nobody keeps a glove compartment that clean."

If it was an attempt to hide identity, he thought, it was a futile one. "Ownership's easy enough to find out."

Maggi nodded. She gave him her thoughts on the subject. "It's a stalling tactic. Maybe whoever did this to her needed the extra time to try to fabricate an alibi."

His eyes made her feel like squirming when they penetrated that way. The man had to be hell on wheels in the interrogation room. "So you think this is a homicide, not an accident."

"That's the way the department's treating it or we wouldn't be here." She gave him an expression of sheer innocence.

He crossed his arms before him, looking down at her again. "Okay, Mary Margaret, what do you think the approximate time of death was?"

"Eleven twenty-three. Approximately," she said. He was trying to get her to lose her cool. Even if this wasn't about something bigger, she wasn't about to let him have the satisfaction.

"Woman's intuition?"

"Woman's vision," she corrected. "Twenty-twenty." Before he could ask her what she was talking about, Maggi reached over the body and held up the victim's right hand. The young woman was wearing an old-fashioned analog watch. The crystal wasn't broken, but it was obviously not water-resistant. It had stopped at precisely 11:23.

The CSI team arrived, equipped with their steel cases and apparatus intended to take the mystery out of death. Patrick stepped out of their way as they took possession of the vehicle and the victim within.

Maggi looked at him. "Want me to brief them?"

Something that could have passed for amusement flickered over him. "Asking for permission?"

She served his words back to him. "Trying not to get in your way."

Too late for that, he thought. Now they had to concentrate on getting her out of his way. Patrick gestured toward the head crime scene investigator. "Go ahead. That's Jack Urban."

Stepping around to the back of the vehicle, Patrick took out his notepad and carefully wrote down the license plate number before crossing to the nearest policeman. He handed the notepad to the man.

"See if these plates were run yet," he instructed. "Find out who the car belongs to. See if it was reported missing or stolen in the past twenty-four hours."

The policeman took the notepad without comment, retreating to his squad car.

The soft, light laugh that floated to him had Patrick looking back toward the crime scene. His so-called partner was talking to the head of the CSI team. Whatever she said had the man smiling like some living brain donor. Patrick shook his head. Obviously not everyone found his new partner as irritating as he did.

"I need to make a stop at the bank."

Patrick spared the woman sitting beside him in the front seat a look. It was cold outside and he had the windows of his car rolled up. He hadn't counted on the fact that along with the added warmth he'd be trapping the scent of her perfume within the vehicle.

Citing that they were partners until the captain tore them asunder, something Patrick was counting on happening in the very immediate future, the woman had hitched a ride back into town with him. When he'd asked her how she'd come to the crime scene in the first place, she'd told him that she'd caught a ride with one of the patrol cars.

The officers were still back at the scene, protecting

it from contamination as best they could. With them out of the picture, Patrick'd had no choice but to agree to let her come with him.

He didn't particularly like being agreeable.

He liked the idea of being a chauffeur even less.

"Why don't you do that after hours?" he bit off tersely.

She shifted in her seat. Again. The woman was nothing if not unharnessed energy, exuding enough for two people. She could have been her own partner, and should have been. Anything but his.

Maggi pointed to the building in the middle of the tree-lined block. "C'mon, Pat, we're passing it right now. It'll only take a minute."

She slid a glance in his direction. If looks could kill, she knew she would have been dead on the spot.

"All right, as long as you promise never to call me 'Pat' again."

"Deal." Like it or not, she was going to have to spend some time with him. She wanted it to be as stress free as she could make it. "So, what do you like being called?"

"I don't like being called at all."

No one said the assignments were going to be easy. "In the event that I have to get your attention," Maggi began gamely, "do you prefer 'hey you,' or shall I just throw sunflower seeds at you until I get you to turn around?"

He could see her doing it, too. She had that kind of bulldog quality about her. "Cavanaugh'll do."

"Not even Patrick?"

He slowed down. There was a parking spot almost directly across the street from the bank. Patrick guided the car into it, then pulled up the hand brake. Only then did he turn to look at her.

"Let's get something straight, McKenna. We're not friends, we're partners. We're not even going to be that for very long, so quit coming on like some Girl Scout and stop trying to sound like you're going to be my lifelong buddy."

She sat there quietly for a long moment, trying to get a handle on this man. "Losing Ramirez hit you pretty hard, didn't it?"

The look he shot her was darker than black. "The last thing I need or want is to ride around with Dr. Phil in the car. You want to analyze somebody—"

She held up her hand, not in surrender but to get him to curtail what he was about to say. "Sorry, just making conversation."

"Well, don't."

Unbuckling her seat belt, she turned to look at him. The intensity on her face took him by surprise. "You know, Cavanaugh, someday you just might need someone to watch your back for you."

"If and when I ever do, it sure as hell isn't going to be you."

She paused for a moment, and then she gave him a bright smile. "Roughage."

Had she lost her mind? What kind of a birdbrain were they cranking out of the academy these days? "What?"

"Morning roughage. Does wonders in clearing out all those poisons that seem to be running around all through you," she declared, getting out of the car. She paused to look in for a last second before closing the door. "I'll only be a minute."

Patrick frowned to himself. Even a minute seemed

too long to remain in the car, surrounded the way he was with her perfume. What he needed right now more than solitude was air. He got out.

When she looked at him curiously, he muttered, "I need to stretch my legs."

She pretended to glance down at them. "And long legs they are, too."

Not waiting for him, Maggi hurried across the street, wanting to put a little distance between herself and Mr. Personality before she said something she meant and blew everything. She held her hand up, stopping traffic as she darted toward the other side.

She supposed having him this ill-tempered made her job easier. It took away any qualms she might have about spying on him.

"Hey, didn't they teach you not to jaywalk at the academy while you were busy graduating at the top of your class?"

For less than two cents, she'd tell him what she thought of him. Exercising extreme control, Maggi turned around when she reached the curb. "You want to give me a ticket?"

"I don't want you risking your fool neck needlessly." What he wanted to do was give her her walking papers, but there was nothing he could do about that here.

Resigned, and far from happy about it, Patrick pushed the glass door open and crossed the threshold ahead of her. She looked surprised when he held the door for her.

"I see someone must have taught you manners somewhere along the line," she said.

"It's expedient. If I let the door go, you would probably walk into it and make the ER our next stop. We have to get back to the station.''

She refused to let him get to her. She knew that was what he was after, to get to her so badly that she'd march into Reynolds's office and declare that she wouldn't work with him, the way all his other partners had. Except for Ramirez.

Ain't gonna happen, Cavanaugh, she thought as she walked by him.

''You can huff and puff all you want, Cavanaugh,'' she informed him brightly. ''I'm not going anywhere.''

With that, she picked out the shortest line. Patrick stopped by the small table with all the deposit and withdrawal slips, looking annoyed. Mercifully, this wasn't going to take long. Mondays were usually slow.

Except where homicides seemed to be concerned, she thought, thinking back to the crime scene they'd just left. Something like that made grabbing lunch a challenge to intestinal fortitude.

The teller in the window directly to her left screamed.

The next moment, the man standing before the window whirled around.

There was a gun in his hand.

''Everyone freeze,'' he announced loudly. ''This is a holdup.''

Chapter 3

The man's eyes bounced around like pinballs that had just been put into play. He seemed to aim his weapon at everyone in the bank at the same time. Patrick could almost hear the bank robber's nerves jangling.

"Get down!" the man shouted. "Everyone get down on the floor!" His gun moved erratically from person to person, turning each into a potential target, a potential victim. "Now!"

Patrick did a quick calculation. There were fourteen other people in the bank, not counting the bank robber. Five of them tellers. The gunman looked so rattled he could start firing away at any second. It had all the signs of becoming a bloodbath at the slightest provocation.

Going through the motions of dropping down to the floor, Patrick reached for his pistol.

The rest happened so fast he only had the opportunity to absorb it after the fact. Before he knew what she was doing, the partner the department had saddled him with cried out in what sounded like utter panic. His head jerked in her direction. The bank robber stared at her.

Maggi's eyes were wide as they were riveted on the bank robber and she was trembling. Her hands were raised above her head in total submission.

"Omigod, it's a gun." Panic escalated in her voice. "He's got a gun. Oh, please don't shoot me," she implored. "I just found out I'm pregnant. You'd be killing two people, not just one. Me and my baby. I don't want to die, mister. I've got everything to live for. Please don't kill me."

With each word she uttered, Maggi edged closer and closer to the bank robber. She was breathing heavily and still trembling.

"Shut up, you stupid bitch. Nobody's going to die, just do what I tell you." The bank robber looked panicked himself as he trained the gun on her.

"All right, all right—" Maggi's voice hitched "—if you promise you won't hurt me. Pretty please?"

The last two words she uttered were distinctively different from the rest. As she seemed to sag down right in front of him, Maggi grabbed hold of his gun hand. Catching him by surprise, she violently jerked his arm behind his back. In less than half a heartbeat, her own gun was in her other hand. She held it close enough to the robber's temple to get her point across.

"Drop the gun." He did as he was told, cursing her roundly. "Now apologize to the nice people and say you're sorry."

"What the—" At a loss for coherence, the bank robber let loose a string of profanities that only made Maggi shake her head.

"You kiss your mother with that mouth?" she marveled. Relieved that the situation was over, Maggi took a deep breath, trying to get a hold of her own nerves. They felt as if they'd been stretched to the limit. Adrenaline still raced through her veins. "Keep that up and we're going to have to wash your mouth out with soap, aren't we, Detective Cavanaugh?"

As if waiting for some kind of word of concurrence, Maggi raised her eyebrow toward Patrick. He merely grunted as he pulled the man's hands behind him and snapped handcuffs around his wrists. The look he gave her left Maggi short on description. Had she just stepped on his male pride?

The robber winced as the cuffs went on. "You're cops?"

"No, just into a little S&M," Maggi quipped. "We like to carry handcuffs with us." She winked broadly at Patrick, beginning to enjoy getting under his skin. "You never know when they might come in handy."

Using a handkerchief, she stooped down and picked up the man's weapon by the butt. Nothing fancy. She wondered if this was the man's first time. He'd certainly behaved that way.

"Next time you want money from a bank, do it right. Use a withdrawal slip." She tucked the gun in at her belt for the time being, then looked at Patrick. "Want me to call for backup?"

Patrick gave the cuffs a good tug, making sure they were secure. "You mean you're not going to fly off with him to the precinct?"

Maggi lifted a shoulder in a casual shrug. "My cape's at the dry cleaners."

Separating herself from the others, she took out her cell phone and put in a call for a squad car. The second she closed the phone, the bank manager was on her, telling her how grateful he was to her and her partner and asking if there was anything he could do to show his deep appreciation.

"Other than giving away a five-pound box of tens to charity, I'd say hire a security guard. The next time you might not be so lucky."

The man was still thanking her profusely as she crossed back to Patrick and the prisoner. It was hard to say which of the two men glared at her harder.

She didn't do recrimination well. "What's your problem?"

Patrick made the prisoner face the wall as they waited for the squad car to arrive. His voice was cold. "I don't like showboating."

"So I won't invite you to a boat show the next time there's one at the marina. Anything else?"

"Yes, did it ever occur to you that you could have gotten your head blown off?"

"Frankly, I didn't have time to think things through to their grisly end." Maggi moved her head from side to side. "See? It's still attached and in good working order."

"Just barely." The last thing he wanted was to lose another partner in the line of duty. He'd had enough department funerals to last a lifetime.

"That's all that counts." She kept her voice cheerful as approaching sirens grew louder. The cavalry had arrived. "Ah, that's always such a comforting sound." She looked at the prisoner. "Bet you don't think so, do you?"

"Bitch," the bank robber spit out. The next moment, he found himself spun around and held up an inch off the ground. The man's feet came in contact with air as Patrick yanked him up.

"What's your name?" Patrick growled at the man.

The bank robber fought for oxygen and against numbing panic. "Joe. Joe Wellington."

"Well, Joe, Joe Wellington, talk nice to the lady or the next time it won't be soap you'll be tasting in your mouth." Patrick's look was dark, malevolent. "Do I make myself clear?"

"Clear," the bank robber gasped out. His eyes were glassy as they regarded Patrick.

Filled with disgust, Patrick all but threw him down. He then became aware that Maggi was grinning at him like some damn Cheshire cat.

"And just when I thought you didn't like me," she said.

"I don't like you," he replied tersely. She didn't stop grinning. To say it got on his nerves gave new meaning to the word *understatement*. "What the hell are you talking about?"

"You defended my honor. I'm flattered."

He didn't want her making anything out of it. It had been purely reflexive reaction. "I did it to defend the honor of the badge. It wasn't done to flatter you."

"Call it a side effect."

He had no time to retort. The backup she'd summoned arrived that moment.

It was just as well, he decided. The sooner they got back to the precinct, the sooner things would get back to normal. Whatever that was.

"Buy you lunch?"

It was a little more than an hour later and the would-be bank robber had been sent to be processed through the system. Cavanaugh was writing up the report, annoyed at the time this took away from the homicide they were supposed to investigate.

He waved his hand at Maggi as if she were an annoying fruit fly buzzing around his head.

Maggi held up a twenty almost in front of his nose. "Now that I've had a chance to cash my check, I can afford to splurge a little. I feel like celebrating. Join me," she coaxed. She knew how dangerous the situation could have gotten, despite her earlier disclaimer to him. The fact that it hadn't gone badly, that she and everyone else were able to walk away, was a fantastic high she wasn't close to coming down from.

He ignored her and the bill she held up. "Not interested."

"Don't you eat?" She bent down until her face was level with his. The ends of her hair brushed against some of his files. "Can I buy you a can of oil?"

Patrick finally looked up. "Is that supposed to be cute?"

"Relatively speaking." She wasn't going to let him rob her of her moment. So little of what she did these days felt this good. The positive reactions she dealt with all squared themselves away on paper. That never produced a high. "C'mon, Cavanaugh, lighten up. We've still got the rest of the day to face together. It goes better on a full stomach." When he made no attempt to get up, she added, "My dad always says you can't trust a man who won't eat with you."

He laughed shortly. "I take it your father never saw *The Godfather*."

Perched on the edge of his desk now, she hooted. "You *are* a movie buff."

He didn't like giving her points, didn't like her feeling

as if she knew something about him. The less you knew
about each other, the less likely you were to get close.

"I told you, that's my sister's department. You can't
help picking up a few things if it's always playing in
the background."

That was the second time he'd mentioned his sister.
She paused to study him for a moment. "Are you close,
you and your sister?" And then she answered her own
questions. "Silly question, I guess."

The computer network was down, temporarily halting the exchange of information that would allow him
to get the name of the owner of the dead woman's
sports car. Sometimes progress created nothing but
stumbling blocks, he thought with annoyance. He
didn't bother sparing Maggi a glance. "Only if you
think that I'm going to give you an answer."

"So what are you, like, the Lone Ranger?"

It became obvious to him that subtlety was lost on
her. She was probably the kind who had to be dislodged
with a two-by-four or a crowbar. "The position of
Tonto is not open."

Since he didn't look up, Maggi found herself staring
at the top of his head. He had deep, straight black hair,
the kind that tempted a woman to touch, to feather her
fingers through it. She purposely slipped her hands under her as she sat.

"That's okay, I don't do sidekicks—I do partners."

He finally looked up. "Aside from catching bullets
with your bare teeth?" The expression on his face grew
darker. "What the hell were you thinking at the bank?"

Another wisecrack was on the tip of her tongue, but
then, she decided to tell him the truth. She'd acted because she was afraid.

"That he was going to fire on you if you drew your

weapon the way you were planning to." And then, because it was getting too serious, she added, "I didn't want to lose a partner before I won you over with my sparkling personality."

"How did you know what I was going to do?"

"I saw it in your eyes," she said simply. "Sometimes, you can't go in like the Lone Ranger. Sometimes you have to go in like Fay Wray."

He stared at her. "Come again?"

"Fay Wray. The woman in *King Kong*." There was still no recognition in his face. "The screamer."

"You didn't scream."

"No, but I got properly hysterical. Enough to throw him off and get the drop on him." Because it was obviously causing friction, she didn't want to continue talking about the foiled bank robbery. "Anyway, it's over. C'mon, Cavanaugh." Playfully she tugged on his arm. "My stomach's rumbling."

He shrugged her off. "No one's stopping you from going to lunch."

"I hate to eat alone." She would have pouted prettily if she'd thought it would work, but she knew it wouldn't. Cavanaugh wasn't the type to go out of his way to please a woman.

He glanced at her before going back to his report. "Go to a crowded restaurant."

"I'd rather go to lunch with my partner." She didn't like being ignored and he was doing a royal job of it. This time, when she tugged on his arm, it was a hard jerk to get him to look at her again. "Hey, you owe me."

Her words more than her action earned his attention. He raised his head, his eyes penetrating her inner layers. "I *owe* you?"

She could see how he could make someone squirm. She felt like squirming and she wasn't the one who was supposed to be sitting on the hot seat.

"Sure, I told you I'd have your back and I did. Only it turned out to be your front, but—" she shrugged "—same difference. Now, are you going to come with me or do I push that chair of yours all the way to the elevator and *make* you come with me?"

He didn't have time for stupidity. He didn't know why he was bothering to answer her or even acknowledge her. "You wouldn't dare."

She grinned, her eyes gaining a mischievous glint he found oddly arousing. The blow to his gut came out of nowhere. He sent it back to the same address.

"Cavanaugh," she informed him, "I was the kid who never walked away from a dare."

He snorted. "You must have made your parents very proud."

"No, just gray." Maggi's eyes shifted down to the chair he was sitting in, then back to his face. "Your chair's got wheels and I know how to use them."

Patrick had every intention of continuing to say no, but the woman had the tendencies of an annoying gnat. He knew damn well that she'd keep after him until he either really snapped at her or gave in. And he had to admit the truth: he *was* hungry.

"Okay." Hitting the save button on the keyboard, he rose to his feet. "But you've got to stop sounding as if someone put your mouth in the fast forward mode." If it ever stopped moving, it might prove to be a tempting target.

Her mouth was quick to curve. "Deal."

Yeah, he thought, with the devil.

As he followed her out the door, he remembered

reading a passage that said something about the devil having the ability to assume a very pleasing shape. He watched the rhythmic sway of her hips.

Looked like the devil had definitely outdone himself this time.

Maggi offered him his choice of places. He picked a pizzeria that had more seats outside than in. She ate three slices with the December wind chilling her food. He seemed more interested in observing the people on the street than in listening to anything she said.

It was a power play, she knew that. She had invaded his territory and he was suspicious of her. He had no idea how suspicious he should have been, she thought. Or maybe he knew. The worst thing in the world was to underestimate your opponent. And he was that. Her opponent, her assignment. Not her partner. This kept life interesting. And damn complicated.

"You've got a healthy appetite," he commented when she reached for her fourth piece.

"He speaks. Wow."

"Forget I said anything."

"No, please, now that the floodgates have opened up, continue." When he made no comment, she shook her head. "You keep this up and I'm going to be forced to practice my ventriloquist act on you."

"Your what?"

"That's when the sane person makes the wooden creation beside her talk. In other words, putting words into your mouth. Like 'Thanks for the lunch, Maggi. Remind me to return the favor.'"

Patrick stared at her. She'd done a fair imitation of his voice, all without moving her lips.

"Want me to continue?" she offered.

"No, you made your point." He rose, passing a ten in her direction. "You're crazy."

"I said lunch was on me." She was on her feet, striding after him to the car. Catching up, she pushed the money back into his pocket. "Do we have to argue about this, too?"

He felt her hand as she withdrew it from his pants pocket. The tightening in his loins was purely instinctive. And annoying. As was she.

"Why not? You seem to like it."

She pulled open the door on her side and got in. "I'd like a little agreement better." Buckling her seat belt, she sighed. "Tell you what, I'll let you yell at me some more if you want to."

About to start the car, he paused to look at her. "I don't yell."

"Okay, growl. Lip-synch, something. Just talk. Say something, anything."

"Why?" Starting the car, he pulled out of the parking area.

"Because I want to get to know you. Partners should know something about each other and I really don't know anything about you, other than what I've heard and the fact that if these were Roman times, your scowl would put Zeus to shame."

He came to a stop at a red light. "Jupiter."

"What?"

The light turned green again and he stepped on the accelerator. "Zeus was a Greek god, Jupiter was the Roman equivalent."

So he knew something beyond police procedure. He didn't strike her as the kind of man who knew mythology. "Impressive. I'll still go with Zeus. You look more like a Greek god than a Roman god anyway."

She was flirting with him, he thought, but when he shot her a look, McKenna's expression was totally guileless. Was she putting him on? Didn't matter. She wasn't going to last long enough for that to become a problem.

"You were damn lucky today that things turned out the way they did and no one was hurt. Next time, you might not be so lucky."

"I've always been pretty lucky." His profile hardened even more. "Hey, don't underestimate the part luck plays when it comes to our line of work." She thought of the wound that had put her out of commission for a month a couple of years back. She'd kept that bit of information from her father. The man had enough on his mind. Thinking of it, she patted the region several inches below her shoulder. "Two inches to the left and this scar might have been the last one I ever got instead of just one of many."

"Scars? You're talking about scars?" What kind of a woman was she? As far as he knew, women didn't exactly go out of their way to draw attention to something that was considered to be a blemish.

"Sure. Don't you have any?"

"I have enough."

"Where?" she asked innocently.

"Out of the light of day."

For just the slightest second, she caught herself wondering just where on his very hard anatomy those scars were located. The next moment, she roused herself, hauling her mind back into focus. "Then you know what I'm talking about. About luck, I mean."

Turning right, he shook his head. "Mary Margaret, I'm beginning to think I don't have a damn clue what you're talking about most of the time."

She wished he wouldn't use her name, but she knew if she said anything, he would only do it more often. "The subject is luck. The visual aids are scars." Grabbing her jacket and blouse, she undid some buttons and pulled both articles back. "Like this one."

Patrick glanced in her direction and almost forgot to look back at the road. He'd only caught a glimpse, but that provided more than enough fodder. He swerved to avoid rear-ending the car in front of him.

"Damn it, Mary Margaret, you always go exposing your breasts to people you hardly know?"

All she'd shown him was a little more skin than had already been evident. "It's called cleavage and I'm not exposing myself, I'm showing you a scar that's well above the bad-taste line. If I was into exposing, there are other scars I could show you."

Patrick didn't have to look at her to know she was grinning. He heard it in her voice. He was about to ask her just where on her anatomy they were situated, but he didn't need to go there. The interior of the car was warm enough as it was.

Maggi moved the fabric back into place. "Anyway, my point is that luck has *everything* to do with it. And I've been luckier than most."

She not only had hair like a Barbie doll, but the intelligence of one as well, Patrick thought darkly.

"Luck has a nasty habit of running out when you least expect it."

"God, but you are Mr. Sunshine, aren't you?"

"Sunshine was never my department." This time, he took on the yellow light, making it through the intersection before it had a chance to turn red. The faster he got this annoying woman back to the precinct, the better. "That's the realm of cockeyed optimists."

"Would it help you to know that I can back up my cockeyed optimism?"

"How? A Ouija board?"

She glanced at her watch. They'd eaten lunch in less than twenty-five minutes. "We've got a little time left. Take me to the firing range."

"We've still got a homicide to solve," he reminded her.

"This'll only take a few minutes and it might make you feel a whole lot better."

What would make him feel a whole lot better, he thought, was finding out that she was just part of another one of his bad dreams.

Growling an oath under his breath, Patrick turned the car around.

Chapter 4

The fiftyish, barrel-chested man behind the desk at the firing range smiled warmly the moment he saw her walking in, transforming his round face from intimidating to surprisingly boyish in appearance. "Hey, back for more, Annie Oakley?"

Reaching behind his desk, the officer, Miles Baker, produced a box of ammunition before Maggi could make a formal request and slid it across the counter toward her.

Inclining her head, Maggi took the box from him. "Just here to see if my edge hasn't dulled."

Baker laughed. "Even dulled, you'd still be better than the rest of us." His deep-set brown eyes shifted toward Patrick. Since the other detective made no request for shells, he left a second box where it was. "Hey, you ever seen this lady in action?"

Against his will, Patrick thought about the incident at the bank. At the time, he'd been sure she'd lost her nerve. To be honest, McKenna had pulled her weapon out pretty quickly.

He looked at Maggi. "Depends on what you mean by action." He noted that she had the good grace to look just a shade uncomfortable.

Baker raised hamlike hands, warding off any stray thoughts. "Hey, I don't go there."

His denial was a bit too vehement. Patrick was willing to bet the man had had a sensual thought or two about the woman he was grinning at. Baker wouldn't have been human if he hadn't. Besides, Patrick had seen the way the man had brightened the second he'd recognized her.

"I'm talking about with a gun in her hand." Baker kissed the tips of his fingers before spreading them wide again as if to release the phantom kiss into the air. "Thing of beauty to watch."

Patrick still wasn't sure if the officer was referring to the way she shot or just McKenna in general. He supposed, if pinned down, he'd have to agree to the latter. But beauty had little to do with their line of work. If anything, it got in the way.

"Apparently that's why I'm here." Resigned, Patrick looked at what he hoped was his temporary partner expectantly. "Okay, you want to show me something, show me."

Though his expression remained impassive, she knew Cavanaugh was challenging her. Ordinarily she didn't go out of her way to prove anything about herself to anyone. She figured people who did were braggarts.

But this wasn't a case of bragging or showing off. This was a case of proving herself to the man she'd supposedly been partnered with. This was showing him that she could be trusted to at least cover his back when the time called for it. And, in her experience, one trust usually led to another.

At least, that was what she was counting on.

"All right." She turned on her heel to lead the way to the firing range. "Let's go."

"Hey, don't forget these." Leaning over the counter, Baker held up two sets of earphones. "Don't want to go around the rest of the day deaf, do you?"

Patrick doubled back and took both pairs from the officer. He handed one set to Maggi.

"All right, Mary Margaret," he said gamely, "impress me."

No pressure there. Going to the rear, Maggi chose a slot, then donned the earphones before pressing a button that sent her paper target flying down the field away from her.

Patrick watched as the blackened target became smaller and smaller. The woman with the gun made no effort to halt its progress. Just how far was she sending it?

"You planning on stopping that thing anytime soon? Nobody expects you to shoot at a perp fleeing the scene in Nevada."

The target still hadn't gone as far as she could shoot, but Maggi pressed the button to oblige Patrick. The paper target looked little bigger than a suspended stray piece of confetti.

Closing one eye, she took careful aim and fired.

Curious, Patrick didn't wait for her to discharge the weapon again. Holding his hand up to stop her from firing, he pressed the button to retrieve the target. When it came back, he saw that she'd hit it dead center. He felt he had to assume that it was just a freakish coincidence, but for argument's sake, he gave her the benefit of the doubt.

"Not bad," he conceded, releasing the target, "if you've got the time to line up your shot."

Maggi said nothing. Instead, reaching over him, she pressed the button again, sending the target back even farther away than before. This time, Patrick made no comment about the target's proximity but waited until she stopped it herself. And then, just when the target had reached the end of its run, she pressed for its return.

Once the line was activated again, Maggi began firing, sending off five rounds before the paper target came back to its place of origin.

Without a word, Patrick examined the target. She'd sent all five rounds into the same vicinity as the first. Two of the shots were almost on top of each other, the rest close enough to make the hole bigger.

Staring at it, Patrick had to admit to himself that she was impressive. But he'd never admit this to her.

"Not bad," he said again, "if the perp is running in a straight line and not firing back."

He was doing it to annoy her, Maggi thought. He wasn't the first man she'd had to prove herself to, and losing her temper wasn't part of the deal. She loaded a fresh clip into her weapon.

"I guess we'll just have to wait for the right occasion," she told him calmly.

"I guess. We done here?"

She squared her shoulders, feeling a slow boil begin. She could have gone on firing, but obviously it didn't prove anything to this lug. "We're done."

"Good." Patrick took off his earphones and walked back to the front desk.

He was a hard man, Maggi thought, but then she

already knew that. And she also knew that she'd made her point. Taking a deep breath, she hurried back to the front desk and handed in the remainder of the box of ammunition to Baker, as well as the earphones.

Baker looked surprised that she had cut her time so short.

"Fun time's over, Baker," she explained. "We've got to get back to the station."

The officer put the earphones away. "See you around, Annie Oakley," he chuckled.

Patrick stood at the door, waiting for her. "He knows you."

She walked out first. "We've talked."

He had a feeling she talked to everyone and everything, living or not. "So, how long have you had this supervision?"

It was a backhanded compliment. Nevertheless, she accepted it gladly. She barely suppressed the smile that rose to her lips, but Maggi knew he'd think she was preening. She walked briskly beside him to the car.

"I don't. What I had was a father who was on the job for twenty-two years. He put a gun in my hand when I was old enough to hold one and took me out to the firing range." She still remembered the first time. The weapon had weighed a ton, but she'd been far too proud to say anything.

"Some people would frown on that." He passed no judgments himself. People were free to live their lives any way they saw fit, as long as it didn't impinge on others. Or him.

"Yeah, well, my father wasn't exactly your average guy. He wanted me to have a healthy respect for guns and to know what one could or couldn't do."

Patrick heard the pride in her voice, and the affection. It was the same tone he heard in his cousins' voices when they talked about their fathers. He wondered what that was like, having a father you were close to, you were proud of. It seemed like such a foreign concept to him.

"A little bit of knowledge is a dangerous thing," he pointed out.

Her father had taught her how to take a gun apart first, piece by piece, and then clean it before reassembling it. She'd had to wait a long time before he allowed her to handle cartridges.

"Maybe, but enough of it sets you free," she countered.

"Whatever." Getting into the car, he waited until she buckled up. "So, how does your father feel about you being on the police force?"

"He worries." Maggi slid the metal tongue into the groove, snapping the belt into place. "He's a father first, a police officer second. But he's proud of me." She knew that without asking. It made her determined never to let him down. "He's the reason I joined up." She thought of the upbringing she'd had. Blue uniforms populated her everyday world. "I never knew anything else."

Starting the car, he backed out of his space. "What's your mother got to say about it?"

Maggi kept her face forward. "Nothing. She died when I was nine. He and his buddies raised me."

Her profile had gotten a little rigid. He'd hit a nerve, he thought. Miss Sunshine had a cloud on her horizon. Interesting. "His buddies?"

Maggi nodded. Her profile was relaxed again and she

was as animated as before. Just his luck. "The other police officers. I was their mascot."

He laughed to himself, taking a hard right. "That would explain it."

Maggi found she had to brace herself to keep from leaning toward the window. "Explain what?"

"The cocky attitude."

"I don't have a cocky attitude," she informed him. "I just know what I'm capable of and, since you're my partner, I wanted you to know, too," she added quickly before he could accuse her of showing off.

"You shouldn't have put yourself out."

Turning her head, she caught him sparing her a glance. She couldn't fathom what was in his eyes. "Why?"

"Because you're not going to be my partner for that long."

Guess again, Cavanaugh. "You know something I don't?"

Arriving at the station, he pulled into his spot and stopped the car. Sure shot or not, someone who looked like her didn't belong out in the field. It was like waving a red flag in front of every nut case in the area who wanted to get his rocks off. The sooner she wasn't his responsibility, the better.

Patrick got out, slamming the door. "Yeah, I know how long people in your position last, on the average." He took the front stairs to the entrance quickly, then paused at the door. She was right behind him.

Maggi grinned up at him as she walked through the door he held open for her. "Haven't you noticed, Cavanaugh? I'm not average."

Yeah, he thought as he followed her inside the building, *that's just the trouble, I've noticed.*

* * *

"Definitely died before she went into the water," the medical examiner, Dr. Stanley Ochoa, informed them with the slightly monotonous voice of a man who had been at his job too long.

Maggi couldn't help looking at the young woman on the table, stripped of her dignity and her clothes, every secret exposed except her identity and why she'd died.

Poor baby, you look like a kid. Maggi raised her eyes to the M.E. "And we know this how?"

Instead of answering immediately, Ochoa turned to Patrick. A hint of amusement flickered beneath his drooping mustache. "Eager little thing, isn't she?"

"And, oddly enough, not deaf or invisible," Maggi cheerfully informed the M.E. as she placed herself between the two men, both of whom towered over her. She missed the glimmer of a smile on Patrick's face. "Now, how do you know she didn't drown?"

"Simple. No water in the lungs. She wasn't breathing when she went over the side."

"Because she was already dead. Makes sense." Maggi looked at the gash on the woman's forehead. It looked as if there'd been a line of blood at one point. If she'd bled, that meant she'd still been alive when she'd sustained the blow. "That bump on her head—did she get it hitting her forehead against the steering wheel when she went over the railing?"

Ochoa dismissed the guess. "Might have, but at first glance it looks deeper than something she could have sustained from that kind of impact."

Patrick's face was expressionless. "The air bag was deployed."

Maggi bit the inside of her lip. She'd forgotten that detail and knew it made her look bad in his eyes. She regarded the victim again. "Could the air bag have suffocated her? She's a small woman."

Again the M.E. shook his head. "No, suffocation has different signs. This was a blunt force trauma to the head. Something heavy."

Because Cavanaugh wasn't saying anything, Maggi summarized what they'd just ascertained. "So someone killed her, then put her into the sports car and drove her into the river to make it look like an accident."

Ochoa nodded. The overhead light shone brightly on his forehead, accentuating his receding hairline. "Looks like."

Patrick had been regarding the victim in silence, as if he was conducting his own séance with her. He raised his eyes to look at the overweight medical examiner. "Anything else?"

"Not yet. I'm waiting on the blood work results and I haven't conducted the autopsy. Check back with me tomorrow."

Patrick was aware that Maggi wasn't beside him as he reached the door. Turning around, he saw her still standing by the table. He thought she was studying the victim for enlightenment until he saw the expression on her face.

With an annoyed sigh, he retraced his steps. "We don't mourn them, Mary Margaret, we just make sure whoever did this to them pays the price."

He probably thought she was weak, Maggi thought. The woman's death just seemed like such a sad waste. "Yeah, right." Squaring her shoulders, she walked out of the room.

The moment they were in the corridor, Patrick's cell phone rang. He had it out before it could ring a second time.

"Cavanaugh."

Curiosity ricocheted through her as she walked beside him, waiting for Cavanaugh to say something to the voice talking in his ear. She wanted to figure out the nature of his call. Her real assignment was still foremost in her mind, but she wanted to find the person who'd wantonly ended the life of the young woman on the table in the morgue.

If she was hoping for clues, she was disappointed. All Cavanaugh said before disconnecting was "Thanks."

Impatient, she tried not to sound it as she asked, "Well?"

He wasn't accustomed to answering to anyone. The only partner he'd ever gotten along with had always given him his space, waiting for him to say something but never really pressing him. But then, this woman wasn't Ramirez. What she was was a royal pain in the butt. "That was Goldsmith."

Maggi knew Goldsmith was the officer he'd asked to track down the sports car license. She was surprised that Cavanaugh recalled the man's name. He didn't strike her as the type to put names to people; he seemed more likely to just label everyone "them" and "me." "And?"

The more she pushed, the more he felt like resisting. It wasn't a logical reaction, but this woman was pressing all the wrong buttons. Buttons that weren't supposed to be being pressed.

"C'mon, Cavanaugh, stop making me play twenty questions. Who does the car belong to?"

"Congressman Jacob Wiley."

She vaguely remembered the last election. Mind-numbing slogans had littered the airwaves, as well as

most available and not-so-available spaces. But one of
the few people she'd genuinely liked was Congressman
Jake Wiley, "the people's candidate," according to the
literature his people distributed.

"The family values man?" She glanced over her
shoulder toward the morgue, reluctant to make the connection. Her father had taught her long ago not to jump
to conclusions. There could be a great many explana-
tions as to what a young, pretty girl was doing dead in
a car that belonged to the congressman.

"One and the same," Patrick confirmed. He was already heading out the door again.

Maggi had to lengthen her stride to catch up.

Congressman Jacob Wiley had a build reminiscent
of the quarterback he'd once been. Blessed with an engaging smile that instantly put its recipient at ease, he
flashed it now at the two people his secretary ushered
in. He'd been informed that they were from the local
police and there was a hint of confusion in the way he
raised his eyebrows as he rose from his cluttered desk
to greet them.

Wiley extended his hand first to Maggi, then to Patrick. "Always glad to meet my constituents so I can
thank them in person for their vote." His tone was
affable.

Patrick's eyes were flat as he took full measure of
the man before him. He found the smile a little too
quick, the manner a little too innocent. "To set the
record straight, I didn't vote for you."

"But I did," Maggi said to cut the potentially awkward moment. "You'll have to forgive my partner,
Congressman. He left his manners in his other squad

car. I'm afraid this is official business. We need to ask you a question."

"Ask away." Lacing his hands together, Wiley sat on the edge of his desk as if he was about to enter into a conversation with lifelong friends. "I believe in fully cooperating with the police."

She held up the digital photograph that had been printed less than half an hour ago. "Do you know this woman?"

Patrick watched the congressman's eyes as he took the photograph in his hands. There was horror on his face as he looked at the dead woman. "Oh, God, no." He turned his head away.

"Are you sure?" Patrick pressed, his voice low, steely. "She was found in your car."

Light eyebrows drew together in mounting confusion. "My car? My car's right outside." He pointed toward the window and the parking lot beyond.

Patrick's expression didn't change. "Navy blue sports car. Registered to you."

A light seemed to dawn in the older man's face. "Oh, right." As if to dissuade any rising suspicion, the man explained, "I have more than one car, detectives. I've got five kids, three of them drive. Of course, there's my wife," he tagged on. "But she prefers the Lincoln." He paused, sorting out his thoughts. "And then, sometimes I let one of my people borrow a car when they're running an errand for me."

Patrick made a notation in his notepad, deliberately making the congressman wait. "So at any given time of the day or night, you don't know where your cars are."

Wide, muscular shoulders rose and fell beneath a handmade suit. "I'm afraid not." Maggi began to take the photograph back, but Wiley stopped her at the last moment. "Wait, let me look at that again." The air was still as he studied the face in the photograph more closely. After a beat, the impact of death seemed to fade into the background. And then recognition filtered into his eyes. "This is Joan, no, Joanne, that's it. Joanne Styles." Wiley looked first at Maggi, then Patrick. "She works for me."

"Worked," Patrick corrected, taking the photograph back.

Disbelief was beginning to etch itself into the congressman's handsome face. "What happened to her?"

Patrick gave him just the minimal details. "She was found in the river this morning, in your sports car. It appears she went over the side of the road sometime last night."

Veering to the more sympathetic audience, Wiley looked at Maggi. "She drowned?"

"Someone would like to have us believe that," Patrick interjected, his eyes never leaving the man's face.

Confusion returned. "Then she didn't drown? She's alive?"

"Oh, she's dead all right," Patrick confirmed emotionlessly. "But she didn't die in the river. She died sometime before that."

"I don't understand."

"Neither do we. For the moment." Patrick pinned him with a look. "Where were you last night, Congressman, if you don't mind my asking?"

The congressman's friendly expression faded. "If you're suggesting what I think you're suggesting, I do mind your asking."

"Just doing our job, Congressman," Maggi interjected smoothly, her manner respectful. "Pulling together pieces of a puzzle. It might help us find Ms. Styles's killer if we could reconstruct the evening.''

''Yes, of course. Sorry,'' he apologized to Patrick. ''This has me a little rattled. I never knew anyone who was a murder victim before. I was at a political fundraiser at the Hyatt Hotel.'' He looked at Patrick and added, ''With several hundred other people.''

''Was Ms. Styles there?'' Maggi prodded gently.

''I imagine so, although I really couldn't say for certain. All of my staff was invited,'' he explained.

''Looks like those several hundred people certainly didn't help keep her alive, did they?'' Patrick asked.

''If we could get a guest list, that would be very helpful. Could you tell us who was in charge of putting the fund-raiser together?'' Maggi felt as if she was tap-dancing madly to exercise damage control.

''Of course. That would be Leticia Babcock.'' Picking up a pen, Wiley wrote down the name of the organization the woman worked for. Finished, he handed the paper to Maggi. He glanced at Patrick, but his words were directed to the woman before him. ''Anything I can do, you only have to ask.''

Patrick took the slip of paper from Maggi and tucked it into his pocket. His eyes never left the congressman's face. ''Count on it.''

Chapter 5

Hurrying to catch up to her partner, Maggi pulled the collar of her jacket up. It began to mist. The weather lately had been anything but ideal.

"You get more flies with honey than with vinegar, Cavanaugh."

Patrick reached his car and unlocked the driver's side. He looked at her over the roof. "I'm not interested in getting flies, Mary Margaret, I'm interested in getting a killer."

She blew out a breath as she got in on her side. "I wish you'd stop calling me that."

Patrick closed the door and flipped on the headlights. The sun had decided to hide behind dark clouds. They were in for a storm. "It's your name, isn't it?"

Her father had named her after his two sisters. She wished he'd been born an only child. "Yes it is. That doesn't mean I like hearing it—" Maggi turned in her seat to glare at him as she delivered the last word "—Pat."

The nickname she tossed at him was fraught with bad memories. Only his father had ever called him that, when the old man was especially drunk and reveling in the whole myth of "Pat and Mike," something Patrick gathered had come by way of a collection of Irish stories about two best friends. According to Uncle Andrew, a number of Irish-flavored jokes began that way, as well. In any case, he and his father didn't remotely fit the description of two friends, and it was only when he was in a drunken haze that his father could pretend that he'd created a home life for his family. In reality, home life was just barely short of a minefield, ready to go off at the slightest misstep.

Maggi sighed, trying to regain some ground. "All I'm saying is that the congressman was a great deal more cooperative when you weren't glaring at him."

He started up the car and got back on the road. "That's what you're here for, right? To win him over with your sunny disposition."

"Attila the Hun's disposition could be called sunny compared to yours."

To her surprise, she heard Patrick laugh softly to himself. "Looks like our first day isn't going very well, is it?"

She trod warily, afraid of being set up. "Could be better," she allowed. Maggi caught his grin out of the side of her eye.

"It'll get worse."

"If you're trying to get me to bail out, you're wasting your time."

"And why is that? Why are you so determined to work with me?" he wanted to know.

"You mean other than your sparkling personality, charm and wit?" She saw his expression darken another shade. The man could have posed for some kind of gothic novel, the kind given to sensuality. He'd be damn good-looking if he wasn't into scaring people off. Upbraiding herself, she curtailed her own impulse toward sarcasm. "I was assigned to you, Cavanaugh, and I don't back away from my assignments, no matter how much of a pain in the butt they might be."

Maggi watched his eyes in the rearview mirror. Instead of becoming incensed, he looked as if he was considering her words. "Fair enough."

She knew she should let it go, but she couldn't. A door had opened, and she didn't know when it could be opened again. She needed to move as much as she could through it.

"No, what's fair is if you give me a chance here," she told him tersely. "I've shown you that I don't fall apart in tense situations and that I'm a dead shot and all in under eight hours. If you were anyone else, that would definitely tip the scales way in my favor."

The woman could get impassioned when she wanted to. That was a minus. He'd always found that emotion got in the way of things. "I'm not anyone else."

She sank into her seat. "So I've been told."

Something in her tone worked its way under his skin, made half thoughts begin to form. It took a little effort on his part to ignore them. He had no idea why. "Make the best of it, Mary Margaret. What you see is what you get."

Not hardly. If that were the case, then there would be no need for her to go undercover to investigate the allegations Halliday had received from an anonymous source. The allegations that made Cavanaugh out to be a dirty cop on the take.

Even if she wasn't on the job, just one look would have told her that what you saw was definitely *not* what you got when it came to Patrick Cavanaugh.

Their next stop was the offices of Babcock and Anderson, which organized and handled the arrangements for fund-raisers of all types. The professional firm was run by Leticia Babcock, president and sole owner. There was no Anderson.

"I thought it sounded more aesthetically pleasing to have two names on the card," Leticia Babcock, a tall, slim woman in her mid-thirties informed them when they asked after the whereabouts of her partner. "Makes it sound as if the company has been around for ages." Because they'd requested to see the guest list, she scrolled through her records as she spoke to them. "Ah, here it is." She beamed. Stopping, she tapped the screen with a curved, flame-red nail. "We raised more than was originally hoped for. The gala was an amazingly rousing success. The congressman was very pleased."

Maggi could all but see the dollar signs in the other woman's eyes. "Congressman Wiley?"

"Yes." The dark-haired woman sat back in her chair, sizing up her visitors. "He was the one who came to me to organize it. Very generous man. Not bad-looking, either." Momentarily ignoring the tall, somber man standing beside her, she winked broadly at Maggi. "Too bad he's married." With a careful movement orchestrated to avoid chipping a nail, Leticia hit the Print key. The printer to the left of the highly polished teak desk came to life and began printing the list.

"That doesn't stop some men," Patrick indicated.

Leticia laughed. The sound carried no mirth. "Didn't stop my third husband, that was for sure. But I hear the congressman's a straight arrow." She sighed again and shook her head, as if lamenting the missed opportunity. She held out the pages to them. "Believe me, I left him enough of an opening."

Patrick glanced at down at the list the woman had provided for them. The names went on for several pages. And everyone was going to have to be checked out. He debated giving that assignment to McKenna, let her run solo with it.

"Five hundred guests," Maggi told him. "Don't bother counting them."

She was quick with numbers, he thought. Handy trait to have around. He looked at Leticia as he tapped the list. "He said his staff was there."

A small, slightly superior smile twisted her lips. "Yes, they were."

He watched the woman's eyes, looking for some telltale flicker. "Is that normal, to invite your reelection staff?"

"Not really, but like I said, the congressman's a very generous man." She ran down the benefits of attending. "There was a great deal of good food to eat. Some of those staff members probably ate better than they ever have in their lives. Not to mention networking."

"Networking?" Maggi asked before Patrick had a chance to.

"Yes, there are a lot of important, influential people attending these things. Everyone likes to be seen 'caring' about a popular cause. Doesn't hurt to be around them. You never know where your next big break is coming from.'' She looked from Maggi to Patrick, her manner terminating the session. "If there's anything else I can do for you, let me know.''

He wasn't ready to leave just yet. Patrick took out the photograph of the dead woman and held it up to the organizer's face. "Did you see this woman at the party last night?''

Leticia shivered, making no move to take the photograph in her own hand.

"Not that I remember.''

The very air had climbed up inside their lungs as they waited for her to go on.

"Is she…dead?''

"Very,'' he replied grimly, tucking the photograph away again.

"Thanks for your help,'' Maggi told the woman as they walked out. Patrick made an inaudible sound that could have passed for "Goodbye.''

Outside the window, Maggi could see that the mist was getting heavier. She hoped it would hold off until she got home for the night.

She glanced at the papers he was holding. "Looks a little daunting.''

"Looks can be deceiving.''

Part of her wanted to ask if Patrick was on to something, but she knew he was just pulling her chain or maybe giving her some kind of encoded message. She wanted no part of either. As he pressed for the elevator, she looked at the list over his shoulder. "So, where do you want to start?''

He folded the list in half twice before lodging it beside the photograph. He never even looked at her. "At her apartment.''

* * *

When she wasn't busy working or partying, Joanne Styles had spent her time in a tiny, cluttered studio apartment about two-thirds the size of the one Maggi had lived in when she was in San Francisco.

Standing in it now made Maggi entertain a very odd sense of déjà vu coupled with the thought "there but for the grace of God…"

Except that she would have never let her guard down enough to have someone do to her what had been done to Joanne.

Maggi supposed that was her inbred leeriness. It came from being raised in an atmosphere of law enforcement agents. Looking back, she knew that it was her leeriness that had gotten in her way with Tyler, urging her on to keep a part of herself in reserve, not allowing him to see all of her.

Lucky thing, too, considering the way that had turned out, she mused.

Patrick noticed the expression on his partner's face as she stood looking around. She seemed a million miles away. He ignored her for a moment, then heard himself asking, "What's wrong?"

"Nothing." Maggi took a moment to rouse herself before turning to squarely face him. "Just trying to put myself in her shoes, that's all."

He supposed there was nothing wrong in getting a female's perspective on all this. "Can't hurt."

She raised her eyes to his, humor playing along her lips. "Mellowing?"

She wore some kind of gloss, he realized, something that caught the overhead light and made her lips shimmer.

He was noticing the wrong things, Patrick told himself.

Not bothering to answer her, he nodded toward the laptop that stood open on the small, pressboard desk. There was every indication within the room that Joanne would have been returning to her apartment.

"She had a computer. Maybe there's some interesting e-mail that might tell us something. We can take it up to the lab," he said.

Maggi closed the lid and unplugged the computer. She spotted a carrying case haphazardly thrown under the desk and tucked the laptop into it. "Why the lab?"

"To read it." When she looked at him quizzically, he added, "There's probably a password they'll need to get by."

"I can get you through that," she said.

Patrick stopped rifling through the victim's closet. "You're a hacker?"

She shrugged carelessly. "I've been known to get into some systems."

He hadn't thought to catch McKenna in a contradiction so soon. "I thought you believed in the straight and narrow."

"I do." With the laptop safely put away, she began to go through the shallow center drawer. "I was also younger once."

Squatting, he looked from the victim's collection of shoes. Twelve pair. Shoes were obviously a weakness. Nothing unusual about that. "Guess not everyone starts out as a plaster saint."

"Guess not."

Maggi closed the center drawer. The desk wobbled dangerously and continued to do so with every move she made as she went through the other two drawers. It was the kind of desk that started out as pieces packed into a cardboard box along with simplistic photographs that were meant to be directions. It couldn't have been any cheaper if it had been constructed out of orange crates. "Looks like being a congressman's staff assistant doesn't pay all that much," she commented.

"Maybe she was in it for the fringe benefits."

Having found an album tucked into the rear corner of the closet, Patrick flipped through the plastic-covered pages until he found something worth looking at. He held up a page with a photograph mounted in the center. It displayed several young people, all smiling broadly and obviously celebrating. In the midst was the congressman. He had his arm draped around two staff members, one a male, the other was Joanne. A banner in the background proclaimed Wiley Is *Your* Congressman.

Maggi moved forward to look at it. Joanne seemed so happy. If this was the last election, that meant it was taken only a few weeks ago. "And maybe he's just a nice boss."

"Maybe."

From his tone, she knew he didn't believe it.

By the time they returned to the station, they had one more piece of information beyond the address book that Maggi had found in Joanne's desk and her laptop. Ochoa had called from the coroner's office to tell them that their victim had also been seven weeks pregnant.

Maggi watched as the rain teased the dormant windshield wipers of his car. They had just pulled into the precinct parking lot when he had gotten the call.

A baby. The killer had gotten two for the price of one. Her own charade in the bank came back to her. *You'll be killing two if you kill me.*

She sighed. "Puts a whole new spin on this, doesn't it?" she commented as Patrick put away his cell phone.

He opened the door. A whoosh of cold air and the smell of rain came in with them. ''That it does, Mary Margaret, that it does.''

She started to tell him again how much she hated to be called that, but then let it go. Some things in life remained the same. The more she voiced her dislike, the more he'd use the names. She was better off just putting up with it. With any luck, she'd find what she needed and terminate this charade Internal Affairs had assigned her before she gave in to the urge to strangle Cavanaugh.

A sense of urgency hovered over her as she hurried up the stairs into the building.

Patrick walked into his apartment, pushing the door shut. It slammed behind him, shuddering in the jamb. He stood in the dark for a moment, absorbing the solitude. And the quiet.

Especially the quiet.

Any way he looked at it, the week had been very long. He and McKenna had canvassed most of the people on the fund-raiser list as well as all those in the victim's address book.

Fortunately, that list had turned out to be a great deal shorter.

Unfortunately, although some of her girlfriends knew she was involved with someone, no one had a name for the mystery man. For all her perky, former cheerleader appearance, Joanne Styles chose to be rather closemouthed when it came to her love affair.

All he and McKenna could gather was that the mystery man had been relatively new in the young woman's life. So new she was afraid to talk about him because of the fear she might jinx it.

At least, that was what she'd told her friends. His money was still on the congressman. In that case, Styles might have been afraid to name him because Wiley had threatened to end the affair if anyone found out about the two of them. After all, he was the family values poster boy.

There was something about the man's wide smile that just rubbed him the wrong way.

He was letting his personal prejudice color his thinking, Patrick upbraided himself. But maybe it wasn't prejudice. Maybe it was a gut feeling. Like the gut feeling that he'd be a whole lot better off without Mc-Kenna as his partner.

As his thoughts shifted to her, he turned the light on. It just seemed wrong to have thoughts about her in the dark. McKenna was still working with Styles's computer, but so far, all the e-mail she'd managed to pull up was unenlightening. If Styles had communicated with her lover/possible killer, it wasn't from her own laptop. The mail there represented communications from and to former college friends and her family, all of whom lived back East somewhere.

He and McKenna had met with the member of the family who had flown out to claim the body. He had to admit that McKenna was better at talking to the distraught older sister than he was. It wasn't the dead that made him uncomfortable; it was the living.

The body had been released earlier today. There was no more information coming from the coroner's office. They'd learned as much as they could there. Besides the victim's own DNA, there was no one with whom to match the fetus's DNA. They had possible motive, but so far, no suspect they could remotely pin down.

Everyone, according to her friends and co-workers, liked Joanne.

Except for one person, he thought grimly, making his way out of his tie and into the kitchen. The father of Styles's baby. The man who had terminated them both.

Tossing the tie onto the back of a chair, Patrick opened his refrigerator. There was nothing except beer in it, but that was all right. Beer was all he wanted. Beer and some peace and quiet.

Going back into the living room, he sat down in front of the television set and left it off. He was vaguely aware of the sounds of cars beyond his window, tires passing through puddles as they made their way somewhere. Concentrating, he could block out the sound.

He couldn't block out the phone.

When he heard it ring, he stiffened. Taking another long gulp from the bottle, he debated letting the phone ring. Most of his work-related calls came through his cell phone. The telephone might mean telemarketers. Lately they had no shame, calling from early until late and invading the weekends. He told himself he needed to get caller ID.

But the telephone was also reserved for family or if there was some kind of an emergency. He stared at it, willing it to stop.

When the ringing went to the count of four, he yanked up the receiver. If it was a telemarketer, he promised himself one hell of a venting session. He could use someone to chew out after holding in his temper this entire week. His new partner had certainly tested him.

"Hello!"

"Patrick, you're barking." His sister's soft voice

filled his ear, the very sound of it soothing him. "Anything wrong?"

He sighed and then relaxed as he sank back into the cushions of the sofa. "Just a homicide case that refuses to cooperate."

"I haven't heard from you all week." Patience didn't add that she worried when she didn't hear from him. Patrick wasn't the type to weather guilt trips and she wasn't the type to bestow them. "How are you?"

"Busy. Tired."

They worked him too hard, she thought, and he never let anyone help him. She loved her brother dearly, but he made her crazy. She wished he was a little more like her cousins.

"Right, the homicide case. You work much too hard, Patrick. When are they going to give you a partner?"

At the mention of the word *partner,* he frowned. This was his haven and he didn't want to think about her when he was at home. "They did."

"Oh?"

He heard curiosity filling her voice. Good old Patience, as nosy as ever.

"Yeah, maybe that's why I need help," he muttered more into his beer than into the receiver.

They both knew what he was like. A hard man to please. That, unfortunately, he got from their father. Patience knew better than to say that to him. But she could say something.

"Give this one a chance, Patrick. Eduardo worked out after you stopped riding him."

"No way in hell this one's going to work out. She's a damn pain in the butt."

Patience's interest immediately increased one hundredfold. He could hear it in her voice.

"She?"

Too late Patrick realized his mistake.

Chapter 6

"Your new partner's a woman?"

Patrick could almost hear the wheels turning in his sister's head. "Temporarily."

"Temporarily?" He couldn't tell if it was confusion or amusement in her voice. "You mean it's a guy dressed as a woman? He's undercover?"

Served him right for opening his big mouth. Trouble was, around his family, he wasn't as vigilant as he was with everyone else. "No, I mean that she's my partner temporarily."

"Until you send her running for the hills and screaming," Patience said.

Patrick took another sip from the amber glass bottle before answering. "She doesn't have to scream."

If he thought he'd closed the subject, he should have known better. Patience had only begun exploring. "What's she like? Is she pretty?"

He frowned as an image of Maggi came unbidden into his head. "That has nothing to do with it," he fairly growled.

"Then she *is* pretty." Now she was grinning. He knew she was grinning. Damn, give Patience an inch and she constructed a regular road out of it. "On a scale of one to ten, what is she?"

An eleven.

The thought came out of nowhere and he shrugged it off as if it were some kind of killer bee buzzing around his head, looking for a tender spot to leave its stinger and die. So what if he noticed that McKenna was a step away from drop-dead gorgeous? He was a detective. He was supposed to notice things. Like the way McKenna's eyebrows drew together every time he called her by her first two names.

Or the way her mouth curved when she thought she was one jump ahead of him on something.

He took a longer drink from his bottle, as if that could wash away the image.

"A huge pain in the butt," he answered Patience. "Not unlike a certain sister can be some of the time. Like now."

"I like her already. What's her name?"

That she professed to like McKenna sight unseen didn't surprise him. Patience liked everyone. In his estimation, she was way too friendly. He worried about her. A lot.

"Don't get too attached," he warned. "She's not going to be around long enough for you to need to learn her name."

"Something you said?"

If only. McKenna appeared to have the hide of a

rhino. A definite contrast to her soft skin. He frowned. The beer was making him lax, leading his thoughts around in circles.

"Patience, you know I work better alone."

"No," she contradicted firmly, "you don't. You only think you do." A note of concern entered her voice. "You've got to stop thinking of yourself as a loner, Patrick."

"I *am* a loner."

They'd gone around about this before. It seemed to him that Patience refused to accept the fact that outside the family, he had no desire to meet anyone halfway.

"You're only a loner until the right woman comes along."

The conversation had taken a sharp turn. "Hey, hold it a second, how did this jump from being about work to my private life?"

Patience sighed softly. "Patrick, you don't have a life."

"That's what makes it private." He finished off his beer and thought about making dinner into a two-course meal by getting a second bottle. "Look, Patience, I'm dog tired and I feel like I've been chasing my own tail for a week—"

"Wouldn't have to do that if there was someone else to chase."

She was like an iron butterfly, soft but strong and determined. He wasn't in the mood for this tonight. "Enough."

"Okay then. Uncle Andrew says to say hi."

"Hi," he mumbled back, knowing there was more to come. With Andrew, there always was, but then, that was his way, and though words hadn't been said to the effect, he loved his uncle, both his uncles, far more than he ever had his own father.

"He also wants to know if you plan on showing up at his table ever again."

Well, that didn't take long, Patrick thought. He eyed the distance between the sofa and the kitchen, wondering if the trip was really worth it. For two cents, he could just sack out here on the sofa and forget about the second beer—he was that tired.

"I'll be there when I'll be there."

"That's what I told him."

He smiled to himself. "Good girl." He paused. Maybe he was just tired, but he thought there'd been something in her voice, something he couldn't place, ever since she'd called. "Everything okay with you?"

"Same as always," she told him cheerfully. "Up to my hips in dogs and cats and the occasional reptile."

His eyes battled to stay open, but he wasn't completely convinced. She sounded a tad too cheerful. "But you're okay."

"Couldn't be better."

Like a small stiletto, guilt slid through him, making tiny slits. "I could drop by tonight."

"What, and have your death on my conscience? No thank you. You sound like you're half-asleep already. Everything's fine, Patrick. Get your rest. I'll talk to you soon."

He let out a long sigh. He was damn tired, but that didn't negate his responsibility. His sister had been the recipient of some very unwanted attention by a man whose African Gray Parrot she'd successfully treated. When this admirer sent a dozen long-stemmed roses to her, she thought he was just grateful that she'd cured the bird, but other gifts followed even after she'd politely but firmly refused them. Was the man bothering her again?

"As long as you're sure everything's okay."

"Patrick, it was a harmless incident. I made too much of it. Fifteen years ago, Steven Jessen would have been called a persistent admirer, nothing more. These days people immediately assume someone with more than a mild interest in another person is a stalker. Forget it," she insisted. "I have."

He wasn't sure if she was just saying that to put him at ease. "Then he hasn't—"

"Nope, he hasn't," she countered quickly, "and I'm sure he won't. Any interest he had in me evaporated when he realized that I came with my own personal section of the Aurora police department." The last time he'd paid a visit to her pet clinic, she'd prominently displayed the group family photograph she had of her brother, cousins and uncles, all in police dress uniforms. That was more than a month ago and Steve hadn't been back since. "But, if you're feeling chatty, we can get back to the subject of your new partner. What did you say her name was again?"

"I didn't. Good night, Patience."

Patience laughed. "Good night, Patrick."

Just before he hung up, he heard dogs barking in the background and absently wondered if his sister was still in the clinic or had gone upstairs to her suite of rooms. Her own two German shepherds made enough noise to sound like a huge pack of dogs.

As far back as he could remember, Patience had always gravitated toward animals, turning them into pets and lavishing her affection on them. Different strokes for different folks, he supposed. As far as he was concerned, a pet rock represented too much work.

Patrick woke up with a start, so much sweat dampening his upper torso it was as if he'd spent the past three hours of troubled sleep on the top rack of a broiler instead of his own bed.

His nightmare was back. With a difference. Now it wasn't Ramirez who he saw being shot down in front of him. It was the woman.

McKenna.

Maggi.

Halfway through the dream, the crack house he and his partner were entering dissolved into the front of a bank. The same bank where she had risked her life to disarm the robber. Except that this time she didn't wrench the gun out of the man's hand. This time it discharged with the bullet hitting her in the forehead the way it had Ramirez.

His heart pounding, Patrick shot the robber dead as he raced to her side. But it was already too late. Maggi died in his arms, her green eyes staring up at him lifelessly. Staring into his soul.

Ripping things out.

He realized he was still breathing hard.

Patrick scrubbed his hands over his face, forcing himself to get a grip.

This just wasn't going to work. He'd tried, given it more time than he'd thought he would, but it just wasn't going to work.

Having a new partner was bad enough. Having a woman as his new partner was far worse. He'd grown up feeling too protective of his mother and sister to switch gears at this point in his life. And feeling protective about McKenna was just going to interfere with the way he responded to situations. He'd be too intent on watching her back to pay the right amount of attention to everything else. All it took was a moment's hesitation and all hell would break loose. He already knew that because of Ramirez. Because he'd been one step behind his partner instead of right there beside him.

It just wasn't going to work.

Four hours later, he was still saying the same thing, except out loud now and to the only man with the authority to make things right.

Patrick cornered his captain as soon as the man walked into the squad room. "It's not going to work."

Captain Reynolds waved him into his office and closed the door behind him before sitting down at his desk and leisurely opening up his container of imported coffee. He studied Patrick over the rim of the paper cup.

Reynolds forced a smile to his lips. "I'm assuming you're talking about your new partner."

"It's not to going to work," Patrick insisted again, his jaw clenched. He didn't want to live with another death on his conscience and she struck him as someone who could easily wind up dead.

The coffee was obviously too hot. Reynolds placed it back on his desk. "It's not that I don't respect your judgment, Cavanaugh, but given your track record as far as taking on new partners goes, I'd say your opinion is a little less than reliable in this matter."

His back against the wall, Patrick tried to strike up

a deal. "Look, I've always told you I work better alone, but if that can't be the case, at least give me another guy."

"McKenna comes highly recommended. She's got commendations up the wazoo from San Francisco—"

Commendations didn't impress him. It was all a matter of politics. Patrick cut his superior short. "I don't care if she's got a letter from the mayor, I don't want to work with her."

"Why?"

Patrick hated explaining himself, but he knew it was the only chance he had to get McKenna reassigned somewhere else. "Having a female around takes the edge off."

Reynolds grinned, as if amused. He blew on his coffee before taking a tentative sip. "This is a side of you I didn't know about. I didn't think you noticed women, Cavanaugh. I would have been a little worried if it wasn't for the fact that I don't think you really notice anything except the job you're working on." Taking another sip, longer this time, Reynolds replaced the container on his stained blotter. "Not that I'm complaining, mind you. You're damn good at what you do—lucky for you," he tagged on.

Patrick could read between the lines. "You're not going to reassign her, are you?"

"Nope."

Ordinarily he didn't push. But then, ordinarily he didn't ask for favors, either. He might as well go all the way. "Can I ask why?"

"Because I like having the best work for me and everyone else is happy in their little niches."

"I'm not happy," Patrick growled.

Reynolds shrugged. "You are never happy, that goes without saying." Obviously needing to keep the peace and give Cavanaugh a false sense of hope, he added, "Okay, tell you what. Give it a few more weeks. If you're still butting heads, I'll see what I can do. I have to say I'm surprised, though."

"Why?"

Draining half the container, Reynolds wiped his mouth with the napkin he'd brought in.

"Usually it's your partner in here, begging to be reassigned. I guess she doesn't find you as hard to work with as you find her. Either that, or she's got a hell of a lot more stick-to-itiveness than most of her predecessors."

She had a hell of a lot more something all right, Patrick thought, but he didn't know exactly what the label for it was.

"Whatever."

Annoyed, disgusted and more than vaguely unsettled, Patrick strode out of the office. He hated wasting time and he'd just wasted a precious amount of it trying to reason with a man who was far more interested in the kind of PR he could generate with the public than he was about the actual internal workings of his department.

His mood black, Patrick decided to go back to the morgue to review the original autopsy report on Joanne Styles to see if anything out of the ordinary struck him this time.

The morgue was deadly quiet. There were no autopsies in progress at the moment. The M.E. had handed Patrick his own copy of Joanne's autopsy before leaving the room. Patrick made himself as comfortable as possible, sitting down to read at a desk that was equally likely to hold the coroner's lunch as it was a victim's final effects.

The silence enveloped him as he read words that he'd gone over time and again already. Concentrating to the exclusion of everything else, the noise almost made him jump.

Maggi marched in at the far end of the room, hitting the door with the flat of her hand and sending it flying open. The door banged against the wall, summoning his attention.

She looked as if she were breathing fire. Her eyes had narrowed, boring small, burning holes into him before she ever reached him.

All in all, he had to admit she looked rather magnificent, like one of those paintings he'd seen by that artist who reveled in strong, beautiful, scantily clad women warriors. All she needed was a spear and a mythical steed.

It had taken Maggi several minutes to find out where Patrick was in the building. Her temper had increased with every second that passed and was now a hairbreadth away from reaching critical mass.

Facing him squarely, she demanded, "Who the hell do you think you are?"

He was as calm as she was angry. "Pay stub says Patrick Cavanaugh."

For two cents, she would have doubled her fists and beat on him even though the blows probably would have hurt her more than him.

"Don't get smart with me, Cavanaugh. I just heard you asked the captain for another partner."

Since the door was closed, she'd had to have heard that from Brooks, the only one in the squad who could read lips. Probably trying to cull favor with her, Patrick thought darkly.

"Asked, didn't receive."

Despite the fact that he'd been trained not to look away from a dangerous animal and he definitely placed his new partner in that category, Patrick lowered his eyes back to the folder on the table.

Incensed, resenting the way he insisted on treating her, Maggi swept the folder aside with the back of her hand. Pages rained down onto the floor. Her eyes blazed, daring him to pick them up. The pages remained where they were.

"Do you realize what kind of implications your asking for a new partner has? It makes me look incompetent. That you don't trust me to watch your back."

He felt something inside him stirring in response to the look on her face, to the fire in her eyes. He banked it down. Just pure animal reaction.

"All it says is that we're incompatible," he told her mildly, "and you wouldn't be the first partner to find yourself in that position." He bent down to pick up the pages, then placed them into the folder.

"If you have a problem with me, you *come* to me, you *talk* to me," she insisted. "You don't go behind my back and talk to the captain." She would have thought that someone like him would have respected that kind of a code. He wasn't a team player, he was a loner. Loners didn't run to their superiors with something.

He shrugged, his disinterest rankling her. "Like I

said, we're incompatible. If we weren't, I would have talked to you.''

''Why?'' Maggi spread her hands on the desk before him as she leaned into his face and demanded an answer. ''Why are we incompatible? How do you even know? We've only been working together for a little more than a week and I haven't gone against you once, even when I felt you were wrong.''

His interest was aroused despite himself. ''When was that?''

Maggi waved away his question. ''Doesn't matter. I'm your partner—you're supposed to talk to me.''

He looked at her, his gaze steady. ''I can't talk to you.''

Her voice softened slightly. ''Well, you're going to have to try, Cavanaugh. Because I am your partner and I am not going anywhere.'' She paused, needing an answer, something to hang his reactions on. If she understood, she could fix it. She needed him to trust her. ''Is it because I'm a woman?''

Her face was too close, invading his space. Patrick leaned back in his chair, balancing it on two legs. ''Partly.''

Furious, Maggi struggled to swallow the scathing curse that rose to her lips. That wasn't going to do anything but lower her to his level, the bastard. Old-fashioned prejudice. She should have known. Cavanaugh was a throwback, a Neanderthal. Well, she wasn't about to let that get in the way of her assignment.

She held out her arms for inspection. ''Look, two arms, two legs, all the same working parts as any other partner.''

He looked at her pointedly. He'd never had a partner

with a twenty-five-inch waist before and he was willing to bet that her legs were a hell of a lot better looking than Ramirez's had ever been. Not to mention the obvious differences.

"Not really."

She met his look head-on. Sex, he was talking about sex. That was never going to be a problem between them. "That doesn't enter into this."

His eyes never left hers. "Doesn't it?"

Suddenly she heard a strange rushing noise in her ears. Maggi blocked it out, refusing to flinch, to give.

"No. I'm not letting it, and you shouldn't, either. We're not dating, Cavanaugh, we're working together. I know partners tend to get closer than some married people, but you certainly don't strike me as someone who'd leave himself open to that. You probably never even learned Ramirez's first name or knew anything about him."

His expression never changed. "Eduardo. He had a wife and three kids. Anything else you want to get wrong about me?"

She blew out a breath. Maybe the man did have feelings and she'd just stepped on them.

"Okay, look, I'm sorry. We'll start over." Before he could respond, she extended her hand to Patrick. "Hi, I'm Detective McKenna. According to the captain, we're supposed to be working together. You watch my back, I'll watch yours. You have any questions, any problems, call me. Anytime. We'll work something out. Deal?"

He regarded her hand for a moment before silently gripping it with his own.

Ochoa popped his head in. "Hey, you two just about

through in here? You're making enough racket to raise the dead." He pretended to look over to the steel drawers that were the temporary resting places for the bodies he had yet to examine.

"Just leaving, Dr. Ochoa." Maggi looked at Patrick pointedly. "See you later, *partner*."

The doctor paused to watch as the young detective made her exit. Sighing, he shook his head wistfully. "That woman's got one mighty fine rear view." He glanced at Patrick. "Wonder if she makes that much noise when she's making love."

Patrick rose. "I wouldn't know."

And it was something he damn well wasn't planning on finding out.

Chapter 7

It was the last booth in an out-of-the-way coffee shop that still believed that the only ingredient necessary for a decent cup of coffee was caffeine. John Halliday, the head of Internal Affairs, had elected to meet with her here for a progress report.

Maggi kept her eyes on the door rather than on the heavyset, aging man sitting opposite her. She was afraid someone she knew might walk in. To the untrained observer, she and John probably looked like a father sharing an early cup of black energy with his daughter before they hurried off to their separate worlds.

She warmed her hands around the cup, knowing that Halliday was waiting for an answer. She didn't have one to give him. It was lack of evidence she was finding herself up against, not proof of innocence. Exoneration by default was not what they were looking for.

"So far, nothing," she told him. "The man puts in

a long, full day, then goes home." The surface of her coffee shimmered, catching the weak overhead light just before she brought the cup to her lips. It was hotter than it was good.

The thin lips beneath the shaggy mustache drew together in a tight frown. "Are you getting close to him?"

"Not yet." And it wasn't for lack of trying. The half shrug beneath her gray jacket was curtailed frustration. "He's like a fortress."

Halliday's brown eyes were steady as they regarded her. "Are you familiar with the story about the Trojan horse?"

Maggi laughed softly to herself. "I guarantee that if Cavanaugh had been inside that fort with the Greeks, he would have burned the Trojan horse down before he'd ever allow them to bring it inside." She hoped Halliday knew better than to think she was throwing in the towel at this point.

"That's why I figured you were the best one for the job."

"Because I'm a woman?"

"Because you're good," he countered. His eyes swept over her in a manner she found almost unnervingly impartial. He was dissecting and reassembling her in the space of time it took to draw a long breath. "Of course, being an attractive woman doesn't hurt, either."

The coffee was growing on her. She took another long sip. "Thanks, but I don't think Cavanaugh's noticed."

Halliday's amusement surprised her. "Trust me, Maggi, dead men notice that you're attractive."

She tried to read between the lines. If he was looking for someone to go above and beyond the regulations, he'd selected the wrong woman. She wasn't about to give new meaning to the term "undercover" just to get the assignment done.

"You're not suggesting—"

"No," Halliday interrupted quickly. "I'm not. Just use a little of what they used to call feminine wiles in my day."

Right, as if that would work on a man like Cavanaugh. She grinned. "I think they still call them that, but I'm not sure I have them."

The look he gave her told her that he knew better. "And if I believe that, there's a bridge out there with my name on it."

Maggi finished her coffee and placed the cup down on the cracked saucer.

"You never know, there might be." Her smile faded as she glanced at her watch. It was getting late. The less explaining she had to do to Cavanaugh, the better. "I should get going." Sliding to the end of the booth, she sighed before she got up. "I'm beginning to feel like a spy."

Halliday signaled the waitress for a refill. "That's good, because you are."

Spies were only glamorous in the movies, Maggi thought. In real life, they felt ambivalent and gritty because of the secrets they were forced to carry around with them. Lines began to blur the moment people entered into the picture. Her assignment and her loyalties had been crystal clear when she'd started out, but now part of her couldn't help feeling like a voyeur.

That was because she was ascribing her own set of values to Cavanaugh, she reminded herself. And that was probably a fallacy that would lead her down the wrong road. Cavanaugh wasn't her. If he'd had her values, he wouldn't be under suspicion for being on the take to begin with.

"See you around." Rising, Maggi made her way past the waitress.

Patrick didn't bother glancing up when she walked into the cubicle. He could tell it was McKenna by the sound of her heels making contact with the vinyl flooring. She had a certain gait, just distinct enough to stick in his mind. He found that annoying, too.

"You're late."

"Stopped to get you breakfast." Maggi set down a white paper bag with a doughnut-shop logo imprinted on the side on his desk.

Breakfast. It reminded him of his phone call with his sister the other day and the fact that he hadn't been by his uncle's house for breakfast in several weeks. Retired, Uncle Andrew liked to gather his family together around the table whenever possible. Cooking was his passion now that his days on the force were over.

Patrick assuaged his conscience by reminding himself that he'd put in an appearance at Thanksgiving, although that had been partially a matter of self-preservation. Not to have shown up might have brought about a family schism. In all likelihood, his uncle would have sent one or more of his cousins to his apartment to drag him back to the table. Uncle Andrew took his holidays seriously.

He caught himself wanting to smile but resisted the urge. Instead, he moved the bag she'd brought to the side as if it were an annoyance that had fallen in his path.

"I don't do breakfast."

She'd picked up the jelly doughnuts on her way out

of the coffee shop to give herself an alibi. Even so, it bothered her to have him reject her offering.

"Save it for lunch, snack, wear it—I don't care." Reining in her temper, she sat down in the cubicle and swung her chair around to face him instead of her desk. What the hell was his problem, anyway? "I'm just trying to be nice here."

"No need."

The words were curt, meant to shut her out. Again. She felt like pounding on him.

Whoa, get a grip, Mag. You're not going to get anywhere if you lose your cool.

"You know," she began, measuring out her words, "you are a damn hard man to get close to."

This time, he raised his eyes to her. "We're not supposed to be close, Mary Margaret. We're just supposed to be working together."

"That doesn't seem to be going all that well, either, Paddy."

If she meant to get a rise out of him, she failed. He merely nodded toward the exit. "You know the way to the door."

This wasn't getting her anywhere. Determined to gain his confidence, she did a complete one-eighty and focused her attention on the homicide they were handling. "Okay, so where are we on the Styles case?"

Patrick never missed a beat. He indicated the time line on the back wall of the cubicle. They'd pieced it together from information they'd garnered since the body had been found.

"My money's on the congressman." He looked at her pointedly, waiting for her to contradict him. Waiting to cut her argument down.

She surprised him.

"I tend to agree, especially since we found out that Mrs. Wiley didn't attend the party and several other people thought they saw Wiley with Joanne at least once during the course of the evening. That makes his performance in the office about not recognizing her immediately a little suspect." She stopped, his scrutiny getting to her. "What are you staring at?"

Patrick shrugged, the movement careless. "Nothing. Just a little surprised that you're willing to come around, that's all."

"I'm not 'willing to come around,' Cavanaugh. I'm willing to let the evidence speak to me." Of all the prejudice, bigoted, thickheaded chauvinists, why did this one have to be her assignment? "What do you think—I've got a crush on the man and refuse to see any other viewpoint than the official party line?"

There was just the slightest hint of a smile on his lips. Or was that a badly concealed smirk? "Something like that."

"One, I don't get crushes." Even as she set him straight, she had a feeling her words were falling on deaf ears. "Two, I'm a police detective and a damn good one. That means I deal in facts and do my job to the best of my abilities."

"Nice to know." Leaning back in his chair, Patrick studied her for a long moment, trying to see beyond the long, blond silky hair and the mouth that always seemed to be moving. The mouth that was so quick to smile and generate a warm, seductive atmosphere around her. "Okay, if this was your case, what's your next move?"

"This *is* my case," she reminded him tersely. "But if you mean what would I do if I were the primary on it, I'd go back to see the congressman again, ask him a few more questions. Try to see if maybe I could jog his memory a little in light of the fact that at least three people saw him talking to Joanne Styles at some time during the party.'' She waited for him to shoot down her suggestion and braced herself to rebut him.

Instead, he rose from his chair. ''Sounds like a plan to me.'' With that, he began to head for the door. He stopped only long enough to look over his shoulder. ''You coming?''

''Yes.''

The man was a trial, she thought as she grabbed her coat. A real trial.

''Of course I might have talked to her,'' Wiley allowed less than forty-five minutes later. He'd prefaced their audience by saying he only had five minutes before heading out for a meeting.

Wiley took a long drag of his cigarette before continuing. Beside him, a tall, slender air purifier was doing double duty in an attempt to help clear the air.

''But you have to understand, I talked to a great many people during the course of that party. During the course of any party. That's both the up- and downside of my position. I have to glad-hand a great deal. After a while, the names and faces begin to swim together.'' Though he made a point of looking at both of them, more than half his words were directed at Maggi. ''Unfortunately for me, I don't have one of those photographic memories so I have to pretend that I know everyone to keep from offending someone. Sounds a little shallow, I know, but in my line of work I try to offend as few people as absolutely possible.'' He flashed a quick, disarming smile. ''Every vote counts, you know.''

Tapping his cigarette ash into the full ashtray on the corner of his desk, he seemed to note the way Maggi watched him. His grin was almost sheepish. "Yes, I know, it's a terrible habit."

There was no judgment intended on her part. "I was just thinking that this is supposed to be a smoke-free environment." According to state law, all public places of work in California were to be kept smoke free.

"Busted," Wiley admitted. He nodded at the tall, silent column. "Hence the air purifier. I'm really trying to cut down, but with the pace of the campaign and the stress of the job, I'm finding it difficult. But I guess it's better than drinking, and I never let myself be photographed with a cigarette." He looked as if he was debating snuffing out the cigarette, then decided not to. "Don't want to be a bad role model for the kids." The grin grew more sheepish. "I try to limit myself to five, but sometimes I cheat by emptying out the ashtray. That makes it look as if I haven't had any and, well..." His voice trailed off as he looked at Maggi.

Maggi's smile in response was soft, easy. "I understand."

To Patrick's disgust, his partner was really beginning to sound as if she was awestruck by the man. He would have thought after what she'd said in the office, just before they left for here, she could see through this tin demigod.

"Let me empty that for you," she offered.

Then, before the congressman could demur, Maggi took the ashtray and threw its contents into the wastepaper basket beside his desk. Wiley smiled at her.

It wasn't the smile of a predator, Patrick thought, trying to be fair. But with little effort, it could have been.

"If you don't remember speaking to her, then just how did she get into your car, Congressman?" Patrick wanted to know.

Rather than looking annoyed or cornered, Wiley simply spread his hands out in puzzled consternation.

"I really don't have an answer to that." All he could do was reiterate what he'd previously said. "As I already told you, I allow my staff access to my cars."

"There's no log, no record?" Patrick pressed.

The sheepish grin was back. That was for people like McKenna, Patrick thought. He just wasn't buying it.

"I'm afraid I'm lax that way."

From what he'd learned, Wiley was a very organized man. What he maintained didn't jibe with the established image.

"Can you remember who had it last?"

Wiley shook his head. "You'll have to ask my office manager, Travis Abbott. He handles the everyday details for me. But I just want you to know that everyone on my staff is trustworthy," he added as if he felt honor-bound to make the statement. "I've never had a pair of cuff links stolen, much less a car."

Maggi could feel herself being led further and further away from the heart of the original discussion. "This is a lot bigger than car theft, Congressman," she said.

The congressman sobered. "I know, murder." His hands folded before him, he shook his head. "I still can't believe it, one of my own people. It's so ugly."

"Uglier still when the victim was pregnant," Patrick told him.

Wiley's eyes widened in shock. "Pregnant? She was pregnant?"

"Coroner says seven weeks." Patrick's voice, like his expression, was grim.

Wiley covered his mouth, as if to keep back words wreathed in horror. "My God, that poor girl."

There was appeal in his eyes as he looked at Maggi, although it wasn't clear to her just what he was appealing to. She chalked it up to confusion.

"I had no idea." The congressman took another drag of his cigarette, a long one this time. Ashes hung suspended on the end of it, defying gravity. "I had no idea," he repeated quietly.

Just then, there was a knock on the door and a pert brunette they'd interviewed several days ago stuck her head in. She nodded toward them, then looked at Wiley.

"Sorry to bother you, Congressman, but you have a meeting with Mr. Donovan in less than half an hour and really should be going. Todd has the car waiting for you out front."

"Right." He rose, still appearing a little dazed. He extended his hand to Maggi out of purely ingrained habit.

As Patrick watched, Maggi brushed her hand against her jacket before shaking Wiley's hand. Had she done that because her hand was damp and she didn't want Wiley to know? Damn it, the last thing they needed now was a case of hero-worship getting in their way.

"I'm sorry I can't be more help," Wiley apologized.

"Don't underestimate yourself, Congressman," she said sweetly. "You've been a great deal of help."

Wiley smiled, nodded at Patrick and then hurried away to the waiting car.

Patrick lingered a moment before leaving the office. And then he walked out the door, struggling to hold on to a temper that seemed to come out of nowhere, flaring. As he punched the button for the elevator, he turned on her and demanded, "What the hell was that?"

"What?" She braced herself.

"Back there." He jerked a thumb at the office they'd walked out of. "Cleaning up after him, wiping your hand so that it wasn't offensive when you shook his. Are you opting to fill the dead girl's place?"

She stared at him, torn between taking umbrage and just laughing at him. "If I didn't know better, I'd say you sounded jealous."

Leave it to a woman to come up with the most ridiculous take on something. Her accusation almost didn't merit a response, but he decided to put her in her place. The elevator arrived and he walked in, jabbing for the first floor before she got in behind him. "To be jealous, I'd have to care."

"And you don't."

"All I care about is how the department comes off, having you do pirouettes around the man who likely killed what might very well have been his pregnant mistress." Arriving at the first floor, they got out.

Maggi hurried to keep up, silently damning his long legs. She was going to have to start working out again if she was going to finish this assignment in good condition.

"He didn't know she was pregnant," she told him as Patrick unlocked the car. "You can't fake that kind of look."

He got in but didn't buckle up. "You can fake any kind of a look, any kind of response."

Something drove her to egg him on. He was irritating the hell out of her. "And you'd know this why? Because of your vast acting experience?"

"Look, the guy's an operator. I'm not saying he's

not a good congressman, but he's a man married to a demanding wife, and this pretty young thing bats her eyes at him, making his blood rush and just like that—'' he snapped his fingers ''—he's off to the races.''

''I still say he was too stunned when you told him about the baby. That was real.'' About to buckle up, Maggi stopped. A strange look appeared on Cavanaugh's face, one she couldn't begin to read. ''What?''

Instead of saying anything, Patrick let actions do his talking for him. Very slowly, he extended his fingers and just barely touched her cheek, all the while looking into her eyes. Holding her prisoner.

Maggi felt her breath stop in her lungs.

Any demands she might have made as to what the hell he thought he was doing never made it to her lips.

Time stood still. Her pulse didn't as it went into rapid overdrive, hammering hard. When he finally leaned in to her, she felt herself going into a complete meltdown even before his lips touched hers.

At the last moment, he drew back. Disappointment created a huge void in her.

His eyes were knowing, as if he didn't need her to agree to the kiss. He was right and he knew it.

''Made you believe I was going to kiss you, didn't I?'' he asked.

Maggi felt as if she were stepping out of the *Twilight Zone* and still not sure if she would find solid ground or empty space beneath her feet. She stalled for time, trying to pull herself together.

''What?''

''Just now, you thought I was going to kiss you. Even though nothing's gone down between us, even though we mix together like oil and water. You still thought I was going to kiss you.''

Maggi's breath returned in tiny dribbles and she husbanded it before saying in what she hoped was a normal voice, ''The thought crossed my mind.''

''Because I wanted it to.''

And maybe, just maybe, he added silently, because the idea was not exactly abhorrent or foreign to him, either. It had buzzed around in the back of his mind now like an annoying itch. One he instinctively knew that, if he scratched, would just increase. He'd been testing himself more than the theory he was tendering to Maggi.

''And you weren't even predisposed to believe I'd do that. Wiley already knew you were buying his act, hook, line and sinker.'' When she cocked her head, silently asking for an explanation, he said, ''You were practically playing his maid, for God's sake, dumping out his ashtray like that.''

''I was playing detective,'' she countered with every fiber she could muster.

Damn, but he'd just about undone her. She should have pushed him away, should have laughed in his face, not just sat there holding her breath.

Waiting.

She should have had more than doughnuts for breakfast. Sugar always did make mush out of her brain.

Patrick's expression told her he wasn't buying what she was selling. ''And how's that?''

It was her turn to play out the line and reel him in. ''We need Wiley's DNA, don't we? To see if it matches the baby's.''

''Yes, but—''

''Think the lab can get something useful from one

of these? I'm assuming there's got to be a little bit of saliva on at least one of them.''

And then, before he could ask her what she was talking about, Maggi opened her hand and produced three of the butts that had been in the congressman's ashtray.

Chapter 8

He stared at Maggi's opened hand. On her upturned palm, a smattering of ashes were mixed with the remnants of three cigarettes, smoked all the way down to the filters. "How did you get those?"

"I palmed them. From Wiley's ashtray." Taking out her handkerchief, she placed the evidence in the center, then carefully folded it and placed it back in her pocket. She made a mental note to have her jacket cleaned.

Patrick shook his head as he turned over the engine. "Damn but you're more resourceful than I gave you credit for."

Satisfied with herself, Maggi smiled. She supposed that was as close to a compliment as she was going to get from the man. "I'm a lot more things than you give me credit for. Apology accepted."

He studied her for a moment, then they left the parking area. "Hacker, thief, anything else I should know about you?"

Yes, that I'm really here to spy on you. The thought exploded in her chest with the force of a magnum bullet. She kept her face impassive and brazened it out. "Lots of things. You'll learn as we go along."

He had no idea why he found that promise sexy. Maybe it was because he found the woman sexy. Maybe because he'd rattled more than just her cage with that near kiss. He hadn't allowed it to come to proper fruition, not from any lack of interest on his part, but from a strong sense of survival. Sex had no business here, or in his life right now.

All he wanted was to be a good cop. Everything else, beyond his existing family ties, was just so much extra complication he wasn't willing to take on. And a relationship, any sort of a relationship, meant complications.

He set his mouth grimly and stared straight ahead as he wove his way through the traffic. "Let's get these to the lab."

His curt tone took her by surprise. Maggi tried to tell herself this made her job more challenging, more interesting, but right now she was getting more frustrated.

Nothing good ever came easy, her mother used to say to her. Too bad the woman hadn't lived long enough to make her own words come true, Maggi thought. One way or another, she was going to get some good out of this. She was either going to out a dirty cop or save the reputation of a clean, albeit ill-tempered, one.

She tried not to notice how the silence ate its way further into the interior of the car.

Processing the DNA evidence took longer than either one of them was happy about. While they waited, they went back to investigating the people who'd known Joanne, trying to catch a break, trying to find out if anyone knew the identity of her mysterious lover in case the DNA samples Maggi had brought turned out not to be a match.

When the call came from the lab, they lost no time in getting there.

For once the regular technician appeared too overwhelmed with work to give in to his normal flair for drama. Instead, he merely handed Patrick the sheet of paper that was the end result of testing and typing.

"Close," he pronounced.

Patrick looked at the summary. At first glance, it made no sense to him and might have just as well been written in Greek. "What do you mean, 'close'? It's either a match or it isn't."

Harry Everett paused to take a drink from the capped bottle of water that seemed to be in endless supply by his desk. "I mean the baby's DNA is not an exact match to what you gave me, but it's definitely in the same family."

"Same family, you mean like a brother or sister?" Maggi asked. She glanced at Patrick and wondered what he was thinking. He'd been so certain Wiley was the baby's father.

Harry leaned back in his chair. It creaked in response. "Son, daughter, mother, father. You know, the old definition of family."

"So it's not the congressman." Maggi deliberately kept an innocent expression on her face. She could tell by the rigid set of Cavanaugh's chin that this annoyed the hell out of him.

Harry's eyes shifted back and forth between two pages as he made one last comparison. "Doesn't look like it.'' He moved the printed page back, clearing the space for the next assignment he had to tackle. ''Anything else I can do for you?''

''This'll do, thanks,'' Patrick muttered as he folded the sheet of paper and slid it into his breast pocket. He looked at Maggi as they left the lab and came to the only conclusion left to them. ''If it's not the father, it's the son.''

They'd interviewed Blake Wiley briefly, along with everyone else. Apparently he deserved a second look.

''Wiley's son is part of his staff,'' Maggi mentioned, thinking out loud. Before Patrick could say they already knew that, she told him something she didn't think he knew. She'd done her homework. ''Only because he can't seem to find work anywhere else. It's one of those clichéd success stories. Dad makes good, son makes trouble. Doesn't have enough backbone to do anything on his own, can't handle living in the shadow of his famous father. Spends his whole life looking for himself when he hasn't gone anywhere.'' She smiled at him as they stopped by the elevator banks. ''Have I impressed you yet?''

He frowned at her as he pressed for the down elevator. The doors opened instantly. The car hadn't gone to another floor while they were in the lab. ''Takes a lot to impress me.''

Maggi reached and pressed for the ground floor before he could. ''I'll keep working on it.''

Talk about getting under his skin. She'd managed to accomplish that in a record amount of time. ''Why? Why would you want to impress me?''

Maggi gave him a half truth, just to see what he would say. ''Because you're my Mount Everest. I don't climb to high places—they tend to make me dizzy—

but everyone's got to have a challenge and you're mine.''

"Why?"

She laughed. When the elevator door opened again, there were several people waiting to get in. They threaded their way through.

"You know you're beginning to sound like an inquisitive five-year-old?'' She saw that the observation didn't win any points with him. This time, she told him the truth, or a least a tiny piece of it. ''Because I never met anyone who didn't like me—eventually.''

Patrick noticed it had started to rain again. This kind of weather drove men to suicide. Or to relocate. He raised his collar. ''So you're saying that you're out to get everyone you meet to like you?''

"More or less.'' She made the shrug look careless, but she had told him the truth. Because in an odd sort of way, it mattered to her. She *did* like to have people like her.

He looked around for the car. Seeing it, he started to lead the way. A steady light drizzle accompanied him through the crowded lot. ''It's an impossible dream.''

Hurrying after him, she raised her voice. ''Hey, we've all got to have goals to keep us going. If it were easy, it wouldn't be a goal. It'd be a fact of life, and that's no fun.''

Turning, he looked at her for a long moment, not knowing what to make of her, or the feelings that stirred up inside him. Since he was treading on unfamiliar ground, he retreated and found another path. ''We've got a murderer to catch.''

Maggi smiled at him. ''That we do.'' She gestured toward the car. ''Lead on, Macduff.''

He said nothing, merely shook his head as he walked the rest of the way to the car.

She reached it first, waiting for him to open the doors. Once he did, she got in, quickly shutting the door and keeping the fine mist out. "By the way, when do I get to say I told you so?"

Buckled up, he refused to look in her direction. "Not anytime soon if you want to keep on living."

"I'll take that under advisement."

Unable to stop, he glanced at her. "That includes smirking."

"I wasn't smirking."

His frown deepened. Now she was lying outright. "Your mouth was curving."

"I smile a lot, or haven't you noticed?"

Turning, he looked behind them as he backed out. The rain made everything three times as hazardous. It seemed to him that no one knew how to handle a little precipitation in California. "Well, don't, it's distracting."

"What, smiling or smirking?"

"Both."

Maggi settled back in her seat. A bolt of lightning creased the brow of the sky. It looked like they were in for it. "Okay, then you try smiling."

Busy with watching the road, he thought he hadn't heard her correctly. "What?"

"If we both frown," Maggi explained, "there'll be no yin and yang."

He knew she was making another pitch for camaraderie. He needed a friend like he needed an extra toe. Both made navigating difficult. "There's not going to be a Starsky and Hutch, either."

Maggi's mouth dropped open. "You know about Starsky and Hutch?"

Another mistake. He sighed. "Do you *ever* stop talking?"

"Do you ever stop being grumpy?" she countered.

He wondered what the manual said about strangling your partner and if it ever fell in the realm of justifiable homicide.

Locating Blake Wiley proved to be relatively easy. They found him closeted with his secretary, examining the shape of her ear. She was on his lap at the time and he was using the taste approach. He was none too happy to see them and unhappier still when they sent his secretary back to her desk.

"Look, I already told you everything I know," he protested.

"Notice how he's telling the wall and not us?" Maggi said to Patrick.

For once, Patrick played along. "Why is that, do you suppose?"

Maggi got into Blake's face. "Could be he's afraid of making eye contact, afraid of what we might see if he did."

"My contacts," Blake retorted flippantly. "You'd see my contacts and nothing else. My father can have you up on harassment charges, you know."

"Hiding behind Daddy?" Patrick asked, deliberately baiting him. "Don't you get tired of that? Don't you ever wonder what it's like to stand up on your own two feet instead of letting him carry you?"

Blake became incensed. "You don't know what you're talking about."

"Don't I?" Patrick pressed.

The door to Blake's office flew open. "What's going on here?" Congressman Wiley asked as he entered.

"Does he always come in without knocking?" Patrick asked Blake. "No respect for your privacy, is there?" He was rewarded with an irritated, sullen look, directed not at him but at the congressman.

"Blake, what are they asking you?" Far from the smiling man they'd encountered the other two times, Wiley appeared worried as he looked from his son to the two detectives.

Patrick answered him before Blake could reply. "We're having an interesting conversation with your son." His eyes indicated the door behind Wiley. "You don't have to be here, Congressman. He's not a minor."

Blake snorted. There was nothing but contempt in his eyes as he looked at his father. "My father'll tell you I'm not very bright, either. At least, he doesn't think so."

Wiley clenched his hands at his sides impotently. It was clear that he wanted to say more but felt he couldn't. "Stop talking, Blake."

As Maggi watched, Patrick shook his head. "Now see, that might have been your first mistake, Congressman. You named him Blake. If you'd called him something ordinary, like Jim or Bill, he might have stood a chance in this world. But right there, you doomed him. You made him stand out for all the wrong reasons." Patrick glanced at Blake. "And he didn't like it."

Wiley appeared at a loss. "What the hell are you talking about?"

He noted that Maggi looked both surprised and impressed at his dabbling with psychology. "Just a little theory my partner and I were working on." He dropped the friendly tone. "The rest of it goes that your son here killed Joanne Styles."

Indignation reddened the congressman's cheeks. Or was that fear? Maggi wondered.

"That's ridiculous," Wiley cried.

"She was carrying his baby." Maggi had interjected so quietly, at first it was as if the congressman hadn't heard her. But when his eyes shifted toward her, she saw no surprise in them.

Figured it out, did you, Congressman?

Blake shifted in his seat as if it was suddenly becoming warmer than he liked. "Small detail I forgot to tell you, Dad." Though his mouth twisted in a mocking smirk, there was genuine fear in the younger man's eyes as they moved from person to person.

"Not another word," Wiley warned. "I'll get Christopher on the line." Picking up the telephone, he looked at Patrick. "He's not saying anything until I can get my lawyer in here."

"He doesn't have to say much." Maggi's tone was polite but firm. "We have the DNA, sir." Wiley looked sharply at his son. "He didn't give us his, we have yours."

Wiley looked stunned, then incredulous. "Mine?"

She could see the denial that was about to come. "You really should cut down on smoking, sir."

The light dawned, ushering in outrage and desperation. "You had no right to take those cigarette butts."

"I'm afraid that once you throw something out, it becomes public." Then, in case he'd forgotten, she added, "You had me throw out the cigarette butts. Our lab found that the baby's DNA was close enough to be tagged in the family." Both she and Patrick looked pointedly at Wiley's son.

Blake gripped the armrests hard enough that the leather groaned. "So I got her pregnant. That doesn't prove I killed her."

Patrick didn't bother talking to Blake. It wasn't the son who was pulling the strings here. "Now that we know what we're looking for, it'll speed things along. Just a matter of time, Congressman. Science has made wonderful strides. Even somebody as thickheaded as me knows that," Patrick said.

Maggi couldn't help wondering if Cavanaugh had thrown that in for her benefit.

"Can't hide from the evidence," Patrick continued. "Your son's best bet is to make a full statement now." He looked at Blake, getting his message across. "It might go easier on him if he cooperates."

Wiley closed his eyes for a moment and Maggi could see that he was genuinely suffering. Life had gotten out of hand for him.

When he opened his eyes, he looked ten years older. And determined. "All right, what's it going to take to make this go away?"

Patrick cocked his head as if he hadn't heard correctly. "What?"

"You heard me," Wiley said, exasperation echoing in his voice. He reached into his inside pocket for his personal checkbook. "What's it going to take? How much money do you want to just walk away from this?"

Maggi held her breath. This couldn't have gone any better if she'd orchestrated it. When Patrick looked at her, she spread her hands as if to say she was leaving the show up to him. She wasn't sure if his skeptical expression was intended for her or Wiley.

"Are you trying to buy us?" Patrick's emotionless tone gave nothing away.

"A little bluntly put, but yes." Wiley saw the look on Maggi's face. "Don't look so surprised. Everyone has a price. What's yours?"

Why wasn't McKenna saying anything? Patrick wondered. Why wasn't she protesting and tossing the offer back in Wiley's teeth? Patrick had no idea what kind of a game she was playing. He would have sworn that, despite the fact that she was a royal pain in the ass and irritatingly smug, his new partner was honest. But maybe that was something she'd wanted him to believe.

He kept her in view as he told Wiley, "I'm going to forget you said that, Congressman, because McKenna here seems to think you stand for something."

The desperation grew. Wiley struggled to keep it in check. He was a man on a tightrope, afraid of a misstep, afraid of falling onto the rocks below. "I *do* stand for something—family values—and I'm trying to keep my family together. This'll kill his mother and sister."

Despite the sincerity in Wiley's voice, Patrick wasn't buying it. "And this wouldn't have anything to do with keeping your campaign on track, or making sure that the opposition doesn't have any mud to fling when you're up for reelection?"

"No, damn it, it doesn't." Wiley's temper flared before he could get it under control. "Sorry." With effort, he tried again. "Don't you understand? He's my son. If he can't make it out in the work world, what chance is he going to have in prison?"

Almost trembling, Blake still spit out, "Your faith in me is touching, Dad."

The comment seemed to push the congressman over

the limit. He turned on his son. "If you'd ever given me something to work with, maybe I'd have some faith." Shutting his eyes, he seemed to center himself. The next moment, he was placing the checkbook on the desk, ready to write. "Now, what'll it be?"

Patrick placed his hand over the checkbook. "The truth, Congressman."

Wiley stared at him, frozen in disbelief.

"Since you're willing to buy our silence, you obviously know more about the situation than you've told us." He told Wiley something they both knew. "Knowing makes you an accessory after the fact."

"You're just trying for a bigger payoff." One look at the congressman told them that the man fervently hoped he was right. The alternative was something he couldn't deal with.

"Yeah," Patrick allowed, "I guess I am." He saw the look on Maggi's face. Did she think he was going to take Wiley up on his offer? How dumb did she think he was? Or did she have him pegged as a corrupt cop? Was that how they did things in San Francisco? "In a manner of speaking," he said slowly, his tone impassive, his eyes darkening. "I don't like liars, Congressman. And you lied."

"I'm not lying now. You've got a choice. You either take what I'm offering and walk away, or I'll ruin you," he promised. "I've got friends in all sorts of places, Detective, and I can make life hell for you."

Patrick looked unfazed. "We all make our own hell, Congressman." He took out his handcuffs. "And it looks like you've made yours."

"It was an accident," Blake suddenly burst out, jumping to his feet and getting in between Patrick and his father.

"Shut up, Blake." Wiley's voice rose an octave.

Maggi held up her hand to silence the congressman. To encourage his son. "Let him talk."

Blake began to sob, his voice bordering on hysteria as he said, "She wanted to get married, said if I didn't marry her she'd go to my father, tell him how I messed up. Again."

She knew it was absurd and that Cavanaugh would ridicule her, but she couldn't help it—she felt sorry for Blake.

"So you killed her?" Maggi prodded gently.

Wiley caught his son's arm, as if to physically pull him away from the confession. "Blake—"

Blake yanked his arm free. "What's the use?" His eyes shifted to Patrick. Imploring. "He said it'd go easier if I told the truth."

"Wait for Christopher," Wiley pleaded.

But it was too late for that. Years too late. Blake suddenly looked like a deflated doll. "I'm tired of taking orders, Dad."

They needed the confession before Wiley got to his son and sent for their lawyer. "How was it an accident?" Maggi coaxed.

Blake sank back down in the chair. "We argued. She came at me, beating me with her fists. I hit her." He looked at Maggi, his eyes begging her to believe him. "Just once, that's all, just to get her to stop. I didn't want to hurt her." He swallowed, remembering. "She lost her balance, fell, hitting her head on the coffee table. She wasn't breathing." Tears flowed down his cheeks, for himself, for the dead woman. "I tried to revive her, I did, but she just didn't come around. There was no pulse." He licked his lips nervously. "I panicked and called my father." He didn't look at the congressman but kept his eyes fixed on Maggi. "He told me what to do. I put her into the car, drove to the river and pushed it over the side." He looked at them, some of the terror he'd lived with evident in his eyes. "It was an accident," he ended helplessly.

Wiley was quick to pick up the slack. "You can see it wasn't premeditated. My son didn't want to kill her. He was just being inept, as always. What good would it do to arrest him?"

Patrick couldn't tell if the man was serious, if he really expected them to go along with what he was saying. "I'm afraid you've forgotten the way the system works, Congressman. Shame on you."

"God damn it, man, just let me give you this money." Quickly he wrote down a figure that would have assured them both of a life of leisure from this day forward. He held it up to Patrick. "You and your partner can split it any way you want to." When Patrick made no move to take the check, Wiley demanded, "What do you make?"

"Not nearly enough to put up with this kind of garbage," Patrick assured him. Taking Blake by the arm, he drew him up to his feet. "Blake Wiley, you're under arrest for the death of Joanne Styles." Putting the cuffs on him, Patrick glanced at Maggi, then nodded at Wiley. "You want to do the honors with the congressman?"

"Me?" Wiley demanded, stunned. "On what charge?"

"Take your pick. Obstructing justice, accessory after the fact." Patrick looked at him pointedly. "Bribing an officer of the law. And that's just for starters. Now, I hate reading the Miranda rights, so I'd appreciate it if you'd both listen closely."

As he began to recite, Patrick motioned Blake out of the office. Maggi followed close behind with the congressman. She spared him the indignity of being handcuffed.

All up and down the hallway, staff members emerged to stare incredulously at the strange parade as Patrick's voice droned on.

"You have the right to remain silent. If you give up that right, what you say can and will be held against you. You have the right to an attorney. If you cannot afford an attorney, the court will..."

Chapter 9

It took them hours to wade through the paperwork, the onslaught of lawyers and the sea of news reporters who'd swarmed in like sharks in a feeding frenzy. None of this fanfare tarnished Maggi's feeling that, in the end, this had been a job well-done. They had solved a homicide in a relatively short time. So many crimes went unsolved years after they had taken place.

The case also helped push other feelings into the background. Feelings that were now crowding her, elbowing out a place for themselves beside the satisfaction. Feelings of ambivalence over her true purpose for being here. Things had blurred since she'd come on the job.

Everything had been fine when she'd thought Cavanaugh was guilty, when she'd been pretty much assured by his aloof attitude that he was what the department feared he was.

But now she wasn't so sure.

She wasn't even half-sure. He'd turned down one hell of a substantial bribe right before her eyes.

Maggi sat at her desk, staring at the last page of the report she'd finished filing. Not seeing it at all.

Granted, the scene with the congressman could have played out as it had because she'd been there and she was, as far as Cavanaugh was concerned, still an untried commodity. Even allowing him to believe that she wasn't as straight as she'd initially let on might not have convinced him to take a chance. To accept the liberal bribe that had been waved under his nose. After all, how did he know she wouldn't turn him in?

The irony of the situation was not lost on her.

Something in her gut told Maggi he wouldn't have taken the bribe even if she hadn't been there to witness it. Something in her gut and in his eyes.

But the look in his eyes could have been faked, she argued. Cavanaugh might be more of an actor than was evident. As for her gut, well, she had her suspicions it was unduly influenced by other things. Things she wasn't even going to visit until after they'd died away.

Rising from her desk, she stretched, exhausted. She couldn't even remember the beginning of the day. It felt as if it had taken place a decade ago. Her stomach reminded her that lunch had been an unsatisfactory hamburger and dinner was only a thought. Still, the idea of falling straight into bed held a great of appeal.

"Want to go and grab a couple of beers to unwind?" When she jumped in response to the sound of his voice, he stepped back, afraid of colliding with her. "Hey, you okay, Mary Margaret?"

Turning, she looked at him. After all the evenings she'd tried to get him to come out with her, to perhaps maybe open up a little after hours, only to be flatly turned down, this invitation out of the blue caught her completely off guard.

"I didn't know you were there. Just tired," she explained when he looked at her dubiously.

He put his own interpretation on her words and started to leave. "Okay, rain check, then."

She made a grab for his arm. When he looked at her quizzically, she let the sleeve go. "No, a beer sounds great. I just didn't think you unwound."

"Even machines power down."

Her mouth curved. "So, is that what you are, a machine?"

"Some people think I am." He started to leave and looked at her expectantly. "You coming or not?"

"Coming," she responded. "Definitely coming." She found she had to hurry to keep up. It took effort. Cavanaugh had to be a laugh riot on a date, she thought. "Ever think of cutting down your stride? Not everyone has legs like a giraffe, you know."

He grinned. "Most people think of necks when they think of giraffes."

Her eyes met his. "Most people don't see the whole picture."

Patrick was already heading down the hall. "But you do."

She couldn't help wondering if he was baiting her. The evening ahead promised to be interesting at the very least. "I try."

"We'll see," he murmured, as if irritated once again.

Was he was putting her on some kind of notice, or just making conversation? In either case, tiny volts of electricity sparked the adrenaline in her veins to flow faster as she stepped into the elevator car beside Patrick.

* * *

They didn't go to the local police hangout the way she'd expected. Was he taking her to his place instead? Somehow, she didn't think so. He didn't strike her as the type who liked having his inner sanctum invaded.

Driving ahead of her, he led Maggi to a small bar, closer to where he lived. Fading neon lights proclaimed its name for all interested parties: Saints and Sinners, except that the second *S* was burned out, turning it into Saints and inners, which was a joke all its own. The bar was part of a strip mall that had seen better decades. Even in the dark, it evidently needed renovation.

After stopping her car beside his in the all but empty lot, she got out and took a longer look at the bar. The building had a sadness to it she found hard to shake. Did Cavanaugh have that same sadness?

She was getting too philosophical, she upbraided herself. What she needed was sleep, not a beer. But maybe he'd feel more inclined to share something with her tonight, closing the case and all. Sleep was just going to have to wait.

Maggi fell into step beside Patrick. "So this is where you hang out at the end of the day?"

He deliberately avoided giving her a direct answer. To hang out depicted a pattern, and he had no routine other than work and sleep. Everything else was just happenstance.

"This is where I go for beer if there's none in the refrigerator."

He was watching her as much as she was watching him, she thought. Was he sizing her up, wondering if he could let her in beyond the first layer of his armor? Or was he just trying to figure out if she was worth the effort of bedding?

She couldn't tell. Nothing in his eyes gave him away. She hoped there was nothing in hers that would betray her.

He led the way inside, holding the door open for her. Once he let it go, the room wrapped itself around her, shutting off the outer world. Making her a part of this one.

She saw three people sitting at the bar. But when she began to walk toward an empty stool, he motioned her toward one of the small tables. Taking a seat, he held up two fingers for the bartender to see. The tall, world-weary, broad-shouldered man behind the counter nodded, putting up two bottles of beer for the waitress to bus over to their table.

Maggi waited until the woman withdrew. She took one long sip to fortify herself. She needed a little push tonight to do what she had to do. Setting the bottle back down, she raised her eyes to his. "Did you mean it?"

"Mean what?" Patrick asked. He couldn't help wondering what made her tick, what made a woman like her opt to put her life on the line every day as she got out of bed.

The thought of her getting out of bed, of being in bed in the first place, sent hot pulses snaking through his body. He chalked it up to a pure physical reaction and reminded himself that he didn't act on those unless there was the promise of no repercussions. Being with McKenna would guarantee repercussions. He knew that without being told.

"Back at the congressman's office, when you called me your partner." She'd been surprised when he had. Surprised and oddly pleased. She shouldn't have been, she told herself, but the feeling had remained for more than a moment.

He shrugged, taking a drag from the bottle he preferred to the usual mug of beer. He liked wrapping his hand around the amber glass, feeling its weight. There was something basic about that. He liked basic things.

When he set the bottle back down again, he laughed. "I couldn't exactly call you my pain in the butt, now, could I? We were supposed to be a united front."

She studied his face and found herself getting sidetracked by its planes and rugged angles. "So I still haven't passed inspection as far as you're concerned."

He didn't answer right away. Instead, Patrick's ice-blue eyes swept over her. Maggi felt as if her clothes melted away. The thought sent shivers of anticipation up her spine. It'd been a long time since she'd been with a man. Maybe too long. But long or not, Cavanaugh couldn't be a candidate. There was a huge conflict of interest involved.

Lacing his hands behind his head, Patrick leaned back, his eyes still creating havoc inside the pit of her stomach. "Mary Margaret, I'm pretty willing to bet you could pass any inspection you wanted to."

She blinked, trying to sound urbane, feeling she was grasping at straws. "Are you coming on to me, Cavanaugh?"

He savored the seductive note in her voice, knowing it could go no further. He was still having trouble accepting her as his partner. Anything else couldn't begin to enter into it.

But a man was allowed fantasies.

His voice was as low as hers. "Just stating the obvious."

The job. She needed to get her mind back on the job, not on what it would feel like having his hands run along her body instead of just his eyes. She dug deep for a question.

"Weren't you tempted?" Too late she realized what he would think she meant and hurried to add, "When Wiley offered you that bribe."

His eyes remained on her face, raising her body temperature by slow increments. She shifted in her seat. "Were you?" he responded.

She wondered if drinking a single beer could make you feel unnaturally warm. She couldn't blame the rising heat or sensation of depleting air on an undue press of bodies. She'd rather think it was the beer than the company.

"I asked you first."

Distancing himself wasn't easy, but then he specialized in the not easy. "You give in once, they have you forever. They get control of your life."

The way he worded it reinforced her feelings that Patrick felt at odds with the immediate world. The man was a loner with a capital *L*. She sincerely doubted anyone would ever get complete control over this man. Not his work, not his family. He went through life solo even in a crowd. She found that rather sad.

Hoping to score a piece of information, another piece to the puzzle that was Patrick Cavanaugh, she said more than asked, "And control is important to you."

"Control," he told her, his eyes pinning her in place, his voice a whisper, "is everything."

Maggi wasn't sure exactly how it had happened. One moment, Cavanaugh was talking to her, the next moment, he was blowing the room apart.

He'd leaned in over the tiny, scarred table and was kissing her.

Or maybe she leaned into him. She wouldn't have

been able to testify as to the exact chain of events if she was on trial for her life. All she knew was that it had happened. And that she was ultimately grateful there was a table between them, that no other body parts were touching except for their lips, because she knew that restraint wouldn't have been a viable option for her if they were.

It barely was now.

A hunger had crawled up from her belly, clawing its way forward and seizing her in its viselike grip, disintegrating almost everything else in its path. Making confetti out of her resolve.

Her heart began to hammer audibly in her ears, drowning out the soft drone of voices until it was completely gone.

He tasted of beer. And sin. The path to which was tempting her beyond her wildest imagination.

She wanted to touch him, to place her hands about his face. Instead, Maggi gripped the sides of the wobbly table, anchoring herself to something real, something tangible, before she was completely swept away.

As she was afraid she would be.

He wasn't sure why he'd let his guard down and kissed her.

Maybe it was the word "tempted" that had triggered him. Because he had been.

Tempted ever since he'd proved his point to her in the car eons ago, halting a kiss at the very last possible moment. Wondering what it would have been like had he gone through with the aborted movement. It had been hovering about in the recesses of his mind all day.

Each time he thought of their almost kiss, the curiosity only became more pronounced.

And now he knew.

Kissing her was like stepping through some kind of time portal. A rip in the fabric of time that took him back to the days when he hadn't quite realized that the world was a hard, unforgiving place where bad things instead of good happened. Back to a time when he'd believed in the kind of world that his uncles tried to create, not the one that existed.

She made him want things.

Want her.

Abruptly he pulled back.

Dazed and struggling very hard not to be, Maggi looked at him with wide eyes that initially refused to focus.

"Afraid of what you found out?" she finally managed to ask, brazening the moment out. Surprised that she had a voice at all. And grateful that they were sitting, because the consistency of her body had turned to mostly sticky liquid.

He searched her face for a clue before asking, "What do you mean?"

"That you're human."

His laugh was short, dismissive. "Annual physical tells me that."

Maggi shook her head, hoping the man didn't have a clue as to how far he'd unraveled her. "No, your annual physical tells you that you're still breathing. The human part's trickier."

He surprised her by smiling at her comment. "You sound a lot like my uncle."

Good, he was talking family. The pleasure of that was dampened by the pragmatic feeling that she knew she needed to burrow in a little further, that this was the way to get him to trust her, bit by bit. "Andrew or Brian?"

He looked mildly surprised that she knew their names. "Doing a little digging into my life, Mary Margaret?"

She was almost getting used to the sound of that, of her names being waved at her like a red flag. Her annoyance had gone down several notches over the course of the past few days.

"Don't have to. You're a Cavanaugh, you come with a pedigree."

Which was also why she'd been told to tread lightly. Because, maverick or not, Patrick Cavanaugh had strong family ties, ties that went back several generations in the police department. Had he been anyone else, the investigation that was launched would have been public. But there were too many possible waves here to make swimming easy, hence the covert approach.

She nodded. "My father used to work with your uncle Andrew and he knew your uncle Brian, as well as your father."

He seemed not to hear her when she mentioned his father, but she had a feeling he did. Had there been bad blood between the two? Did that affect Patrick in some manner, turning him against the force to which his father had sworn allegiance?

Questions crowded her head, butting up against the sensations that were still rippling through her minutes after he'd withdrawn his mouth from hers.

Her body hummed, aching. Wanting.

"Want another?" he asked her.

She stared at him, her heart hammering hard again. Was he actually asking her if she wanted him to kiss her again? The word "yes" hovered on her lips, begging to be released.

"Beer," Patrick clarified. The lighting in the bar was several notches below dim, but he could have sworn he saw color creeping up her cheeks. Amusement nudged an elbow in his ribs.

For a moment, she'd thought...

Damn, what was wrong with her? She wasn't some nubile, untried virgin, being led off to the hayloft for her first tryst with the good-looking farmhand. Why was she acting like one?

Annoyed with herself, with him for rattling her this way, she cleared her throat. "No, this was nice, but I think one's a good place to stop." She looked at him pointedly.

Good advice, applied to the beer and to her, he told himself. For once they were in agreement.

Patrick inclined his head. "Well, then I guess we'd better call it a night."

"Right." Maggi was on her feet a little too fast. Wobbly or not, she needed to put some space between them. Fresh air might not be a bad idea, either. "Early day tomorrow." She was babbling, she thought, but she didn't want there to be silence between them right now. Silence was too sensual. "There's probably some *i*'s we forgot to dot and *t*'s we forgot to cross."

"I don't forget to dot *i*'s or cross *t*'s," he told her, throwing down several bills on the table.

Placing his hand at the small of her back, he ushered her out. Making it feel as if this was a date. But it wasn't, Maggi told herself. And it couldn't be.

"Sorry, don't know what came over me. I forgot you were perfect."

"Not perfect," he told her as he opened the door

then let her walk through first. "Just thorough. And careful."

Careful.

That was the key word here, she thought. The word she needed to hold on to. Because she'd slipped back there, slipped and very nearly lost her footing. Fraternizing with the enemy was strictly forbidden and, until she could find proof of it otherwise, Patrick Cavanaugh was still the enemy—a dirty cop who made them all look dirty by association. And cops like that had to be routed from the force and punished for the tarnish they caused and spread. She needed to remember that.

Flipping her collar up, Maggi turned around to look at him. The wind had picked up and the smell of more rain wafted through the air. The parking lot was all but empty. They might as well have been the last two people on the earth. It felt that way.

She took a deep breath, as if that could somehow fortify her against the man before her. "Thorough and careful," she echoed, letting amusement play along her lips as she thought of what had just happened inside the bar. "Always?"

He looked at her, at the way the light from the streetlamp was playing off her lips. He could taste just the barest hint of her lipstick. Something light, sweet, mingled with the bitter taste of beer.

He felt that tightening in his gut again and deliberately concentrated on shaking it off.

"No," he said quietly, "not always."

The wind picked up the words and feathered them across her face.

For one very long moment, she felt as if there was a war going on, a war she was destined to lose no matter which way it went.

If she gave in, allowed herself to be pulled in, she faced a huge ethical and moral dilemma. If she did the right thing, pulled back, everything would remain intact. Except what she was feeling.

The right thing felt all wrong.

Desperately searching for higher ground before she slid down a slippery slope, Maggi shoved her hands into her pockets and cleared her throat. She forced a smile to her lips as she looked at the man she had to remember was her assignment and nothing else. "So, this the way you usually celebrate closing a case with your partner?"

Patrick hunched his shoulders against the wind and mist. "Throwing back a couple of beers? No, not usually." He thought back. "Just a couple of times with Ramirez. He insisted on buying."

That wasn't what she meant and they both knew it. "And the other?"

Looking into her eyes, he smiled to himself. The woman was damn annoying, there was no question about that. So why did he find her, of all people, appealing? "No, never kissed Ramirez. Never even been tempted."

Did I tempt you?

Ripples of excitement undulated through her. She wanted to talk about what had just happened, to explore the sensation it had created and let it titillate her.

Damn it, Mag, you're behaving like a schoolgirl.

God knew she didn't feel like a schoolgirl. She felt like a woman. A woman who wanted what she knew she couldn't have. Moreover, what she *shouldn't* have. Hooking up with Patrick Cavanaugh promised nothing but complications. She had to remember that. She wasn't trying to get on his good side to form a lasting partnership, she was trying to draw information out of him. To get him to trust her enough to let something slip.

The bitter taste of bile rose to her mouth.

"It's late," she murmured. "We'd better get going. My father'll be standing at the window, watching for me." A fond smile played on her lips. "Trying to pretend he's not worried."

Patrick looked at her, mildly surprised. He would have thought she lived alone, with maybe a pet for company. A dog. She didn't look like a cat person. "You live with your father?"

"No, not anymore. I just promised I'd stop by on my way to my apartment, that's all."

"Not anymore?" he questioned.

"I did for a while. I came back to take care of him after he was shot." She still remembered how she'd felt getting the call. Like a mule had kicked her in her stomach. Which was why she let her father fuss over her. Everyone had their own way of dealing with tension. "Friendly fire," she said incredulously. "Technically, anyway."

About to walk away, Patrick jerked to attention. "What did you say?"

"Friendly fire," she repeated, wondering why he was looking at her so strangely. "The bullet came from a police-issued weapon, but they found one of the dead 'suspects' holding it. He must have gotten a hold of the gun somehow during the scuffle. It was a raid," she explained. "My dad was one of the backup cops on the scene." The look in Patrick's eyes told her she'd said something that had caught his attention, something she didn't realize she'd said. A lightning review of the conversation assured her that it had nothing to do with her cover. But still it was something. "What's the matter?"

Maybe something. Maybe nothing. "That's how my partner got killed," he told her. "Friendly fire."

"Except that in Ramirez's case, it really was so-called friendly fire," she pointed out. "Isn't the officer who did it undergoing counseling right now?"

Patrick raised his brow, obviously surprised.

"Hey, I like to know what I'm getting into. I asked around when I found out you were going to be my partner."

Patrick nodded absently. It was plausible. What still didn't feel plausible or right was Ramirez's death, over and above the obvious. More than a month later, there was still something about the way it had gone down that didn't sit right with him.

He told himself he had to let it go, to put that out of his mind. Just as he had to put the longing that was attempting to wrap long tentacles around him out of his mind. Because he knew he'd be out of his mind to give in. McKenna was his partner and that was bad enough. Making her anything more was crazy and asking for the kind of trouble he didn't need or want.

"See you," he tossed over his shoulder as he abruptly walked away.

"Count on it, Zorro," Maggi murmured, staring after him.

Who was *that masked man?* Had he just kissed her like that to throw her off? Because she certainly felt thrown off. No, kissing her to throw her off would have been the action of a man accustomed to winding women around his little finger. She'd be willing to bet her next year's pay that wasn't Cavanaugh's style.

So what the hell was going on here?

Damned if she knew.

Suddenly feeling very drained and weary, Maggi got into her car and drove to her father's home. She planned to pay a quick visit and then go straight to her apartment. What she needed right now, she counseled herself, was sleep. Things would be back to normal in the morning.

Or so she told herself.

Chapter 10

Morning came and went. Maggi put the evening before out of her mind and concentrated on her job. Both the one she was supposedly doing and her covert one. With no new homicide to work on, Reynolds made it a point to tell them that it was an ideal time to catch up on long-overdue paperwork.

As far as Maggi was concerned, there was never an ideal time to catch up on paperwork, especially when the cases initially had belonged to someone else.

The day dragged on longer than it should have. When she saw Patrick getting up from his desk, his computer shut down for the day, her antennae gratefully went up.

She swung her chair around to bar his way out of the cubicle. "Where're you going?"

Very deliberately, he took hold of her armrests and repositioned her, then walked out of the cubicle. "I'm taking off early."

Maggi was on her feet. "Hot date?"

Turning around, he looked at her. "No."

"Then what?"

Was it him, or did she sound eager? Maybe she just wanted to get out like he did. Sitting, shuffling papers all day could be mind numbing. It was for him. "Did it ever occur to you not to ask questions?"

"Not really," she told him cheerfully. "Knowledge is a wonderful thing."

"Curiosity killed the cat."

Looking down, she indicated her legs. She wore a skirt that showed them off to a far-from-modest advantage. It took Patrick a beat to draw his gaze away.

"Two legs, not four. I'm safe." Determined to learn what he was up to, leaving early like this, she gave it her best shot. "I thought that unless you're off on a trip to your proctologist to have that stick you've been harboring surgically removed, since there's no grisly homicide staring us in the face right now, maybe you'd like some company."

He wasn't looking forward to what he was about to do and it left him in a less-than-amenable mood. "I'm going to see Alicia Ramirez to see how she's getting along. And no, I wouldn't like some company."

Her eyes skimmed over his face, trying to read between the lines. She thought she detected something. A reluctance he was trying to hide from her. Maybe even from himself.

"But maybe you need some," she countered. "Alicia's your partner's widow, right?"

"Yeah. So?"

He sounded almost belligerent. She would have backed away if this wasn't about something bigger than just her own feelings.

"So it's still in the early days since he was killed. Your heart's obviously in the right place, but you really don't have the softest touch, Cavanaugh." She pretended to be cocky. "My touch is very soft. She might want a woman around."

Alicia Ramirez came from a large family. Her emotional support system was assured. He was going over for a different reason. He'd already put this off for too long. "I'm sure she's got plenty of women around."

"Then *you* might want a woman around." He looked at her sharply and she added, "To take over when the going gets awkward."

He supposed she might have a point. Though he liked Alicia, this wasn't something he looked forward to, just something that had to be done. His sense of honor demanded it. "You certainly have no problem taking over."

She laughed. "Funny, that's what my father always says."

He nodded. "Smart man."

"Yeah, he is," she said. There was no mistaking the affection in her voice. He couldn't remember ever feeling that way about his own father. Earliest memories involved hearing his father shouting and his cowering in his closet, trying to get away from the sound.

Maggi looked over to the secretarial assistant they had covering the front desk. "Terrance, if the captain asks, I'm taking a couple of hours personal time."

"Very good, Detective." The young man's bright hazel eyes shifted toward Patrick. "You, too, Detective?" His meaning was less than veiled.

"Apparently," Patrick muttered, even though he had already told Terrance earlier that he was going to be leaving early.

Patrick walked out of the room without another word.

Maggi grabbed her purse and hurried after him. If nothing else, this assignment was certainly keeping her on her toes physically. "Are we going together?"

Patrick was already on his way out of the building. "No."

He didn't need to be in an enclosed space with her. The effects of last night at the bar were still very present in his mind. He needed to dissipate, not reinforce, them.

She was almost trotting to keep up. "Then give me the address in case we get separated."

"We're not going to get separated," he snapped, then added as he slowed down, "no matter how much I try."

The backhanded admission nudged a smile from her. "Just trying to help, Cavanaugh."

They weren't going to go there, to some area of mutual dependency. He'd made the mistake of forming a relationship with his last partner and he wasn't about to leave himself open to that again.

"Get this straight, Mary Margaret, I don't need your help."

"Fair enough." But she stood her ground. "Then maybe Alicia Ramirez might."

There was no getting rid of the woman, he thought. And maybe, just this once, she was right. He wasn't at his best dealing with emotional situations or emotional women. He already knew that. With a sigh, Patrick rattled off the address to her.

Alicia Ramirez was a petite, dark-haired woman with huge, sad eyes that brightened when she saw her late husband's partner standing on her doorstep. She smiled warmly at him, opening the door all the way.

"Patrick, please, come in." Too polite to ask, Alicia looked at the woman beside him with a silent query in her eyes.

"This is Detective McKenna. She's—"

About to say that she was his new partner, Patrick couldn't quite get himself to do it. Perforce, life always went on, but for those left behind when the train pulled out of the station again, it was a difficult thing to accept. He didn't want to make it any worse for Alicia than it already was.

"I work with Detective Cavanaugh," Maggi explained, extending her hand to the woman. "I just wanted to tell you how sorry I am for your loss."

Bright tears shone in Alicia's eyes as she took Maggi's hand. "Thank you. Did you know my husband?"

"No," Maggi replied honestly. "But I heard very good things about him."

"That's because he was a very good man." Alicia led the way inside. The two-story house was in the kind of perpetual comfortable disarray that having three children under the age of ten sustained.

The kitchen was a little better, Patrick thought. The counters were cleared, the sink empty. It looked as if Alicia Ramirez was reclaiming her life a room at a time. Progress was slow.

"I—we," he amended, bringing Maggi into it because the situation begged for it, "didn't come to put you out," Patrick protested as Alicia insisted on serving them each tea. Obligingly, he accepted the cup she'd poured and kept it sitting in front of him on the table. "I just wanted to see how you were managing."

Alicia took a seat between them. Wrapping her hands around her cup, she took a sip of the dark liquid and let it warm her before answering.

"I'm managing." The smile on her lips was sad. "The kids keep me busy and my sisters come by every day to help out." She raised her eyes to Patrick. "I still can't—" Alicia pressed her lips together. Grief stole the last few words away from her.

He'd come to the conclusion long ago that he'd rather face bullets than tears. He hadn't known how to handle them when he'd seen his mother crying, when they had sprung up in Patience's eyes the time she'd turned to him for consolation. All he knew to do was fight what had caused them. Which was why at the age of ten, he'd pitted himself against his father and why he'd fought a bully teasing his sister in the schoolyard when he'd been one half the bully's size.

But there was no one he could take on here. Only a formless entity, a sadness that couldn't be vanquished with any amount of blows. He gave Alicia his handkerchief. A helplessness pervaded him that he neither tolerated nor knew what to do with.

Out of the corner of his eye he saw Maggi reaching across the table, putting her hand over Alicia's.

"It's okay to cry," Maggi told the woman softly. "It takes about a year for the tears to stop coming unexpectedly."

Alicia dried her eyes with the handkerchief. "You lost someone?"

"My mother." She was nine at the time. Sometimes it still felt like yesterday. "Only time I saw my father cry. Took me six months to stop blaming her for dying. Took longer to stop crying every time I thought of her." Maggi offered the other woman an encouraging smile. ''It's rough, but it passes into something you can live with,'' she promised. ''Something you can handle instead of having it handle you.''

Alicia nodded. Folding it again, she offered the handkerchief back to Patrick along with an apologetic smile. ''I'm sorry, you didn't come here to see this.''

Patrick took the handkerchief, shifting slightly in his discomfort. He cleared his throat. ''Actually, I came to see if you needed anything.''

Alicia cocked her head slightly, not following him. ''Needed anything?''

Though it was invading a private area, it was easier for him to talk about finances than trying to handle the woman's tears.

''I know that Ed must have left debts.'' His late partner had had trouble hanging on to a dollar. There was always some new venture, some surefire scheme that called to him. Patrick knew that he was treading on the woman's pride, but children were involved. And he felt responsible. If he'd just been a little faster, there would be no tears in this household. ''If you need any money, Alicia, you just have to ask.''

To his amazement, Alicia laughed softly. ''Money is the one thing I don't need.'' He looked at her, puzzled. ''Eddie was very smart when it came to money. He made a lot of good investments, put the money in the bank. First Republic,'' she murmured, her voice dying out. The sadness threatened to take her over again. ''If only he was as smart about what he did for a living.'' And then she sighed. ''That's not fair. He loved being a policeman.''

She looked at Maggi. ''Said it was what he'd wanted to be ever since he was a little boy. The only thing that meant more to him were me and the kids.''

Alicia looked over toward the framed photograph on the mantel. It was of a handsome man wearing a dress uniform and a huge, bright smile. Her breath hitched. Another round of tears threatened to come and she struggled to hold them back.

The doorbell rang a second before they heard the sound of the front door being opened and someone calling out to Alicia.

"I'm in here," she called back. Overhead they heard the sound of small feet pounding down the stairs. "That's Teresa, one of my sisters," Alicia explained. Her mouth curved. "They take turns baby-sitting me. Teresa brings ice cream for the kids. They get excited every time she comes over."

Patrick was already rising. He'd overstayed his visit. "We'll get out of your hair."

Alicia was on her feet. She looked at Patrick's untouched cup of tea. "No, really, you can stay if you'd like."

If he saw her indicating the tea, he gave no sign. "Like I said, I just wanted to see how you were doing and to make sure that you knew if you needed anything, all you have to do is ask."

Alicia paused to kiss his cheek and then give him a grateful hug. After a beat, he closed his arms around her in response, though he was obviously a man uncomfortable with displays of emotion. "He was lucky to have you," Alicia said.

Maggi noted that Patrick's discomfort seemed to heighten. She slipped between them as Alicia released Patrick from the hug. "It was nice meeting you, Mrs. Ramirez."

"Alicia, please." She walked with them to the front

door. "And if you're ever in the neighborhood," she told Maggi, "you're welcome to stop by."

"Thank you." Maggi squeezed her hand. "I will."

They nodded at Alicia's sister as they passed her and let themselves out.

Maggi stepped off the front step, then turned to Patrick. "Don't much like tea, do you?"

He hoped it hadn't been overly obvious. "I'd rather drink poison."

She laughed. The sound was oddly comforting to him. But then it faded as she asked, "When are you going to stop blaming yourself?"

"What?"

She disregarded the sharp note in his voice. "I saw it in your eyes when she said Ramirez was lucky to have had you as a partner." He looked angry, like a bear whose wound was being probed. She didn't let that stop her. "I read the report, Cavanaugh. There was nothing you could do."

That wasn't the way he saw it. Ramirez had a family, a wife and kids who had depended on him. He didn't. "He took the bullet meant for me. I was supposed to be the one walking into that crack house first."

"You said it was friendly fire. What are you saying now—that you were supposed to be the one killed by our own side?"

"I was talking about fate, not intent." He waved his hand. Why was he trying to explain it to her anyway? There was something more important on his mind right now. "Never mind. Look, I'm going to go back to the station. You go home."

Maggi felt as if she as being dismissed. *Not that easy, fella.* She glanced at her watch. It was a little after five.

"You're off duty. Technically." She was beginning to get the impression that Cavanaugh felt he was never off duty. Which conflicted with her reasons for being assigned to the case in the first place. If he was so dedicated, could he really be dirty? "Why don't we go somewhere and I'll buy you a beer to wash the taste of that tea out of your mouth?"

It was tempting. So was doing something else to rid his mouth of the taste that was there. But right now, something bothered him more than the rebellion of his own hormones. What Alicia had told them wasn't sitting right with him.

"Some other time."

She deliberately moved in front of him, blocking the way to his car. "What's on your mind?"

Annoyed, he had to repress the desire to physically move her out of his way. "What?"

"I'm starting to know you, Cavanaugh." The funny part of it was, she was. What's more, she liked what she had learned. He exhibited all the warmth of a clay statue, but it was obvious that he cared about the welfare of his late partner's family. He got points for that. "I can see the little wheels in your head turning. Something's bothering you. What is it?"

"Other than a nagging partner?"

He'd called her his partner again. He was getting used to her. That was both good and bad, depending on what side of her guilt she was standing on. "Goes without saying."

Maybe two heads were better than one. At the very least, maybe he could use her as a sounding board. Just thinking of that surprised him. The whole concept of sharing his thoughts was foreign to him because he'd always gone it alone, always relied on his own instincts.

But maybe this time he was too close, too involved to be impartial. He cared about Ramirez, and about the welfare of the man's family. "Okay, I'll take you up on that beer."

Score one for the home team. "Great. Do I get to choose the place this time?"

"No."

"Didn't think so." She nodded toward his car. "You drive, I'll follow."

He was already getting in. "Wouldn't have it any other way."

Maggi bit her tongue to keep from commenting.

Chapter 11

This time Patrick took her to a place with more light, more noise, more anonymity. If she was interpreting body language correctly, no one here seemed to know him by name or by sight. The noise around them guaranteed their privacy.

She was secretly grateful he hadn't brought her back to the bar they'd been to last night. What had happened there was still very fresh in her mind and the velvety darkness would have only aided and abetted the desire that still hummed through her. A booth with a proper-sized table between them was a lot better.

She was also secretly disappointed.

Maggi waited until the waiter brought over their beers, bottles again, before she said anything. She had a feeling that if she didn't initiate the conversation, Cavanaugh would go on sitting there, not a syllable leaving his lips, until he decided it was time to get up and go.

"All right, I'm all ears."

She saw the way his eyes swept over her. For a second, she could almost feel them touching her as they passed. Her mouth grew a little drier. She felt less like a partner and a great deal more like a woman.

"Figuratively speaking," she felt bound to add. "Something's been bothering you since we were in Ramirez's house. What is it?" When he didn't begin to speak, frustration raised its head faster than she knew it should have. The man really knew how to press her buttons. A lot of them. "Talk to me, Cavanaugh. That's what I'm here for."

Even as she uttered the words, Maggi couldn't help wondering if the man she was sitting opposite had any idea how true those words were. That was what she was here for, to get him to talk to her. To wheedle into his confidence, not as a partner but as a spy.

She felt an unwanted shiver creeping through her system and banked it down.

Patrick sat for a long moment, regarding the neck on his bottle of beer. He hated what he was thinking. He wasn't outgoing, but his late partner had gotten to him, gotten his trust. Facing the possibility that he'd been fooled wasn't easy for him.

Finally he looked up. "He didn't have that kind of money."

"Ramirez?" she guessed.

He nodded slowly. "He always needed money. He was always into something that would get him rich, quick. Anytime he did anything right, anytime something panned out for him—and it wasn't often—" Patrick emphasized "—he told me about it. Told everyone about it. That man couldn't keep his mouth shut. That was just his way."

He needed to believe in his partner, she realized. It made Cavanaugh a little more real to her, a little less like some remote, two-dimensional being. It also made her want to help him hang on to his memory of the man.

"Maybe his wife's not asking for anything because of pride."

Patrick shook his head. "Alicia's not like that."

"You'd be surprised how much pride someone can have when it comes to preserving the reputation of someone they love." Patrick looked at her sharply. She'd only been throwing out words. *What are you thinking, Cavanaugh? Have I set off something in your head?* "A man's not a good provider for his wife and kids," she continued, pretending she hadn't noticed his reaction, "that brings his stock down."

He wasn't convinced. Something felt wrong. "It wouldn't have been something she would have kept from me." He thought of Ramirez. The first thing he remembered was the man's wide grin. The second was the sound of his voice, going on incessantly. Not unlike the woman in the booth with him now. "Partners get close. They spend a lot of time together—it's hard not to."

"And the two of you got close." It was hard picturing him getting close to anyone, Maggi thought. Maybe that was why he was resisting the idea they were silently waltzing around, because he'd gotten in close and put his faith in someone. And that someone had died.

He looked at her. "As close as I've ever gotten to someone who's not a member of my family."

His steady gaze held her prisoner. Needing to pull

back, Maggi tried to lighten the moment. "So I've got something to live for."

"Maybe."

There was no way to know what he was thinking now, she noted. His clear blue eyes gave nothing away.

Maggi struggled to keep her mind on the object of all this. "You do know how to put someone in what you think is their place, Cavanaugh." Maggi leaned forward, playing out her line, trying to reel him in a little closer. Ignoring the slight spasmodic twinges running up and down her conscience like a short circuit. "Okay, so if you were privy to everything Ramirez did that was aboveboard, maybe this wasn't."

"What are you saying?"

The man looked as if he could shoot lightning bolts from his eyes. She suddenly felt sorry for anyone on the wrong side of his temper. "That maybe Ramirez was getting something on the side. It's not the kind of thing he'd share with a partner."

Anger flared like unguarded flames. "You're saying he was dirty?"

She kept her voice light, low. "I'm spinning theories, not trying to get in a fight."

Patrick sucked in his breath. His voice had a dangerous ring to it as he said, "He wasn't the type."

Maggi didn't budge. "Everyone's the type if the situation is dire enough."

"Now you sound like Wiley." There was no missing his disgust.

"No," she insisted, "I sound like a realist."

Patrick started to leave the table. She grabbed his wrist. If looks could kill, she figured the one he shot her would have left her mortally wounded. But now

that she'd gotten on to something, she was not about
to back away.

"Follow me on this. The man had three kids, a wife,
a mortgage, maybe a shoe box full of other debts. You
said he was always getting into things that didn't pay
off." Reluctantly Patrick sat down again. She continued
holding his wrist. "Somebody offers to give him a little
money to look the other way. He's a good guy but he's
got creditors breathing down his neck, that kind of
thing. So he does it." Seeing that she had his attention,
Maggi slipped her hand from his wrist. "It's a one-
time thing. Or so he tells himself. Except that once he's
in, he's in. Like you said, he had no more control over
the situation. It had control over him. So he goes along
with it, putting aside money for the kids' college funds,
a vacation, something pretty for his wife. And all it
takes is not saying anything.

"But his conscience eats at him until he says 'that's
it, I've had it.' Now whoever slipped Ramirez that
money gets nervous. They know they've got a liability
on their hands—"

"They?" He looked at her closely. Did she know
something she wasn't telling him? After subjecting him
to days of useless information and endless rhetoric, was
there actually something useful she was holding back?

"Or he," Maggi allowed. "She, whatever. Bottom
line is Ramirez has to be eliminated before he talks."

He hated to admit it, but the scenario fit. "And he
gets killed."

"And he gets killed," she echoed.

He gazed at her intently. "So you think this is an
inside thing?"

She raised her hands from the table, palms up. "I'm
only spinning theories," she repeated. "But it does

GET 2 BOOKS FREE!

To get your 2 free books, affix this peel-off sticker to the reply card and mail it today!

MIRA® Books,
The Brightest
Stars in Fiction,
presents

Superb collector's editions of the very best books by some of today's best-known authors!

★ **FREE BOOKS!** To introduce you to "The Best of the Best" we'll send you 2 books ABSOLUTELY FREE!

★ **FREE GIFT!** Get an exciting surprise gift FREE!

★ **BEST BOOKS!** "The Best of the Best" brings you the best books by some of today's most popular authors!

GET 2

HOW TO GET YOUR
2 FREE BOOKS AND FREE GIFT!

1. Peel off the MIRA® sticker on the front cover. Place it in the space provided at right. This automatically entitles you to receive two free books and an exciting surprise gift.

2. Send back this card and you'll get 2 "The Best of the Best™" books. These books have a combined cover price of $11.98 or more in the U.S. and $13.98 or more in Canada, but they are yours to keep absolutely FREE!

3. There's no catch. You're under no obligation to buy anything. We charge nothing – ZERO – for your first shipment. And you don't have to make any minimum number of purchases – not even one!

4. We call this line "The Best of the Best" because each month you'll receive the best books by some of today's most popular authors. These authors show up time and time again on all the major bestseller lists and their books sell out as soon as they hit the stores. You'll like the convenience of getting them delivered to your home at our special discount prices . . . and you'll love your *Heart to Heart* subscriber newsletter featuring author news, horoscopes, recipes, book reviews and much more!

5. We hope that after receiving your free books you'll want to remain a subscriber. But the choice is yours – to continue or cancel, anytime at all! So why not take us up on our invitation, with no risk of any kind. You'll be glad you did!

6. And remember...we'll send you a surprise gift ABSOLUTELY FREE just for giving THE BEST OF THE BEST a try.

SPECIAL FREE GIFT!
We'll send you a fabulous surprise gift, absolutely FREE, simply for accepting our no-risk offer!

Visit us online at
www.mirabooks.com

® and TM are registered trademark of Harlequin Enterprises Limited.

BOOKS FREE!

Hurry!

Return this card promptly to GET 2 FREE BOOKS & A FREE GIFT!

The Best of the Best ™

```
Affix
peel-off
MIRA
sticker here
```

YES! Please send me the 2 FREE "The Best of the Best" books and FREE gift for which I qualify. I understand that I am under no obligation to purchase anything further, as explained on the back and on the opposite page.

385 MDL DRTA   185 MDL DR59

FIRST NAME	LAST NAME

ADDRESS

APT.#	CITY

STATE/PROV.	ZIP/POSTAL CODE

Offer limited to one per household and not valid to current subscribers of MIRA or "The Best of the Best." All orders subject to approval. Books received may vary.

THE BEST OF THE BEST™ — Here's How it Works:

Accepting your 2 free books and gift places you under no obligation to buy anything. You may keep the books and gift and return the shipping statement marked "cancel." If you do not cancel, about a month later we will send you 4 additional books and bill you just $4.74 each in the U.S., or $5.24 each in Canada, plus 25¢ shipping & handling per book and applicable taxes if any.* That's the complete price and — compared to cover prices starting from $5.99 each in the U.S. and $6.99 each in Canada — it's quite a bargain! You may cancel at any time, but if you choose to continue, every month we'll send you 4 more books, which you may either purchase at the discount price or return to us and cancel your subscription.

*Terms and prices subject to change without notice. Sales tax applicable in N.Y. Canadian residents will be charged applicable provincial taxes and GST. Credit or Debit balances in a customer's account(s) may be offset by any other outstanding balance owed by or to the customer.

BUSINESS REPLY MAIL
FIRST-CLASS MAIL   PERMIT NO. 717-003   BUFFALO, NY

POSTAGE WILL BE PAID BY ADDRESSEE

THE BEST OF THE BEST
3010 WALDEN AVE
PO BOX 1867
BUFFALO NY 14240-9952

NO POSTAGE
NECESSARY
IF MAILED
IN THE
UNITED STATES

make sense." And it did, she thought, now that she'd put it out on the table. She only had to prove it. And then she had to see if perhaps Cavanaugh was a hell of a lot better actor than he let on and was actually part of all this. Damn, but this job was making her paranoid. "Puts a different light on 'friendly fire,' doesn't it?"

The theory put McKenna in a whole different light as well, he thought. "You're a lot darker than I thought you'd be."

"It's the lighting," she cracked, taking a drag from her bottle.

Why did she do that? he wondered. Why did she say something flippant to throw him off, keep him off balance? He didn't like it. "You know damn well what I mean."

Maggi sobered. "Yes, I do. I'm just not sure if it's a compliment or not."

"Neither am I." Leaning back, he contemplated the mouth of the empty bottle. He didn't like what she was saying, but he was too good a cop not to admit that, at least from the outside, it made sense. "We'd need proof. Evidence."

"Definitely."

He didn't know whether he wanted to dig deep and ruin a man's reputation because of principles. Ramirez had been one of the few people he'd allowed himself to call friend.

She saw the doubt on his face as he warred with his thoughts. Was he worried that an investigation would lead to his own dirty hands? Or was he just concerned for a man he'd privately considered a friend?

Instinct told her that if Patrick was dirty, he wouldn't contemplate shining a light on someone else so close to him.

But maybe that was what she wanted to think.

She hated admitting the possibility that her personal feelings were obstructing what she had to do. She needed distance here, at least for a few hours.

"Look, we're not going to settle anything tonight," she pointed out. "You can think about it and tomorrow, if you still agree there's some chance Ramirez was killed to keep him quiet, I'll help you dig."

He raised his eyes from the bottle. "You?"

"Well, you're going to need to get hold of bank records, information on file, things like that. We already know how proficient you are with a computer, so I figure you're going to need help."

There was no use protesting that he could manage alone, not when he was up against technology. Still, he didn't want her working with him, not on this. A man had to draw the line somewhere. How did he know he could trust her? "This isn't your concern."

Her eyes told him that she wasn't about to budge on this. "It's about a cop on the police force. How *isn't* it my concern?"

He thought of Ramirez, of seeing the life drain out of the man even as he held him in his arms, willing him back to life. "It could get ugly."

"I can do ugly."

"Not hardly," he said under his breath. For now, he wanted to table the discussion. "You hungry?"

She cocked her head. "You offering to buy or taking a survey?"

Something tightened in his gut. He figured it was in protest against hunger. "The former."

"Then I'm hungry." Maggi settled back in her seat, not bothering to suppress the smile on her face as he signaled for the waitress to come over.

Tiny, baby steps.

*   *   *

The telephone was ringing when he walked into his condo over an hour later. He and McKenna had gone their separate ways after dinner, although he'd had to struggle against the urge to ask her over to his place. The pretext of a nightcap wasn't even remotely in his thoughts. What he wanted was to find out if her skin was as smooth as it seemed. All over. If that look in her eyes hid a wildness instinct told him was there.

For a simple man, Patrick knew life had gotten incredibly complicated for him, and this bone about Ramirez was hard enough to chew on. He didn't need more.

Except Maggi was tormenting him. Need tormented him. A basic need as old as time. That's all it was, he told himself, taking off his holster. All he wanted was a little gut-wrenching, toe-curling, sweaty sex, nothing more.

The fact that he was contemplating having it with his partner made his mouth curve. Never thought he'd catch himself thinking that.

The phone kept ringing, an irritating noise scratching at the perimeter of his mind. Patrick thought of letting the machine get it, but his natural sense of urgency and order forced him to walk over to it and pick up the wireless receiver.

"Cavanaugh."

"Just wanted to put in my bid early for Christmas day."

The familiar voice drew out a smile as Patrick sank down on his sofa. The second he did, he felt as if he'd collapsed. He'd warred with a host of emotions that had made him more tired than a full day out in the field.

He put his feet up on the secondhand coffee table Patience had picked up for him at a garage sale. "You don't have to put in a bid, Uncle Andrew. It's a done deal, you know that."

"No, I don't," the other man informed him. "I didn't think I'd have to call and ask to see you, but apparently it looks like I have to. Your sister's looking well. She tells me she hasn't seen much of you, either."

Patrick grinned. There was something comforting about listening to his uncle's harping. He'd missed it. "Work. You know how it is."

He heard his uncle sigh and knew there was more than a little nostalgia echoing in the sound. "Yeah, I know how it is. Still doesn't give a man an excuse to cut out his family."

"No cutting," Patrick assured him, then teased, "trimming maybe."

"If I asked to see your clock-stopping mug at the table in the next say, three or four days, what do you think my chances would be?"

"Fair to good."

"But not perfect."

There were no birds on his uncle's antennae, Patrick thought fondly. Sometimes he wondered why the man opted to take early retirement. Andrew was still as sharp as ever. "No, not perfect."

Andrew hesitated for a moment. "You know, Patrick, if a case you're working on is giving you trouble, I'd be happy to have you bounce a few things off me. The brain still works pretty well."

Patrick glanced at a stack of mail on the corner of the table. It was beginning to pile up. He supposed he'd have to get around to going through it one of these days, before a utility company decided to shut off something he found useful. "So I've heard, but I just wrapped up a case."

Patrick could hear the trap snapping as soon as he made the admission. He'd been set up.

"Well, then, I guess you've got no excuse not to come over."

The private part of him liked leaving himself a little leeway, although he did enjoy going to his uncle's house for breakfast. His thoughts shifted to the conversation he'd had at dinner. "I'm working on something else right now."

"A new case?"

He heard the interest in his uncle's voice. Not being part of the force anymore, Uncle Andrew still had more connections than anyone Patrick knew. Maybe he'd heard something useful. But it was still too early to think of letting more people know about this. It chaffed him that McKenna was in on it.

"Not exactly." He paused. "I'll let you know if I need to ask you hypothetical questions."

"My best area," Andrew assured him. "Tomorrow's Saturday. Unless something comes up, you don't have to be in to work. Always a place for you at the table. Breakfast is eight-thirty. Try to make it."

"I'll try."

Patrick made himself a promise to do more than just try as he hung up. If his job kept him grounded, being around his uncle and cousins reminded him why he was still doing what he did, that there were times when the good guys actually did outnumber the bad.

With a sigh, he reached for the stack of mail.

"To what do I owe this unexpected pleasure?" Matthew McKenna moved back out of the way as he opened his front door farther. "Why didn't you use your key? You don't have to knock. This is still your house."

"I know and I appreciate that, Dad, but I didn't want to barge in." She winked. "You might have been entertaining a lady."

He shut the door, following her into the living room. "The only lady I want to entertain keeps making herself scarce." He looked at her pointedly.

She took off her jacket and tossed it on the side of the sofa. "Oh, Dad, don't act like I never come by."

His smile was fond. "Not nearly enough, Mag-pie, not nearly enough."

Maggi knew he wasn't trying to make her feel guilty, but she felt it just the same. Juggling family and work wasn't easy. "You and Mom should have had more kids."

He looked over toward the array of framed photographs on the wall along the stairway. They chronicled his life together with the two women who'd meant the most to him, his wife and his daughter. "Yes, we should have, but I'm afraid the good Lord didn't see it that way." He smiled at her. "He gave us all of heaven wrapped up in one little girl."

She gave him a warning look. "Dad, you keep that up and I'm leaving."

He laughed, raising his hands in mock surrender. "I'll behave. Is this one of your whirlwind visits, or can you stay for dinner?"

Her father's idea of dinner was taking something out of the freezer and introducing it to the microwave. "Already ate."

He was on his way to the kitchen to get her one of the diet soft drinks he kept on hand for her. "Alone?"

As she talked, she began to gather up the newspapers he'd left where he'd read them. The man needed a maid, she thought. "There were people in the restaurant."

"You went to a restaurant by yourself?" Returning, he handed her a can. "Why didn't you give me a call? I could have met you—"

He was fishing and she knew it. She tossed him a tidbit. "I wasn't by myself."

He beamed at her with satisfaction. "So, you did go with someone."

After placing the newspapers in the recycle bin, she turned around and looked at him. Amusement played along her lips.

"Were you this heavy-handed when you were investigating a crime?"

He shrugged carelessly, making himself comfortable on the sofa. "It's the father thing, brings out the clumsiness. I just want to see you happy."

"I *am* happy." Picking up the can again, she sat down opposite him. "I'm also curious."

"Oh, so this isn't just a casual visit. You've got questions. About?"

She looked at his left hip, remembering what had gone through her mind when she'd stood over him in the hospital, not sure if he was going to make it despite what the doctor had assured her. Her father had been shot in the shoulder and the hip and his chances were not the best. Twenty-nine or not, she wasn't ready to be an orphan yet.

"Are you sure that was an accident?"

His brows drew together. "You mean did I see the guy who shot me? No. There was a lot going down that day, Mag-pie. Shots were flying everywhere. One second, we were making a good bust, the next minute, all hell broke loose. The guy we were coming for had reinforcements. There were shooters everywhere. They matched the bullet I caught in my chest to the gun some dead punk was holding in his hand. Why?''

"Just trying to get a few things straight in my head. You said it was a policeman's service revolver," she reminded him.

"If you're asking me how the scum got a hold of it, I can't help you." He told her what she knew was in the report. "The guy it belonged to caught a bullet in the head."

This information had bothered her then and it bothered her now. "Why take his gun when there were obviously so many others on the scene?"

He lifted his right shoulder, letting it fall again. "A sick sense of humor, maybe. Or he lost his own weapon. Who knows? All I know is that every day I thank your mother for watching over me." He nodded upward. "Another inch over and we wouldn't be having this conversation." And then he looked at her more closely. "Why *are* we having this conversation?"

Talking to Cavanaugh had made her start to compare the two incidents. Both had been deemed as tragic mistakes. Both men had been shot with service revolvers, but that was where the similarities ended. Or did they? She couldn't get past the feeling that maybe there was a connection of some kind.

"I can't really put it into words, Dad. It's just a feeling I have."

"About?" he prodded gently.

"That maybe this is part of something else."

"Like what?"

She couldn't tell him about Ramirez, or her assignment, but she could talk to him about what had happened to him. "Like maybe someone tried to get you out of the way—you said the bullet almost cost you your life. Or if not out of the way, then at least off the force." She could feel an excitement building in her, but it had no outlet yet. "Is there anything you might know that could be a danger to someone?"

He laughed and shook his head. "You've been watching that TV show about the CIA again, haven't you?"

Maggi bit her tongue. Her father had no idea that she worked undercover for Internal Affairs and she meant to keep it that way. She wasn't sure exactly how he would take it, even if her motives were pure.

"Yeah, maybe I have. But if you think of anything, give me a call."

"You'll be the first to know." He dug himself out of the sofa and rose to his feet. "Now come in the kitchen and keep me company while I have my dinner. You can have some if you want."

She really hadn't eaten all that much at dinner. "What are you having?"

"Stroganoff. The brand you like," he added.

"Got an extra one in the freezer?"

He grinned. "Don't I always?"

She'd lost her taste for frozen dinners since she'd grown up, but here there was a bit of nostalgia attached to it. She felt like being nostalgic tonight, felt like remembering a time when dirty meant something that needed a little soap and water to come clean. "Okay, you twisted my arm."

He slipped his arm around her shoulder. "I thought I might."

Chapter 12

He'd had better ideas in his time.

Patrick frowned as he turned down a street. One side looked out onto a golf course, dormant now in deference to the inclement weather. The other, to his left, was lined with houses peering over a gray cinder-block wall. He was on his way to McKenna's apartment. She'd gotten to him at a weak point, when he'd been fresh from a visit to his uncle's.

Early this morning he'd swung by Patience's place. He'd picked her up and the two of them had breakfast with the others. Best medicine in the world. Going there helped ward off the darkness that threatened to seep into his soul. Not only did he get to see Shaw, Callie, the twins and Rayne, but two of his other cousins, as well, although Uncle Brian was a no-show.

Patrick hadn't done much talking, but he'd listened. And basked in the normalcy of the gathering. He'd lowered his guard just enough so that when McKenna called to ask him if he wanted to go ahead and start digging into Ramirez's records, he'd said the first thing that had come to his mind—yes.

The next thing he knew, he was listening to directions on how to get to her apartment. The radar that ordinarily saw him through dangerous, dicey moments kicked in immediately.

Dangerous and dicey. He figured she could be placed under that heading, although he was starting to think she belonged in a subcategory all her own.

"Why your apartment?"

"Do you have a computer?"

"No." He saw absolutely no use for one. Gadgets annoyed him. They required patience and reading, not to mention babying. If something was to work, it should do so at the flip of a switch, like a lightbulb or a television set, not because you were armed with an instructions manual big enough to choke a Clydesdale.

"I didn't think so," she said. He didn't particularly care for her smug tone. "The main thing you need if you're trying to get access to computer files is a computer."

He saw the woman five long days a week. Why was he even contemplating giving up his weekend to subject himself to more of the same? "Don't get smart with me, Mary Margaret."

He heard her laugh and instantly saw her in his mind's eye, her eyes bright, her mouth wide. Patrick wondered what the hell was happening to his control.

"Wouldn't dream of it."

He asked for a rain check. She talked him out of it. He placed several obstacles in the path; she knocked them down. The end result was that he found himself here, entering her apartment complex, searching for a parking place.

He told himself if he didn't find one in five minutes, he would just turn around and go back. But then a spot opened up. Grudgingly he took it.

Her ground-floor apartment faced the back of the complex. He had no trouble finding it. Apart from the identifying number on the door, his attention would have still been drawn to it. McKenna's door was completely gift wrapped in gold foil with a wreath topping it off.

The woman obviously had never found the word *restraint* in the dictionary.

Feeling surlier than usual, Patrick rang the doorbell. Christmas carols echoed in response. It figured.

Maggi unlocked the door even before his thumb was off the bell. "Hi, you showed up."

He tried not to notice that she was barefoot and her jeans fit her as if she'd just this moment painted them on. The powder-blue pullover she had on needed at least three inches to meet the top of her jeans. Her flat belly peeked out flirtatiously and made his palms itch.

"Told you I'd be here," he growled in response.

She opened the door wider. "I figured you'd come up with a last-minute excuse."

He gave her a look and remained where he was, on the opposite side of the threshold. "I could go."

Maggi stepped out of the way, her invitation clear. "Staying is easier."

"That's a matter of opinion," he muttered under his breath. He still thought coming here was a mistake, but he'd never been one to back away from something that made him uneasy.

Following her into the two-bedroom apartment, he

made it past the small kitchen before stopping dead. The whole apartment was saturated with toys of all shapes and sizes, wrapping paper and ribbons everywhere he looked.

And smack in the middle of the living room was a floor-to-ceiling Scotch pine jammed into a tree holder, its head slightly bent under the weight of the star affixed to it. There were decorations, multicolored lights and tinsel reflecting back at the viewer from every angle.

If there was a Santa Claus, he would have had less going on in his workshop than was happening here, Patrick thought.

"Someone die and leave you a toy shop?" He turned to look at her. "What are you doing with so many toys? You actually know this many kids?"

She led him to the rear of the room. There was a small desk against the wall. It hosted a computer and flat panel, leaving just enough room for a notepad. The printer sat on the floor to the right of the desk.

"No, not personally," she told him.

He looked around again. Action figures, dolls, stuffed animals. Did she have some kind of toy hang-up? He didn't think he'd ever seen this many toys outside of FAO Schwartz toy store.

Patrick found himself wondering more and more about his new partner and liking it less and less. "Don't tell me Santa Claus is really a woman."

"These are for the kids at St. Agnes Shelter. That's the shelter for abused women and children," she explained. "I'm collecting for them." Innocence personified, Maggi turned her face up to his. "Care to make a donation?"

"I know what St. Agnes Shelter is."

She'd struck a chord, one he would have preferred not having struck. He was intimately familiar with the shelter she'd named. It had been around for twenty years. Long enough for him and his mother and sister to visit once. Flee to, actually. They'd been forced to go that time his father had completely lost control. Patrick remembered because it was shortly after his aunt Rose, uncle Andrew's wife, had disappeared.

His father's drinking binges had gone from bad to worse. When his mother tried to get him to stop, one thing had led to another until he was threatening to kill all of them. Despite that, Patrick knew his mother would have remained with his father, but Patrick had pleaded with her to think of herself and Patience. And told her that he would kill his father if anything happened to either one of them. In the end, more afraid of that than harm to herself, she'd gone, but only after he'd promised to come with her.

So he'd gone to the shelter with his mother and sister and had seen firsthand the sadness that existed in places like that. Everyone tried to cheer one another up, but the sadness had hung on like a steely specter, waiting for them, never letting go.

They'd gone home again, amid his father's promises to his mother that things would change. They had, but not of his choosing. His father was killed in the line of duty less than six months later.

Maggi looked at the dark, brooding man in her living room. Something was going on here, Maggi thought. More than just his cynicism. "Are you all right?"

"Yeah, fine." He waved a dismissive hand at her question. "I was just thinking that maybe I will make a donation."

He shrugged, drawing his eyes away from her face

before he did something stupid he'd regret. And then, because he'd been on the inside, because he'd seen the vacant eyes and the despair up close in children who were old before their time, he added, "That's a good thing you're doing."

An odd note stirred in his voice. She couldn't begin to interpret it. There was a lot of that going on when it came it Cavanaugh, she thought. Somehow, she was going to have to find a way to get closer to the man. So far, she hadn't a clue as to how.

"Thank you. That means a lot, coming from you."

His eyes narrowed as he maneuvered his way around the living room, his path impeded by piles of toys. "What's that supposed to mean?"

"Well, you don't exactly act as if you approve of me."

"You're all right. I mean, as far as cops go." Impatience began to break out of its bonds. "Can we get on with this?"

"Sure." She edged over to her computer, which was on, her cable connection already opened. "Where would you like to start?"

He looked around, at a loss. "How about finding a place to sit?"

"Sorry." Since the sofa was close to the desk, she cleared a place off for him, moving the brigade of stuffed animals closer together and over to one side. She grinned, gesturing toward the spot. "I'm sure that Big Bear and the others won't mind sharing their seat with you."

"Big Bear?" He stared at the large white polar bear with its silly grin and drooping head. "You named the stuffed animals?"

"Not me. The toy manufacturer beat me to it." The

bear looked as if it was going fall forward so she tucked it in beside the stuffed fox. "But I used to whenever my father gave me one." A fond look curved her mouth. "I was an only child—he liked to spoil me."

"Yeah, it shows."

If his words were any more weighed down with sarcasm, they would have made a hole in the floor. "Oh?"

"You like getting your own way."

Maggi tried not to take offense, but it wasn't easy. "That's called a forceful personality."

"That's called being a pain in the—" He sighed. If they were going to do anything productive, although he still wasn't sure what, then this was the wrong way to go. "Sorry, let's start over."

Maggi sat down at the computer, her back to him. "Fine by me."

He paused, unable to wrap his mind around his late partner and the possibility of wrongdoing, especially when his mind kept traveling the short path to the woman sitting at the computer.

The question came of its own accord, as if he had no say over the matter. "You've mentioned your father several times."

"Sorry, does that bother you?"

There was a touch of frost in her reply. He ignored it. "It's just that you never talk about your mother."

Maggi glanced toward the framed photo on the side table. It was of the three of them. The last one she had of her mother. "My mother died when I was nine. Car crash."

He'd heard her tell Alicia about her mother, he just hadn't realized she'd been that young when her mother died. "Sorry, didn't mean to…" Uncomfortable, Patrick let his voice trail off.

"Didn't mean to what, ask me a personal question? No problem. Just means we're getting closer together."

The look on his face was one of annoyed disgust. She would have been a little disappointed if he hadn't reacted at all.

"You're not going to be happy until we're joined at the hip, are you?" he asked.

"If I'm going to be your partner, I need to know how you think," she told him simply. *And if I'm going to get any answers for IA, that won't hurt, either.*

"Why?"

"So I can anticipate your next move. So I can be there to cover your back."

He'd wandered over to the side table and picked up the family photograph. They were all smiling. The smiles looked genuine. In the single shot he had of his immediate family, the only smile in the photograph belonged to Patience, who would have smiled standing next to the devil himself. His sister would probably like McKenna, he thought.

"You keep pushing me out in front and covering my back," he said.

"Sorry, does that bother you?" She turned around to glance at him and was surprised to discover that he was right behind her. "I'd take the lead but I get these Neanderthal vibes from you that tell me you wouldn't let a woman walk in front of you. It's a macho thing, am I right?"

Why the hell were her eyes getting to him when her wagging tongue was rubbing the very flesh off his body? Annoyed, he took a step back. "Which is why a man shouldn't be partnered with a woman."

Maggi sighed, her eyes fluttering shut for a second

as she sought strength. "That is so wrong I don't even know where to begin."

He laughed shortly. As if she was going to ever be quiet. "But you'll find a way, won't you?" He made a decision. "Look, this was a mistake." He began to back away. "I can—"

He was going to say that he could get the information he needed by himself. "Not easily," she interjected.

Ordinarily, what people thought had less than no effect on him, but for some reason, when it came to her, Patrick didn't like being cast in the role of an idiot. "Are you saying I can't get the information I need without you?"

"No," she contradicted. "What I'm saying is that it'll take you longer than if you let me help." She raised her eyes to his. "And I'm betting that you're smart enough to put whatever differences we still have aside to tackle this."

"Whatever differences we *still* have?" Patrick hooted incredulously. "Mary Margaret, there are nothing *but* differences between us."

Maggi tossed her head, sending her hair over her shoulder. She looked at him pointedly. "Oh, I think we found some common ground and it seems to be widening all the time." Before he could comment, she moved her swivel chair back to face the computer. "Okay, let's start out with the basics."

As he stood watching over her shoulder, Maggi called up Eduardo Ramirez's vital statistics via an internal program that had been installed by the Aurora police department some years earlier. The safeguards on it were brand-new. In an instant, they had Ramirez's social security number, his driver's license as well as a thumbnail sketch of his background and education.

In the area designated for any incidents reports, there was nothing. His record was surprisingly spotless, given their suspicions.

"You have access to that?"

She heard the doubt in his voice. Maggi indicated the screen. "You see it, don't you?"

Patrick was beginning to figure out how her mind worked. Sideways, like a sidewinder. "You're not answering my question," he persisted.

Maggi smiled to herself as she took in the information she'd pulled up. "Let's just say that if there's a paper trail of some sort, I can get access to almost anything we might need to clear this up."

She had already gotten into Patrick's banking records the night she'd received her assignment. But if Patrick was trafficking in something illegal and getting paid for it, he wasn't putting the money into anything that showed up on her radar. That fact didn't clear him, just made him harder to pin down. But then, if this mission had been easy, she wouldn't have been here.

"You really weren't kidding about being able to hack into data banks." The look he gave her wasn't quite accusing, just mystified. "Where did you learn how to do this?"

She didn't bother boring him with the fact that she had perfect recall. The kind that made people leery around you. "From a computer genius I knew in high school." She thought of Ronnie Rindle and smiled to herself. "He liked to challenge himself. His aspirations ended when he was caught starting a major upset on Wall Street by moving stock around and having false data show up in accounts." She still got cards from Ronnie at Christmas. "While he was behind bars, he found a new passion. Pottery. Keeps him out of trouble.''

Patrick didn't quite follow her narrative. "And he passed on his mantel to you?"

Ronnie had tried to get her to join him, but she'd politely pointed out the very real danger of what he was doing. He'd been caught the very next day. "No, just gave me a few tips in gratitude."

"Gratitude?"

"He was kind of lonely. I was the only one who called him a genius, not a geek. He was a little odd, but nice."

Patrick had a feeling that she was the type of person who could find some good in almost anyone. They were as different as night and day. "For a felon."

"Reformed felon. Very good sculptor, really." Maggi looked back at the screen. "We've got Ramirez's social security number, shouldn't be too hard for us to get anything else. His wife said something about the money being in First Republic, didn't she?"

"You figure the money's just sitting in his bank account?"

"If your ex-partner got mixed up in this by accident, sure, why not? You make things too complicated, Cavanaugh. Only hardened criminals pay attention to safeguards and details. Besides, if Ramirez was accustomed to blowing money the way you said he was, he'd want it where he could get his hands on it easily enough."

But even now, she was frowning. A scan of the bank's records showed that the joint account held by Eduardo and Alicia Ramirez had less than a hundred and fifty dollars in it.

"This wouldn't take care of a week's groceries for

a family of four,'' Maggi commented. The money had to be somewhere else. But where?

''See if there's another account.''

She'd already tried that. ''Not with his name and social on it.'' Maggi bit her lip, tying again.

''Try his wife.''

''That's what I'm doing.'' Glancing over her shoulder at him, she grinned. ''You know what they say about great minds.''

''Yeah, they're inside swelled heads.'' No one was going to accuse him of thinking like this woman.

Maggi shook her head. ''Definitely need to work on your holiday spirit.''

Patrick pointed at the flat panel. As far as he was concerned, Christmas was just another day, like all the rest. ''Keep your mind on the screen,'' he told her tersely.

Maggi typed, her fingers flying, keying in codes. Watching her, Patrick marveled at how fast she was going. When he typed, it took him more than a minute to find every letter of a word.

Sitting back, Maggi looked at the information she'd manage to pull up. She was far from satisfied. ''Okay, Alicia Ramirez has a checking account with almost a thousand dollars in it.''

He thought of the way the woman had turned down his offer to help. ''I guess it was just her pride, then,'' he surmised.

Still typing, Maggi wasn't ready to throw in the towel. ''Maybe, maybe not.''

There was something in her voice that put him on the alert. ''You find something?''

Yes! ''There's a third account.'' Satisfaction rippled through her as the information began to emerge. ''Neither Ramirez nor his wife is the principle reportable social security number on it.''

He didn't follow and hated feeling dumb. ''Then how did you—?''

She turned the screen at an angle so he could see it, as well. ''I tried to link either one of them up with another account. You know, like maybe in one of the kids' names.''

''And?''

She tapped the top line of the screen. ''You have any idea who Maria Cortez is?''

''No, why?''

''Well, she and Alicia have a joint account together and this Maria's social security number is the one that gets reported to the IRS. And whoever she is, she must be one rich lady.''

Moving aside, Maggi indicated the bottom line of a series of entries, all made in a relatively short amount of time. And fairly recently.

The current balance in the account was close to two hundred thousand dollars.

Maggi shook her head as she looked at the figure. ''If this does represent money that Ramirez was putting away in his wife's name, all I have to say is that the raises in your department must be phenomenal.''

Chapter 13

She was having a hard time concentrating, what with Patrick behind her, moving back and forth like a brooding duck at a shooting gallery. Until now, she would have sworn that the man had been created without any nerves, but this clearly flew in the face of what she thought she knew about him.

It was obvious that what they were discovering about Ramirez bothered him. Why? Because she was getting close to something, or because this was about someone he'd allowed himself to think of as a friend? Did it disturb him because he thought his judgment was poor, or because it was Ramirez, a man he'd liked?

Whatever the answer, the relentless movement behind her began to grate on her nerves. When she hit a misstroke and had to backtrack, she bit off a curse. Trying to hold on to her temper, she glanced over her shoulder. "You know, I could do this a lot faster if you weren't pacing around like that."

Patrick stopped, not because she wanted him to but because he hadn't realized he was pacing. His own display of unrest annoyed him. "I thought nothing distracted you."

"So did I."

Her answer was barely audible and was meant more for herself than for him. She was becoming increasingly attuned to Patrick and not in a useful way. Maggi was afraid that it would make her want to tip the scales and the second she did, she became worse than useless to Internal Affairs.

Patrick pointed a finger at the screen. "Just work."

She caught the vein of distress beneath the royal command. "This is bothering you, isn't it?"

He raked his fingers through his hair, sending it into further disarray. Watching him, she found herself wanting to do the same, but she kept her fingers flying over the keyboard. It was safer that way.

"Wouldn't it bother you to find out you had a crooked partner?"

"Yes," Maggi deliberately turned around to look at him, "it would." She watched his face.

Nothing. Not a flinch, not a twitch, not an uncomfortable look. You're either very, very good, Cavanaugh, or you're innocent.

And she knew exactly which way she wanted to vote. Trouble was, you couldn't vote on facts. They either existed or they didn't. So far, there was nothing she could find to substantiate the rumors against him. But that didn't mean they weren't true, she reminded herself. Just that Cavanaugh was good at burying things.

It didn't take Maggi much more digging to discover the identity of Alicia Ramirez's partner on the joint account. Cortez turned out to be Alicia's maiden name. Maria Cortez was her mother.

Playing on the side of the angels, she asked, "Did Ramirez ever mention or hint that his mother-in-law was well-off?"

Patrick shook his head as he stared at a flickering light on her tree. She needed a new bulb, he thought absently. "He didn't say much about her except that she was a dragon lady and never forgave him for getting Alicia pregnant."

The more she heard about his late partner, the more she liked him. But then, she'd learned a long time ago that nothing was ever black or white. Dirty cops could be nice guys, too. "Pretty open, wasn't he?"

"That's my whole point." The frustration Patrick felt was barely contained beneath the surface. "If he'd gotten into something that wasn't aboveboard, he would have told me."

Still on the side of the angels, she pushed a little further. "Then maybe this is his mother-in-law's money."

He looked at the screen she'd pulled up, his expression darkening. "Not if she was making deposits up to six weeks ago."

She looked at the string of deposits that were listed. They'd stopped abruptly the third week in October. "Why?"

"Because I attended her funeral nine months ago."

Without saying a word, Maggi scrolled back to the beginning of the account. "This account was opened seven months ago."

Damn it, Ed, what the hell were you up to? What were you thinking? He looked at Maggi. It didn't make sense. "So tell me, how does a dead woman open a bank account?"

That she could answer. "It's very simple, really. Alicia goes in, saying she wants a joint account, but that her mother is too ill to come in and sign the papers. Wanting their business, the bank is more than happy to be accommodating. They give her a signature card to take home to mom, Alicia brings it back signed and voilà, a new account is opened, bearing mom's name." She stopped. He had that strange look in his eyes, the one that said he was examining her. "What?"

"How would you know that?" Patrick asked.

"I worked Fraud for a while in 'Frisco. You pick things up." She frowned as she viewed the screen again. There was no doubt about it—this did not look good. Wanting to see what he would do next, she placed the ball back in his court. "Now what?"

Patrick shoved his hands into his jeans. "Now I try to figure out what to do with this." He hated the kind of thoughts he was having. Ramirez had been one of the few people outside his family he'd trusted. Hell, he'd trusted the man more than he'd trusted his own father. What the hell did that say about his ability to read people? He slanted a glance at Maggi. "Those deposits wouldn't happen to be traceable, would they?"

Maggi shook her head. "Cash, every time." And then she paused, looking closer. "Interesting."

"What is?" Patrick leaned more closely over her, his hand on her shoulder as he looked at the screen.

She felt waves of warmth working their way through her, coming out of the blue. Trying to seduce her. *Not the time, Mag, not the time,* she warned herself. The waves kept coming.

Shifting, she got him to remove his hand. "The

handwriting on the deposit slips doesn't seem to match Alicia's.'' She pointed out the copies, then, hitting a button, she enlarged the portion that had caught her attention. ''Hers is neat, precise.'' She shifted back to the deposit slips. ''This is somebody dipping a chicken's foot in ink and making passes on a piece of paper. It actually makes my dad's handwriting look good.''

Patrick's expression was grim as he looked at the samples she pointed out. ''That's the way Ramirez used to write.''

Ramirez made the deposits, probably to keep his wife innocent of what was going on. Maggi sincerely doubted the woman knew what her husband was really up to, other than trying to avoid reporting interest on an account.

Keeping his wife in the dark was one thing. Keeping his partner there was another matter. She was having a difficult time believing that Cavanaugh had no inkling of what Ramirez had been up to. After all, it wasn't as if Cavanaugh was mentally challenged or walked around, oblivious to things.

Maggi decided to go fishing. ''You said he liked to talk. He ever approach you about this, make any vague references to feel you out?''

Patrick looked at her sharply. ''No, he knew better than that.''

She was pushing him, she thought, and he looked like he was on the edge. Maggi shoved with both hands. ''You mean that he knew you were a straight shooter, right?''

He came close to telling her what she could do with her sarcastic tone, but stopped himself in time. He wasn't angry at her. He was angry at Ramirez for betraying him and for being stupid.

"I'm not pure as the driven snow," he informed her tersely. "I've got my share of black marks, but you don't get mixed up in something like that. One way or another, they'll get you."

Her eyes never left his face as she typed in more code. "You talking about the good guys or the bad?"

"Both." Bullets came from both directions. The way he saw it, if the good guys didn't catch you, the bad guys killed you. "Somebody gets greedy, somebody gets nervous." Cursing roundly, he moved away, needing space. Feeling frustrated. "Damn it, why didn't I see it?"

His anguish seemed genuine. So genuine she wanted to comfort him but knew that was both stupid and counterproductive. She needed him like this. If he was emotionally strung out, he was more likely to slip up. *If* there was anything to slip up about.

"Maybe because you're not clairvoyant."

He didn't need or want her sympathy. It changed nothing. Ramirez was dead not because he hadn't gone first into that building but because he hadn't been smart enough to pick up on things. He'd let the man down.

"I was his partner, the guy who was stuck with him for eight, ten, twelve hours a day. I should have felt it. He'd gotten quieter in the end." Patrick blew out a breath. Why hadn't Ramirez said anything? Why? "I just thought he and Alicia were having problems."

"I thought you said he always talked. Doesn't that mean he would have said something to you about it if he was having problems with his wife?"

A broad shoulder rose and fell. "Well, sometimes Ramirez kept a little something to himself. Chewed on it until he was ready to share." Now that he thought about it, things started to fall into place. Ramirez *had* looked as if he wanted to talk just before they'd gone on the raid, but then the man had waved it away. At the time, he hadn't thought anything of it. Maybe Ramirez had wanted to make a clean breast of his involvement. "He'd been preoccupied that last week."

"Maybe debating whether or not to get out."

And the wrong people had found out, Patrick thought, and decided to have him eliminated. He clenched his fists in his pockets. "Maybe."

She stopped pretending to type and turned to give him her full attention. "Any ideas on what he might have been mixed up in and who else might be involved?"

He frowned as he eyed her. "Right now, where I stand, everybody's a suspect." His meaning was clear.

The look in his eyes made her squirm inside, but she kept a mild expression on her face as she raised her hands in protest. "Hey, I'm the new kid on the block. I'm clean."

"This is a virus. It could have spread out in any direction." But he really didn't believe she was mixed up in something. She was the one doing the probing. If anything, he held that against her, but nothing else.

Patrick's words triggered a thought. Her father popped into her head. The accidental shooting had gotten her father off the force. Had that been on purpose? Had her father been about to stumble onto something and been blocked just in time?

"The trouble with conspiracy theories," she said aloud, "is that they start making you paranoid, get you looking over your shoulder all the time."

He thought of the way he'd been fooled. It wasn't

an image of himself he relished. "Maybe that's not such a bad thing."

She laughed shortly, thinking more of her line of work than anything he was facing. "Hell of a way to live."

"Key word here is 'live' and to keep on living." The image of his partner on the ground, already having taken his last breath, leaving behind a wife and three small children, ran through his head. "Maybe Ramirez should have been a little paranoid."

"Maybe he was. Maybe he tried to get out and that's when they had him shot."

She was on to something, he thought. And he needed to act on it. "I think I'll start by talking to Dugan."

"The guy who shot him?"

Mentally he was already out of the apartment and on his way. "Yeah, he's on disability."

Maggi was on her feet. The man definitely didn't know how to segue into anything. "Now? You're going to see him now?"

"Now's as good a time as any."

If he was going to question the man, she wanted to be there. This could all wind up being part of the same puzzle. She began to entertain the idea that maybe someone was throwing dirt on Cavanaugh to avoid any undue scrutiny.

"Give me a second to shut down my computer and unplug the tree."

Instinct told him to keep walking. He stopped anyway. "Why?"

"Because I'm going with you."

"He was my partner." He didn't want her tagging along. It was bad enough he had to put up with it during work hours.

She looked at him before answering, trying to figure out just what was going on in his head. "Yes, and you're mine."

Arguing with her would take up too much time. And he had a feeling that if he opted to walk out, she would be right there on his tail. He might as well keep her in his sights.

Sighing, Patrick gestured at the Christmas tree. "All right, go ahead, unplug it."

To his surprise, she began to crawl under the tree. He couldn't help watching as she snaked her way underneath, her small, tight posterior moving just enough to dry his mouth. He was only vaguely aware when the tree went dark after she hit the switch at the end of the abbreviated extension cord.

"You know, it must be five degrees hotter around this tree. Are you single-handedly trying to fund the energy company?"

Maggi wiggled back out from beneath the tree and rose to her feet. She'd managed to emerge a little closer to him than she'd anticipated. But to take a step back would have shown him that his proximity affected her. She remained where she was, at least for a beat.

"Hey, it's only one month out of the year. And it makes me happy."

The scent of something sweet and heady swirled around him. Cologne? Shampoo? Hadn't the woman ever heard of using scent-free products?

"I didn't think you needed anything to 'make' you happy," he said gruffly. "I thought you came that way."

"Never hurts to have a little reinforcement."

Her smile unfurled inside him like a cat stretching awake before a fireplace. "Whatever you say." If he didn't back off now, he knew he was done for. "Let's get going."

"Right."

Thank God he had backed away, or she would have had to, Maggi thought. She was going to have to remember to leave space between them. Lots and lots of space. Otherwise, the temptation to have no space at all would overwhelm her.

Another time and place, this would have been different, and she might have acted on what she was feeling, but here it wasn't going to work. Anything that might have been between them was doomed before she ever laid eyes on the brooding man. Allowing herself to go further down that road was only asking for trouble.

Why did trouble have to look so damn enticing?

Josh Dugan lived in a small wooden framed house that had once belonged to his parents and looked it. Like an aging former athlete, the two-story building sagged in a number of places and there were shingles missing from its roof.

"Well, if he's in on something illegal, he's not spending the money on home improvements, that's for sure," Maggi observed as Patrick rang the bell. "This place would have to have some major renovations just to be classified as a fixer-upper."

He made no comment, listening instead for the sound of someone coming on the other side. But there was nothing. After ringing again, Patrick knocked, hard.

A woman across the street was walking by with her dog. She stopped to look in their direction, curiosity painted on her weathered face. Pulling her terrier closer, she stopped and called out. "You two looking for Josh?"

Maggi walked down the rickety steps, crossing the wide residential street to reach her. "Yes, you know where he is?"

The other woman lifted her shoulders beneath a worn winter coat that had never been in style. "Gone."

Patrick frowned, joining Maggi. "What do you mean, gone?"

The woman seemed puzzled by the question. "Like, not there. I knocked on his door more than a couple of weeks ago to see if he wanted to come over for some Thanksgiving leftovers—never seem to be able to get rid of the stuff, you know?" she said, looking at Maggi.

Patrick suppressed an impatient sound. "What about Dugan?"

The expression on the woman's face told them she didn't like being rushed. "He wasn't home. Hasn't been home since, far as I can tell." As if to validate the information, she added, "I live across the street."

She pointed to a house that looked as if it had been a mirror image of Dugan's when the builder had finished his work. Now, the second house was in far better condition than the one belonging to the missing policeman. The woman's house squarely faced Dugan's. Her front windows would have allowed her a perfect view of Dugan's comings and goings. Patrick had a feeling she stationed herself at them with fair regularity.

"Do you remember when you last saw Officer Dugan?" Maggi asked.

The woman paused to think. "Just before then. Two and a half, three weeks ago, maybe."

"What was he doing?" Patrick pressed.

She shifted the leash from one hand to the other and

turned up her collar against the late afternoon wind. "Some men came over to see him. Friends from the squad I guess."

Patrick was on it immediately. "What makes you say that? Were they in uniform?"

The woman looked annoyed at the close questioning. "No, I said I guess."

Maggi intervened before Patrick's lack of people skills alienated the woman. "And you haven't seen him since?"

The woman frowned. A longing appeared in her eyes as she looked over to the other house. "No."

"Could you describe the men?" Maggi wanted to know.

Again the woman shrugged. "I dunno. They were men. Average height, dark hair, nothing special. Not like Josh," she added.

"How many were there?"

"Five. I remember because I wondered how they could all get into the car they were in. Like clowns in a circus, you know?"

Maggi nodded. "Did you notice what kind of a car?"

"Some foreign thing. Black, navy, I'm not sure."

It was obvious that the woman had exhausted her supply of useful information. Patrick took out a card and handed it to her. "If you think of anything else, give me a call."

Her hand curved around the card as she looked up at him. There was no mistaking the interest that had entered her brown eyes. "Can I give you a call if I don't think of anything else?"

"You might have to talk to his wife or one of his six kids first," Maggi told her cheerfully as she hooked her arm through Patrick's and drew him away. "Thanks for your help," she tossed over her shoulder.

"Thanks," he muttered to Maggi as the woman walked away.

"Don't mention it." She winked at him. "Told you I had your back." He was suddenly striding ahead of her with purpose, and she hurried to catch up. "Hey, where are you going?"

"To look around Dugan's. We've got probable cause now."

"We also have nothing," Patrick conceded thirty minutes later after they had searched the premises. He'd half expected to find Dugan's body in a pool of blood. It was getting to be that kind of a day. "He might have just gone on vacation."

Maggi stopped rummaging through the man's closet. "I thought he was in the middle of therapy with the department shrink."

"Can't think of better therapy than a vacation."

She caught something in his voice. "You don't believe he went on one, do you?"

"Nope."

Maggi stepped away from the closet and went to check the bureau drawers. "And you'd be right. Unless he went to a nudist colony." When Patrick lifted a brow, she nodded toward the open closet. "Suitcases are still in the closet."

"Maybe he had an extra one."

A half smile curved her mouth. "Men don't have extra suitcases. They also don't go anywhere without underwear. They shove it in at the last minute, but they take it." She closed the last of the drawers she'd opened. "His drawers are full."

He looked at her, curious despite himself. She kept doing that to him, he thought. "How do you know so much about how men pack?"

"Because I used to repack for one."

"Your father?"

"My fiancé."

The information stopped him in his tracks. He refused to speculate why. "You're engaged?"

"Was," Maggi corrected.

A wave of relief came out of nowhere. "What happened?"

She wondered if he'd even understand what she meant if she said, *Que sera, sera.* "My father caught a bullet, I caught a plane. My fiancé stayed where he was, nurturing his career."

"And you're not going back?"

"Nothing to go back to. Since when do you ask personal questions?"

"You must be rubbing off on me. And before you say anything, no, that's not a good thing."

Maggi forced herself to get her mind back on her work. She walked out of the bedroom. "I'm going to give this place another pass. Maybe there's something we're overlooking."

He was right behind her. "Like evidence of foul play?"

Maggi nodded. "Crossed my mind."

He doubted they had missed anything. The house was almost Spartan in its decor. "Easier to just take Dugan for a ride and do away with him somewhere else. Still, he might have decided to take off."

"Easy enough to verify, unless he decided to drive somewhere."

She was talking about her computer, he thought. "Back to your place?"

She was quick to grin. "Took the words right out of my mouth."

"That's a first."

There were other things he wanted to do with her mouth, things that had nothing to do with uttering words, but he kept that to himself. It was getting crowded there, amid all the things he was holding to himself, but he figured it was damn well safer that way. To release them into the light of day might just spell something else for him and he wasn't willing to go there yet.

Maybe never.

Chapter 14

She was getting too close.

Not to any dark, secret underbelly that Patrick Cavanaugh was suspected of having, just too close to the man himself. Too close to emotions that had absolutely no place in this kind of investigation. Not that she would allow them to cloud her judgment or stand in the way of her doing the right thing. She had too much integrity for that.

But Patrick did make it extremely difficult to concentrate, difficult to think of him as possibly being guilty of the allegations anonymously brought against him.

Just after she'd finished her shift, she'd been summoned to meet with her superior over another tepid cup of coffee at yet another out-of-the-way diner. She waited only long enough for the waitress to withdraw before expressing her doubts about the necessity of continuing the charade.

Maggi thought of the way Cavanaugh had looked when she'd suggested his late partner had been on the take. "The man can be colder than last week's toast, but he's a good cop," she insisted.

Halliday poured enough cream into his coffee to turn it a pale shade of tan. "Maybe that's what he wants you to think."

She didn't like the idea that Halliday thought she could be manipulated. "I don't think he 'wants' me to see anything. He doesn't care what I think of him, what anyone thinks of him. He's just out to do his job." It was stupid, but she felt protective of Cavanaugh. Felt the way, she realized, she would about a real partner she cared about.

If Halliday even noticed or was disturbed by her defense of the detective, he gave no indication. "It's early days and no one said he wasn't good at what he does. Maybe it's too soon for him to relax around you, to let his guard down."

She thought of the dark bar and the kiss across a wobbly table. And the way her heart had stood still. "I think he's as relaxed as he's going to get."

"Early days," Halliday repeated.

She felt a little as though she was telling tales out of school, but then, that was what she was supposed to be doing, right? Halliday had a right to know what she and Cavanaugh were investigating in their free time. And it might cast him in a good light. "There's more."

Halliday looked attentive. "Such as?"

Though the booths on either side of them were empty, she still leaned over the table and lowered her voice so that only Halliday could hear. "Cavanaugh suspects his late partner might have been on the take."

Halliday's eyes were flat as they regarded her. "Suspects, or wants you to suspect?"

She didn't want Halliday thinking that Cavanaugh was orchestrating anything. "He doesn't even want himself to suspect and he's been against my getting involved in this from the beginning."

The role of devil's advocate fit Halliday like a well-tailored, custom-made glove. "Because it'll point to his culpability."

"No," Maggi insisted, stopping just shy of being heated, "because Cavanaugh liked Ramirez, because he wants to help the man's wife and kids." She paused for a moment, knowing she was pulling things out of the air, setting them down out of order. "Let me start at the beginning."

Quickly she filled her superior in on what they'd learned about the situation, being careful to skip just how the information came into her hands. She had a feeling that unless there was a trial involved, Halliday didn't care about the means, only the end.

Halliday listened quietly, his hands wrapped around the almost cold cup of coffee. When she was finished, he nodded, as if sorting through the information and slipping the various pieces into different slots in his head. He fixed her with a meaningful look. "There are at least two sides to everything."

"And?" She realized she held her breath and willed herself to draw air back into her lungs.

"And with two sides, things can be turned around a full hundred and eighty degrees."

She knew where he was going with this and part of her actually resented it on Patrick's behalf. "Meaning he's dirty and he wants to draw attention away from himself and onto someone else."

Halliday's look went right through her, clear down to her bones. "Wouldn't that be the way you'd do it if it you were in his shoes?"

She sighed and stared at the table. The Formica surface had long since turned a yellow tinge, showing signs of wear as well as ingrained stains that she guessed were probably older than she was.

"Yes."

Her answer was quiet, swallowed up by the late afternoon din of people stopping by the diner for a quick bite before hurrying back to their lives. Right now, she envied them, envied what she imagined was the simplicity of their lives.

Halliday drained his cup, then set it down. He folded his hands before him, a theoretician stating his argument. "Don't you think it's rather odd that if Ramirez was dirty, Cavanaugh didn't know it? The two worked together for over two years. Cavanaugh isn't exactly fresh off the turnip truck."

No, she thought, he wasn't. He was one of the sharpest people she'd ever met. Which was why she was afraid that sooner rather than later, Cavanaugh was going to catch on to what she was doing.

"But if you're not looking for something, you might not see it," she insisted. And then her eyes widened as she thought she understood. "Is this why you're having me investigate him? Because of Ramirez?"

Halliday was quick to put her theory to rest. "No, we didn't know about Ramirez. But if it is true, it only solidifies our suspicions."

"I don't know. I'm still not buying it."

A hint of a smile played along his thin lips. "Doubt is good. Always doubt."

That was the problem. She was doubting. Doubting

Cavanaugh, doubting herself and doubting her ability to remain impartial no matter what.

If she couldn't properly defend Cavanaugh's reputation, even for herself, the least she could do was find out some information for the man she'd been sent to defame. "What about Dugan?"

There was a pause. The look in Halliday's eyes told her he was debating whether or not to answer.

"We're looking for him," he finally said. "The department's psychologist said he was a no-show for his appointment. That was over two weeks ago. Right now, from what you're telling me, it fits in with the puzzle, that Dugan shot Ramirez on purpose rather than by accident."

A thought came to her. "Maybe he didn't shoot Ramirez on purpose. Maybe he was aiming for Cavanaugh and got the other man by accident."

Halliday considered it. "It's a possibility." He wanted to get her reasoning, see if it fit in with his own. "Why would he be shooting at Cavanaugh?"

Maggi was getting up a full head of steam now. "Because they wanted Cavanaugh out of the way. Maybe they were afraid he was getting too close to the truth and if he found out, he'd turn them in."

Halliday's face was impassive. "Still want him to be innocent, don't you, McKenna?"

Maggi resented the veiled implication that she'd doctor details to suit her purpose. "No, I just want the truth and I don't want a good cop to be sacrificed."

Halliday suddenly seemed weary. "Nobody's sacrificing anyone, Detective. We're both after the truth."

She sincerely hoped so. As far as she knew, Halliday was an honorable man who had managed to keep above the taint that this kind of job dealt with.

But he had planted enough doubts in her mind to have her not only wondering about Cavanaugh, but about Halliday and what he wanted as well. Halliday was close to retiring. Was he after one last spectacular cleanup before he handed in his shield?

She wasn't sure of anything anymore.

It was time to leave. "Let me know if you ever find Dugan," she said, rising.

Halliday nodded. "And McKenna—"

"Yes?"

His eyes held hers and she couldn't shake the feeling that he was probing her. "This is a good thing you're doing."

She allowed the corners of her mouth to curve slightly. "If it's such a good thing, why do we have to keep meeting like a couple of clandestine lovers every time you want to debrief me?"

"It's just the way the system works."

Maggi pressed her lips together. "I'm beginning to think that maybe the system needs an overhaul," she commented just before she left.

She got into her car, feeling disgruntled and gritty. It had been that kind of a day. Just before she'd met with Halliday she and Cavanaugh had gone to see Alicia again, to confront her with what they had found. This time, Patrick hadn't hung back.

"We know about the bank account, Alicia. The joint one you have with your late mother." His eyes had narrowed. "The one that was opened after she died. Why is the account under her social security number?"

Alicia had looked upset, like a good little Catholic girl caught playing hooky instead of going to mass.

"Eddie said it was better that way, that we wouldn't have to pay taxes. I know it was wrong, but—" She stopped, the look on Patrick's face halting her flow of words. "What is it?"

"This goes deeper than just trying to avoid taxes, Alicia."

She'd looked from Maggi to her husband's partner, confusion on her pretty face. "I don't understand."

"We're afraid your husband might have been mixed up in something," Maggi had said tactfully, watching Alicia's expression.

"Something?" Alicia had echoed.

"Shady," Patrick put in.

The woman rose from sofa, her face clouding over. She seemed to understand the implication if not the actual details. "Get out of my house."

"Alicia—" Patrick began.

Alicia pointed to the door. "Get out of my house," she repeated. "You come here and trash my husband's name when he can't defend himself?" Outrage echoed in her voice. "Get out of my house!"

So they had left, convinced that Alicia knew nothing beyond what she'd said. That she'd opened the account because her husband had assured her it involved avoiding taxes and nothing more.

Even now, driving home, Maggi could remember the accusing look on the woman's face. She hated it. Hated anticipating the one she knew she would eventually see on Cavanaugh's face.

It had been one hell of a day.

Matthew McKenna opened the front door on the third ring. In the background, his favorite movie, *Unforgiven,* was playing. He knew the dialogue by heart. It only enhanced his enjoyment of the viewing experience.

The expression on his daughter's face had him forgetting all about Clint Eastwood. Concerned, he ushered her in. "You look like you lost your best friend."

Her smile seemed tired to him. "No, you're still here."

Matthew shut the door behind her. "Don't try to snow me, Mag-pie. What's up?"

She'd driven around for a bit after leaving the diner and Halliday. The adult thing would have been to drive home, but she didn't feel very adult right now. She felt like a child in need of comforting. In need of knowing that there were no monsters in the closet and that things were going to turn out for the best once morning came.

Shedding her coat, she dropped it on the back of the sofa. "I can't tell you that."

Picking up the remote, he shut off the video and then the set. He motioned her to the kitchen. He knew there were things about the job that people kept to themselves. He could respect that, but it was hard when his own daughter was the one involved.

For her sake, he tried to sound chipper. "What'll you have?"

Maggi dropped down into a chair. "A shoulder to lean on and a cup of hot chocolate."

"You've already got the shoulder, you knew that when you walked in. And as for the cup of hot chocolate, this sounds serious." Taking out a saucepan, he poured what he knew by practice was a ten-ounce glass of milk, then turned the burner on low. He sat down at the table, giving his daughter his full attention. "Okay, give me a hypothetical."

She cloaked her words as best she could. "Hypothetically, I think I've lost my way. The investigation

I'm on has me completely turned around and I don't know what to believe anymore.''

Matthew covered her folded hands with one bearlike paw. He wasn't a large man, but his individual features were powerful looking.

He gave her the only advice he could. ''Your instincts, Maggi, trust your instincts. You haven't gone wrong yet. How could you?'' Getting up to tend to the milk, he paused long enough to wink at her. ''You're my daughter.''

She felt a little better even before the chocolate was poured.

Dashing around to get ready, Maggi belatedly registered the ringing in her brain. She dug into her pocket to retrieve her cell and put it against her ear. ''Hello?''

''You up, Mary Margaret?''

Patrick's deep voice filled her ear, sending echoing waves through her, swirling around in her insides. She took a controlled breath before answering.

''Up and at 'em, why?''

''Because I need a ride in and I'm on your way.'' She heard the strain in his voice. He didn't like asking for favors.

''Car trouble?'' she guessed, moving the conversation along. She paused before her reflection in the microwave door to run a hand through her too-flat hair.

''Yeah. Alternator died.'' His uncle had promised to come by this afternoon to take a look at it, just perpetuating the legend Uncle Andrew could do anything when he had to. Not like his own father who'd always put things off and accepted defeat before it ever arrived. To him, Andrew had always been the better man. ''Can you pick me up or what?''

She was tempted to ask him just what comprised an "or what," but had a feeling that would just put him off. "Consider yourself picked up. It'll be a first for me," she heard herself saying, although for the life of her, she didn't know where this had come from. "I've never picked up a man before."

That he could readily believe. Women who looked like McKenna always had men hitting on them. They didn't need to think about picking up men. "Aren't you going to ask for the address?"

"I know where you live. Part of my self-orientation program," she added, picturing the scowl on his face as he thought of having his space invaded. "I told you, I like knowing what I'm getting into."

"And knowing my address helps?"

"Just part of the whole picture, Cavanaugh, just part of the whole picture."

Ramirez had been as invasive as she was. And yet, not quite the same way. He'd also never been remotely tempted to kiss Ramirez. The urge was still very much with him, getting in his way. "Anything else on that canvas I should know about?"

"Not that comes to mind," she told him cheerfully. "See you in twenty minutes."

She made it in fifteen.

Patrick lived in a modern, two-story condo in one of the newer residential areas in Aurora. That he owned property was in itself a surprise to her. From the bio she'd been given on him, she couldn't picture Patrick owning anything—not a pet, not a plant, certainly not a place to live. A home represented ties to something and the image he projected was of someone who wanted no ties to anything.

But she was learning that the image she'd gleaned from his department file didn't really do Patrick justice or cover nearly all the bases. Like the ties she'd discovered he had to his family. Or the fact that being with him in small, tight places did things to her respiratory system over and above the expected result that came of sharing oxygen.

After leaving her car in guest parking, she walked the short distance to his front door. The first thing she noticed was that, unlike a good many of his neighbors, Patrick's door had no wreath or any other sign of holiday decor on it.

No wreath, no lights, no token holly. This lack of festivity was definitely more in keeping with her image of Patrick Cavanaugh.

It struck her as sad.

She rang his bell. The door swung open a moment later. He was still buttoning his shirt. The obligatory tie was hanging out of his front pocket.

"You're early." Turning away, he picked up his gun and holster.

"Just three minutes." She peered into the house. "Can I come in?"

"No."

She raised an eyebrow in response.

"You're not going to be here long enough to come in."

Patrick was already reaching for his jacket and slipping it on. Maggi maneuvered around him to get a better view of the inside of the condo, stepping inside.

"Like you said, I'm early." The place looked neat. That surprised her. It was also relatively empty. That didn't.

Because he disliked it most, he put his tie on last. "You just want to snoop around."

She looked at him over her shoulder. A grin flashed. "Busted."

He tried to ignore the effect it had on him and tried to concentrate on the fact that she was yet again staging an invasion. "No, but that's what you're currently doing to a certain part of my anatomy."

Maggi barely paid attention to the protest. She swung around to face him. "You have no Christmas tree."

He knew he should be annoyed. Why he was amused made no sense to him. "Sharp. I can see why they made you a detective. With observation powers like yours, you could rise all the way to the top."

"But it's Christmas." Even her father put up a tree. He said it was to appease her, but she knew the tree made him think of her mother and the Christmases they had shared.

"Technically," he pointed out, "not for another few days." Patrick tried to remember the exact date on the calendar and couldn't. He glanced over to the wall next to the sink in the kitchen.

"So when are you going to put it up?"

Taking her by the arm, Patrick began to usher her out of the living room and toward the door again. "Does the twelfth of never ring a bell?" She had that look on her face, the one that could undo a knot the size of Baltimore. "Look, Mary Margaret, what do I want with a tree? There's one at my uncle's house. A big one," he emphasized. "That's where I go for Christmas."

"But you need a tree."

She was really getting worked up about this, wasn't

she? He found it oddly amusing. And kind of sweet. Not that he'd tell her. "Why?"

"Because it's a tradition."

He shrugged carelessly. "Maybe I'm not a lemming."

"This has nothing to do with going over a cliff—" Exasperation cut off her words. "What's wrong with you, don't you have a soul?"

For the first time since she'd met him, she heard Patrick laugh. The sound was warm and rich, embracing her like the feel of a sip of brandy going through her system on a particularly cold night. "You sound just like Patience."

"Patience. Your sister." She saw the affection in his eyes as he nodded. She knew it shouldn't mean anything to her to be compared to his sister, but it did. "I think I'd like to meet a female version of you."

He set her straight immediately. "Oh, no, Patience isn't anything like me. Fortunately for her," he said, surprising her. "She's the one who got all the 'soul' in the family. She's been after me for years to get a tree."

And he seemed to care a great deal about what his sister thought. Another surprise. "So why don't you?"

He shrugged again. "Too busy." On his way out the door, he stopped. "Wait, I forgot something."

"Your heart, Tin Man?" she suggested.

He gave her a reproving glance. "No, stay here."

The next moment, he disappeared into another room in the back. She was tempted to follow him but refrained. Instead, she stayed where she was, scanning his place.

She didn't like the thoughts finding their way into her head. The condo was new and she knew what decent houses went for in Aurora. This place was head and shoulders above decent. Not an easy thing to swing on even a detective's salary, given property taxes.

How did he afford a place like this?

There was no getting away from the conclusion, even though she wanted to. She was too good a cop to turn her back on it. Raising her voice, she decided to meet the challenge head-on.

"You've got a nice place here." She didn't bother trying to sound innocent. "Renting?"

"It's mine."

What little bit of hope she had evaporated like standing water in the hot sun. "How much did this set you back?"

Patrick walked out of the other room, a large red and blue wrapped box in his hands. His expression was dark. "Enough." He knew exactly what she was thinking and he resented it. "I also had enough after Patience and I sold our parents' home when my mother died." The house had too many bad memories for either one of them to want to live in it. Selling it was the only option they had.

She hadn't thought of that. "I didn't mean to imply—"

"Yes, you did." Angry, Patrick shoved a large box at her.

She stared at the glitter for a moment without saying anything. "What's this?"

"You asked me for a donation for the shelter's toy drive. Here's a donation." He snapped out his words like machine-gun fire. "It's one of those castles you build out of small building blocks. Good for girl or boy. The woman in the store wrapped it. Thought I'd save you the trouble."

Guilt tap-danced through her. She followed him outside. "I don't know what to say."

"Good." He slammed the door shut behind him. It locked automatically. "Keep it that way."

Chapter 15

Patrick wanted nothing more than to get on with the investigation into Ramirez's dealings, to find some kind of plausible explanation for the large deposits into the account bearing his wife's name.

Because the latter also bore the name of his old partner's late mother-in-law, he knew that kind of redemption of Ramirez's name was doomed. The excuse Ramirez had given his wife was flimsy, a lie for her to hold on to. Patrick knew Alicia loved her husband and didn't want to believe he was mixed up in something dirty.

He needed to get to the bottom of this, but because he wanted to carry out his investigation without attracting any undue attention, it had to be put on hold during work hours.

Like a racehorse pawing the ground at the starting gate, Patrick felt as if he was chafing at the bit, but there was nothing else he could do. Work had to come first.

He and McKenna were involved in a new homicide, one that mercifully wound up being open and shut. A young woman was found dead in her apartment, killed, it turned out, by the man who'd been stalking her. They had the suspect in handcuffs by the end of the day.

The incident made him think of Patience and the unwanted attention she'd garnered from the owner of one of her patients. Patience claimed that the whole thing had gone away after the man had seen a framed family photograph, the one in which they'd all worn their dress uniforms, but it didn't hurt to be too careful. She was the only sister he had.

He put in a call to her during the minimal lunch break he took, warning her to be careful. She gave him her word she would be. There were dogs barking in the background like a canine Greek chorus.

He knew that Patience took the situation a lot less seriously than he did. Patrick had a feeling she wasn't telling him everything, because she didn't want him to worry. However, he had no way of proving it. He hoped he was just being paranoid, but he strongly doubted it.

Some detective he made, he thought darkly now. Couldn't even catch his own sister in a lie.

With a sigh, he shut off the computer he rarely used. Outside the window, day was slipping gracefully into nightfall. Time to go home.

Maggi heard the click and looked Patrick's way. He'd been keeping her at arm's length since she'd stopped by to pick him up this morning. Nothing she said changed the scenario.

"Good work on the Miller case," Captain Reynolds

tossed the compliment their way as he walked past their desks.

"Thanks," Maggi murmured.

Cavanaugh, she noticed, said nothing, just barely nodding his head in acknowledgment. Of course, he didn't seem to need any kind of reinforcement, not like other mortals. He was in a class by himself.

Except that he took insults hard and she had insulted him this morning.

She had fences to mend.

"Want to go grab a beer?" she suggested, clearing off her desk. The squad room was almost empty now. All but one of the other detectives had gone home. She was vaguely aware that Reynolds had stopped to talk to the man.

"No."

"All right, I'll just drop you off home, then—"

He cut her off as he rose to his feet. "I've already got a ride."

Maggi sighed. He'd reverted to the way he was when she'd initially been coupled with him. Worse.

On her feet, she tried to block his way out. "Look, I'm sorry about this morning." She lowered her voice, afraid it might carry, knowing how much he hated having the smallest thing about his life made public. "I didn't mean I thought you were dirty. I guess I just got caught up in this whole conspiracy thing."

His eyes were flat, cold. "Apology accepted."

The hell it was. Maggi frowned as she watched him leave the squad room. "Doesn't sound it."

Barefoot, Patrick straddled the kitchen chair and set down the bottle he'd just gotten out of the refrigerator.

It took its place on the table next to the two empty bottles he'd finished off.

Thinking about the fact that Ed might have been on the take ate away at him.

How could he have misjudged someone so much?

He hadn't made that kind of a mistake since he'd thought of his father as being an honorable man. At least honorable in his own way. That image had been shattered when he'd accidentally overheard his father talking on the phone one day. As he stood in the shadows, listening, he heard his father try to convince Aunt Rose to run off with him. He'd been vaguely aware of some kind of trouble between Uncle Andrew and Aunt Rose. She had turned to his father just to vent. His father, always envious of what his two brothers had, had seen it as an opportunity for something more.

Whether that "something more" had ever happened, Patrick didn't know. All he knew was that he'd felt overwhelming disappointment that his father lacked the kind of family values, family loyalty he'd just taken for granted within the framework of the Cavanaughs. He remembered being disappointed in his aunt Rose, too, but then she'd gone missing shortly after that and things like blame and disappointment took a back seat to family grief.

Patrick took an extra long drag of his beer, savoring the ice-cold bitter brew as it flowed through his system. Looking to anesthetize himself.

He'd been wrong about his father and now it looked as if he was wrong about Ed, too. Showed what he knew. Nothing. Absolutely nothing.

He dragged a hand through his hair, finishing off the third bottle. Blinking, he looked down at the piece of paper on the table. He was working on a list of all the men he knew Ed had interacted with. Half-finished, the list was still long. Ramirez had had a lot of friends. And apparently some deadly enemies.

He heard the doorbell ring and groaned. He didn't feel like having company or talking to anyone. It was the middle of the week, not normally the time for visitors. But then, his cousins had a tendency to drop by without warning.

Maybe a little bit of company might be a good thing. He got up.

"Yeah, yeah, I'm coming," he called out as he heard the doorbell peal for the third time.

He wasn't prepared for what he saw when he opened the door.

It was a tree—a tall, skinny tree, its branches straining against the hemp that had been wound tightly around it. If the tree had taken on human form, he would have classified it as a runway model, all angles and malnutrition.

"What the hell?"

"Well, don't just stand there," a voice from behind the tree retorted. "Let me in."

Now it made sense. Sort of. "Mary Margaret, is that you?"

She peered around the tree she was holding. "Unless you believe in talking trees."

He had no idea why he felt like laughing. He was still incensed over what she'd intimated. At least, it had made a good excuse to be incensed. And a good excuse to keep her at arm's length, where she belonged.

"After being partnered with you, I'm starting to believe anything is possible."

"Good. Now help," she instructed, pushing the tree in his direction.

Patrick caught it in time and dragged the tree over the threshold. It was surprisingly light. Glancing back in her direction, he saw that Maggi had a six-pack of beer in one hand and some kind of aromatic large bag in the other. There was a red dragon embossed on the side. Was the woman moving in?

"What the hell is all this?" he demanded.

"Well, this—" she held up the six-pack "—and this—" she raised the bag "—are peace offerings."

He was willing to accept that, even though he wasn't entirely sure what she thought she was making peace over. But he was more interested in finding out why the woman was dragging around a scrawny tree in her wake. "And the tree?"

"Is something you need. Kitchen this way?" She walked toward the left before he could give her an answer. Patrick leaned the tree against the wall and hurried after her.

He managed to get in front of her. "Why would I need a tree?"

Scooting around him, she set the six-pack down on the table, noting the presence of the three empty bottles. Good thing she'd brought food, she thought. The man obviously had his sights set on a liquid dinner tonight.

"A Christmas tree," she corrected.

"A scrawny one," he pointed out.

"I tried to find a better one," she told him. "But it's almost Christmas. You wait too long, you have to settle."

He didn't want one in the first place. "Answer the question. Why the hell do I need a tree? A Christmas tree," he corrected himself before she could.

Maggi stopped unpacking the take-out dinner she'd brought and faced him. "Because Christmas is about love and forgiveness and being nice to people around you, I thought if you had a tree, you might remember the rest.''

The absolute nerve of the woman amazed him. He frowned and gazed at the tree leaning against his living room wall. ''I suppose you expect me to go out and buy decorations for it.''

''Nope, got those in the car. Extras,'' she explained when he looked at her incredulously. ''I have trouble resisting buying ornaments. They get cuter every year.'' And she had no willpower when it came to that. Over the years she had collected more than enough to decorate two trees and still have ornaments left over. ''So I thought I'd bring over some of them for you.''

The woman obviously took no prisoners. Except for maybe him. ''Think of everything, don't you?''

She grinned. ''I try.'' She folded the empty bag and left it on the counter. ''So, are we friends again?''

''We weren't friends before,'' he said.

Maggi could only shake her head. ''You are a hard man, Patrick Cavanaugh.'' She motioned him to the door. ''C'mon, help me bring in the decorations.''

He debated putting his foot down about that, but there didn't seem to be any solid ground beneath it. She'd come this far. He supposed letting her decorate the damn thing wouldn't hurt. With a shrug, he growled an ''Okay,'' and walked out the front door.

The moment he did, a shot rang out, whizzing by his head. Missing him by less than an inch. He instantly grabbed Maggi's arm and pulled her down, blocking her with his body, the extra service revolver he kept strapped to his calf out in his hand.

There was no second shot.

Patrick looked around. He thought he saw someone

running in the distance. On his feet, he started to give chase.

"Stay here," he tossed over his shoulder.

But Maggi was beside him, matching him footfall for footfall, her own service revolver in her hand. "I'm not a civilian, Cavanaugh."

"No, just a damn pain who never listens," he snapped.

A quick surveillance of the area turned up nothing beyond a teen couple necking in a car in the girl's driveway. By the look on their faces, Patrick had managed to scare ten years out of each of them. He withdrew with a curt apology.

Just then, someone peeled out of the development, tires screeching. Patrick was too far away to get off a clear shot, or even see a license plate. The car was dark, blending into the night. Even its make was obscured.

Disgusted, he holstered his gun. "Now what the hell was all that about?"

The first thing that popped into her head was that he was being set up. Someone had tried to sabotage his reputation and since that wasn't happening quickly enough, they had resorted to plan B, trying to eliminate him. Or maybe that was the original plan, she thought, remembering the circumstances behind Ramirez's death.

She bit back the urge to tell him what she was thinking. She couldn't do that without risking the operation. And if he suspected that she'd been sent by IA to investigate him, he'd probably never speak to her again. She didn't want to risk that, either.

Damn, but this assignment was tying her up in knots, leaving her feeling conflicted.

She speculated the only way left open to her.

"Maybe someone thinks we're getting too close to finding out something about Ramirez."

It made sense. And troubled him, but there was nothing he could do about it tonight. He blew out a breath, centering himself. "You said something about decorations."

His defensiveness was gone. Maggi smiled to herself. At least the shooter had managed to get her closer to Cavanaugh again. And that was a good thing.

"You don't have to do this, you know."

He was addressing the words to her posterior as she stood up on the ladder she'd had him get out of his garage. What the tree lacked in breadth it made up for in height and she intended to decorate every scrawny inch of it. When he'd hooted at it, she'd informed him that the tree needed love and she figured he and the tree would be good for each other.

She gave him the answer he knew she would.

"Yes, I do." Holding on to the top of the ladder, she turned around so she was looking down at him with her back against the steps. She liked being taller. It gave her a certain advantage. "I'm an optimist, but I don't believe in magic."

He didn't trust the ladder and stood holding it, more than vaguely aware that he was bracketing her thighs. "Magic?"

Something warm and soft stirred through her as she gazed down at him. The words, meant to be light, had trouble leaving her mouth at more than a measured pace. Things were happening inside her, things that shouldn't. And she was enjoying them far too much.

"Yes, as in decorations magically going on the tree

by themselves because you sure as hell aren't going to put them on.''

Thoughts crowded in his head that had nothing to do with police work, or shift partners, or even Christmas. ''Think you know me?''

She took a step down, then another, careful not to lose her footing.

Too late for that, Mag, she mocked herself.

She ran her tongue along her lips, trying to fight the dryness. ''I know that much about you.''

The ladder swayed a little as she took another step down. Patrick immediately tightened his hold. ''Careful, the damn thing's rickety.''

''That's okay, so am I.'' The words all but floated from her mouth.

She was too close to him. Too close to do anything sensible. She could hear a rushing in her ears and wondered if that was her blood, making a break for it.

Unable to help himself, to push away the sudden shaft of desire that shot through him, Patrick cupped her face with his hands and brought his mouth down to hers.

She'd lied to him when she'd said that she didn't believe in magic. Because magic was exactly what was happening to her now. Everything about the moment was magic. And it swept her up so quickly she had no time to brace herself against it, no time to fend it off. And no desire to.

''You don't feel rickety,'' he told her, drawing back before he lost his resistance. What he really wanted to do was tear her clothes from her body and make love to her until he'd hopefully had his fill and was over these feelings.

''I thought you were a better judge of situations than

that,'' she breathed. ''My heart's about to hammer out of my chest. Hasn't pounded like this since I tackled that perp running out of the First National Bank in 'Frisco.''

As if to show him, she took his hand and placed it over her heart.

Maggie looked up into his eyes. Her pulse quickened, her loins ached.

Time stood perfectly still.

It was incredible. The woman was the last word in independence, in whatever the female version of macho was, and yet, right now, as he touched her, she felt delicate, frail.

His eyes held hers, knowing he should stop it here before it went any further.

Not that he didn't want to.

The fissures in the walls around his resolve doubled in size, widened until there was nothing to hold the dam back.

Patrick brought his mouth down to hers again. When she leaned her body into his, he knew there was no turning back.

Caution and clothing went flying, tossed to the winds on an impulse that had been waiting in the wings from the very first, waiting for the right unguarded moment. And it had arrived.

Restraint was a byword with him. Every movement he'd ever orchestrated had been carefully thought out, viewed from both sides, sometimes quickly, sometimes slowly, but always examined.

Until now.

Now he wasn't thinking. He was feeling, reacting. Wanting. There was something about this woman that got to him, that intoxicated him beyond logic and negated any good judgment he had. He'd unconsciously felt it from the first moment he'd laid eyes on her. His sense of survival had urged him to try to get her replaced, to push her away. But everything had failed.

And now there was no turning back.

He was glad.

Glad because she tasted like heaven and heaven had seemed like such a faraway place. It had never been anything he'd ever encountered. But she tasted of the promise of heaven and salvation and he wanted both more than he could say.

Maggi yanked the pullover he'd had on, dragging it off his torso and arms and pitching it carelessly aside. She had no idea where because all her attention was riveted to working the jeans off his hips. The black briefs he wore went down with them. He kicked them aside, his body cleaving to hers. He'd already made short work of her sweater and jeans before she'd ever started on his garments.

That left them both nude. Except for the hardware. A by-product of being on the force.

A mischievous smile played on her lips as she looked at him. *Now there was a sexy shot.* "Your weapon, Cavanaugh."

He glanced down. "Oh, you mean my gun."

Kneeling, he quickly removed it, then looked up at her with a grin that she found bone-scrapingly sexy. She wanted him more than she'd thought possible. She tried to chalk it up to abstinence, but knew she was lying to herself. It wasn't the lack of it that made her want to make love, it was the man.

The look in his eyes went right through her. "Since I'm already down here, let me do yours."

Maggi felt as if someone had struck a match and thrown it at her as she nodded.

Patrick unstrapped the holster from her thigh, slipping the leather from her. He carefully placed her secondary weapon beside his own, away from the field of play.

She expected him to rise. He remained where he was, his hands lightly resting on either side of her hips. Maggi felt herself begin to throb even as she moistened.

The next second she was digging her hands into his hair as he opened up gates leading to an ecstasy she'd never experienced before. Lines of flames shot through her like wildfire as she felt his tongue anointing the tender flesh between her legs. And then he was thrusting it in and out, causing shock waves to oscillate all through her.

She reached a climax before she fully realized what he was doing.

Clutching at his shoulder, Maggi dragged him back up to her level. "You don't play fair," she breathed.

"I don't 'play' at all."

He sealed his mouth to hers.

Damn it, he shouldn't want her this way, shouldn't surrender control over his actions to this formless thing that demanded fulfillment. But logic had no place here. Only desire.

The imprint of her body against his as he pressed her to him made him wild. He'd been hoping that once he knew he could have her, whatever he was grappling with would dissipate, go away. Not grow.

And yet it did.

With every kiss, every movement, the passion grew until it threatened to consume him completely. He should have taken her in his bedroom. He took her on the living room floor instead, beside a tree he'd never wanted, lit with lights he'd never asked for.

Kissing her until she was little more than pulsating flesh that twisted and writhed beneath him, he grasped her hands and held them above her head. He took her mouth, savaging it with kisses as he drove himself into her.

The soft sound that escaped her lips filled him with a sweetness. It drove the savagery away.

He stopped for a moment, looking down at her, not knowing what to think, not wanting to think at all.

Watching her eyes, he moved slower, then faster, until he wasn't conscious of making any effort at all. The effort made him. The moment made him. And he raced to embrace it. With her.

Chapter 16

Utterly exhausted, Patrick shifted his weight off Maggi. He felt as if he barely had the strength left for even that. The woman had completely drained him.

Who would have thought?

"If I'd known that was part of the tree-trimming ceremony, I might have gotten a Christmas tree a long time ago," he said.

In response to his carefully measured out words, he heard her laughing. Felt the sound bubbling up within her as her body moved against his.

He'd never known that listening to laughter could feel so good. So sexy.

Without thinking, he gathered her closer to him. "You find that funny?"

Maggi planted an elbow on his chest and raised herself up to look at him. A curtain of blond hair swept along his skin, tightening his gut. Laughter seemed to radiate from every part of her.

"I can't believe we just did this."

Neither could he.

Nor could he believe that he wanted her again. Just looking at her made his body hum, his cravings multiply. Why wasn't he sated? They'd just made love for longer than he could ever remember doing it. He should have been more than satisfied and on his way to being over whatever it was that kept drawing him to her.

What the hell was wrong with him? Why was she affecting him this way?

There was no answer to his question. Logic had left on winged feet.

"Then I guess we'll just have to review the evidence." Patrick cupped the back of her head with his hand and brought her mouth down to his.

This time, she was ready for it, braced, knowing that the wild ride ahead was going to sap her strength and send her mind reeling. This time, she wanted not to be alone in that first car on the roller coaster as it plunged and climbed its way ever faster over the slopes and peaks.

She kissed him back, long, hard. Sensuously.

The ride began slower, and by the time it was over, had brought the blood rushing through their veins to a new fever pitch.

Whatever he did, she did him one better, until by the end, Maggi knew his body better than he did. And in her heart, she had a feeling that he knew hers far better than she ever could. He had found pulse points she hadn't known existed, sent her flying almost out of control with a pass of his hand, with the lightest trace of his lips.

Nothing was sacred, nothing overlooked. Knees, elbows, fingertips, not to mention the soft, sensitive flesh in areas designed for lovemaking and ecstasy.

She sought out his secret places, determined to render him almost mindless with desire and pleasure, the way he had her. And when he moaned, she knew she had him. The thrill she felt increased a hundredfold.

He'd had his share of sexual encounters, but this, this was something new, something he hadn't realized was out there. This didn't just bring with it the burst of a crescendo at the end. This brought something much more with it.

It brought feelings, and with them a sense of protectiveness that he neither wanted nor knew what to do with.

But there was more.

Making love with her released something inside of him. It was formless, without a name, but moved over him like a low-lying fog, claiming him, obliterating his senses.

He felt he was entering a dark alley with only one path of retreat and that was behind him. What was in front was an unknown. He had no idea where to point his weapon, how to protect himself. The uneasy feeling that he was being taken prisoner without being able to defend himself was all too real.

Lacing his fingers through hers, he suddenly switched places with Maggi and, as he watched her, drove himself into her. He saw a host of emotions wash over her face. The same kind that he felt echoing within his own chest.

It scared the hell out of him.

And then there was no time for thought, no time for fear. There was only the race to the final place, the one that released volleys of lights and made everything else insignificant.

When it came to claim him, he felt her arch her back, driving her hips up to his and knew that she had reached a climax with him.

The quest for oxygen commanded his full attention.

Maggi slid off his slick body, her own body damp with the dew of lovemaking. She hardly had the strength to lift her head. He'd taken everything out of her and she had valiantly tried to do the same to him.

She could only hope she had succeeded in some small measure.

But as the euphoria receded into the shades, the reality that came in its wake dragged out questions that were quick to assault her. What the hell was she doing here, making love with a man she was supposed to be investigating?

Had she lost her mind?

The simple answer was yes, but that didn't negate what she had to do—leave as soon as possible.

She felt cold suddenly. "I think I should be going. Just as soon as I find my legs," she qualified.

He didn't want her to leave. Didn't want her to move a muscle. His arm tightened around her without any thought on his part.

"They have to be around here somewhere. I know I saw you come in with them."

It was on the tip of his tongue to tell her she could stay. To ask her if she *would* stay. But the very fact that he wanted her to chased the words away from his lips. This couldn't go any further than it had already gone and if she stayed, it would. He knew it would.

Pivoting herself on her palms, her arms still bracketing him, Maggi glanced over her shoulder. "Oh, there they are."

She was trying desperately to be flippant, but every word she uttered took effort. She couldn't remember ever feeling this drained. Or this happy, as if her whole body was humming a tune.

Dangerous, this is dangerous, not to mention unethical. Damn it, Mag, what were you thinking?

She wished her mind would shut up and let her enjoy the moment, but she knew it wouldn't. She was too disciplined for that.

Where the hell had her discipline been a few minutes ago?

Struggling for control of the situation, Maggi pushed herself off. She reached for her clothes, wishing she had something to wrap around herself other than her dignity, which had serious holes in it right now.

Still she did what she could. Rising, she held her clothes against her and looked down at him, forcing a smug smile she didn't feel to her lips.

"Well, my work here is done." Patrick was still lying on the floor, watching her. Maggi found it difficult not to let her gaze roam. He had one hell of a magnificent body. "Bathroom?"

"Through there." He pointed to the left.

"Thank you," she mustered with as much regal control as she could. With that, she withdrew.

He couldn't tear his eyes away. The M.E. was right, he thought. She made one hell of an exit.

Maggi was the first one to arrive in the squad room the next day. After she'd left Patrick's house, she knew there was no way she was going to fall asleep so she'd stayed up writing a formal report to Halliday, detailing her findings.

One thing she knew for certain: The man was one hell of a lover. The only time she smiled was when she tried to envision the expression on Halliday's face if he read that line.

Sleep had all but eluded her entirely. Every time she would almost drift off, her brain would intrude. There was no denying that she'd broken more rules than she could count and severely compromised herself and the operation. Moreover, she'd tainted any testimony she might offer on Patrick's behalf.

How the hell could she have slept with him?

How could she not? something within her whispered. That had to be the best time she'd ever had with or without her clothes on.

Her mind not on the report on the screen, Maggi stared away. Too bad last night didn't mean anything. At least, not to him.

Not to her, either, she insisted.

The silent argument continued to ricochet back and forth in her brain. Neither side won points.

The moment Patrick walked in, she was on her feet, crossing to him as if she was an arrow shot from a bow. "I need to talk to you."

He looked at her, not quite certain what to expect. Once dressed, she'd bolted out of his house so quickly last night, he was sure she must have broken some kind of speed record. He'd wanted to call her back. Drag her back. But common sense had finally prevailed and kept him where he was.

He'd slept poorly, dreaming of her. She'd be there one minute, gone the next and he'd spend the rest of the dream looking for her. Over and over again. He had no idea what it meant, only that he shouldn't have let last night happen.

There was an expression on her face now he couldn't fathom. He hated being in the dark.

"Okay." He followed Maggi to the coffee area. There were others in the squad room, but they were all in their cubicles, working. Still he lowered his voice before asking, "What's up?"

Maggi took a breath before answering. "I don't want you to get the wrong idea about last night."

His expression gave nothing away. "And what would be the wrong idea?"

"That it was about something." She thought she saw someone coming their way and paused, but the detective walked out. "It was just sex, pure and simple."

He thought of last night. He'd never known the human body could bend like that. She'd left him in awe. "There was nothing pure about it."

"What I mean is that there're no strings, no consequences."

Did she make love like that to every man? An unaccountable jealousy slashed through him before he regained control over himself.

"Aren't there?"

"No." Why did Cavanaugh look so annoyed? "I thought you'd be happy. Isn't that what all men want? No consequences?"

Until the second she'd uttered the words, he would have said yes. Would have thought that *was* what he wanted. But now that she was acting so cavalier about it, he felt his pride wounded.

"Don't presume to know what I want, or lump me in with everyone else."

"I didn't. I don't." She tried to find high ground as

everything sank around her. "It's just that I didn't want you to think there was anything going on."

"I don't think that."

A tiny salvo of regret lodged itself in her chest. *Isn't this what you want? What's wrong now?* "Good."

"Fine," he snapped. "Are we done with this conversation?"

"Completely." Her voice rose. Two could play this game. "Time's up. Nickel's been used."

He frowned. "If you ask me, your brain's been used and whoever used it forgot to put it back."

About to utter an equally mindless retort, she stopped herself and looked at him. "Are you angry with me for some reason?"

"Angry?" Yanking his mug to him, Patrick poured himself a cup of coffee. Even as he did so, he knew he was going to regret it. The coffee here could be used to retar worn-out roads. He glared at Maggi. "Why would I be angry with someone who insists on telling me she knows what I'm thinking?"

Without thinking, Maggi poured a cup for herself. Even as she did, she felt her stomach tightening in protest. "I wasn't insisting."

He laughed shortly. "Obviously you weren't on this side of the conversation."

She glared at him. He was such an ass. Why had she thought there were any feelings there? She wouldn't go to bed with him again if he were the last man on earth. In the galaxy.

"No, I was on the 'done' side." She closed her eyes, running her hand along her forehead. There were little men clog dancing inside her head. "You're giving me a headache."

He set his mug down, last night returning to him in

spades. He could feel his body responding and struggled to keep his thoughts in check. He only half succeeded. "You know the best thing for a headache?"

She raised her eyes to his and guessed at his answer, "A swift execution?"

She wasn't prepared to see the smile. Wasn't prepared for the way it went straight to her gut and unraveled her. "Hair of the dog that bit you."

"That's for a hangover."

His eyes shone as they washed over her. "Same principle." And then a stony expression took over his face as he saw the wary look come into her eyes. "Don't worry, Mary Margaret, I'm not about to jump your bones anytime the whim hits."

As if he could if she didn't want him to. But that was just the trouble. Even with all the obstacles she put in her way, even though she knew it was wrong, she still wanted him to. "I'm not worried about that."

He looked at her, puzzled. "Then what?"

She was worried about what he'd stirred up. About the way she'd compromised herself. And about the fact that she wanted to do it all again, every teeth-jarring second of it.

"Nothing," she bit off. Coffee in hand, she retreated to her desk on legs that were more than a little shaky.

What would Patrick say if he knew that he'd spent last night making love to someone whose primary function was not to be his partner, but to spy on him? Whose very existence in his life was a lie? At the very least, he would have felt betrayed and she couldn't blame him at all.

Maggi knew the right thing to do was to have herself removed from the case, but she refused to go that route. She wanted to clear Patrick's name. Every fiber of her being told her he was innocent of the charges lodged against him. At the very least, she owed him that much.

Patrick stood by the coffeemaker, staring at the back of her head as she returned to her cubicle. The best thing for him to do was go along with what she'd said. He didn't want ties and she was telling him that there weren't any.

So why did he feel so damn unsettled? So damn insulted?

Was it a matter of wanting what he couldn't have, or was it something else? But he'd never been like that before, never felt drawn to secure acquisitions. That just wasn't him.

But even as his mind counseled him to move along, to take the opportunity she'd offered him and forget this had ever happened, he felt himself resisting. Last night had been incredible. Since she didn't want anything permanent, what would it hurt to explore things a little further? To see if last night had been a fluke?

After a beat, he wandered over to her desk and perched on the edge of it. Her fingers flew madly across the keyboard. They moved even more wildly the second he sat down.

"Any faster and you're liable to melt them."

"They're heat resistant." He wasn't moving. She raised her eyes from the screen only because she dared herself to. "What's up?"

"I thought I'd do some nosing around, see if I can pick anything up." She knew he referred to looking further into Ramirez's dealings. "I want you to cover for me in case the captain comes looking around for me—"

"Why don't we just go to the local hangout after work? We're bound to hear more there. We're not in the middle of an investigation. It'd be kind of hard to explain where you are," she pointed out.

After a moment, Patrick nodded his agreement. Starting to rise, he stopped.

"Anything else on your mind?" Maggi asked.

About to say no, he changed his mind. Something was going on here, and he wasn't sure if he wanted it to or not. He figured if he could see how all this felt against a backdrop comprised of the people who meant something to him, then maybe he could make up his mind.

"What are you doing tomorrow night?"

"Christmas Eve? Wrapping a few last-minute presents, why?"

"My uncle Andrew has this Christmas party he's throwing. I thought maybe if you didn't have any other place to be..."

She wasn't sure just who was more stunned to hear the words, him or her. "Are you asking me out?"

"In," he corrected tersely. "I'm asking you in. Specifically, into my uncle's house. If you don't want to come—"

She cut him off. "I didn't say that." She'd heard about the parties Andrew Cavanaugh liked to throw. Boisterous, friendly. Warm. "Are you sure he wouldn't mind?"

"Not Uncle Andrew." He was willing to make book on that. His uncle was always after the next generation to settle down with someone. If he walked in with a woman, Andrew would be rendered speechless. At the moment, because of the improbability of the situation, the idea tickled Patrick. "He always says the more people, the better."

She gave up trying to concentrate on what she was

doing and pushed the keyboard away. "So you're trying to fill a quota?"

"Yes, no." She was getting him all tangled up again. He shouldn't have gone with impulse. Impulse wasn't his forte. "Damn it, woman, I'm inviting you to a Christmas party. You can come or not come—your choice."

Disgusted with himself and the way he was suddenly tripping over his own tongue, he began to walk away.

"Okay," she called after him.

Patrick stopped and slowly turned around. "Okay what?"

Because she didn't want anyone else listening, she got up and crossed to him. "Okay, I'll come. Do you want to give me the time and directions?"

She made it sound as if they were meeting a witness or going undercover. "Eight o'clock. And I'll pick you up."

"You don't have to...."

He blew out a breath. "I said I'll pick you up so I'll pick you up." He pinned her with a look. "Are you always this difficult?"

"No." Her mouth curved. "Not always." She searched his face for a clue. "Are you sure about this?"

"I wouldn't have invited you if I wasn't. I don't do or say things I don't want to."

Her grin grew wider as a warm feeling filtered through her. Telling herself that going to a party at Andrew Cavanaugh's was all in the line of duty, that maybe she would get more insight into Patrick that way, was a crock and she knew it. The upshot of the matter was that she was asking for trouble, but she couldn't help it. The temptation of seeing him surrounded by relatives was just too great.

"Okay, then."

"Cavanaugh, McKenna," the captain called out. Standing in the doorway of his office and holding a piece of paper aloft, he waved them over. "We've got another body."

Back to reality. Maggi sighed. There was something extra sad about having to deal with murder around the holidays.

"Whatever happened to "Tis the season to be jolly'?" Maggi asked.

"Some people have different ways of getting jolly," Patrick speculated.

She was already on her way to the captain's office. "That's got to be it."

Maggi's room looked as if a fashion tornado had been through it. Every dress she owned had been taken out and tried on in front of her mirror before joining the heap. Some had been unearthed three times before being permanently discarded.

In the end, she'd settled on her first choice. A curve-hugging electric blue velvet dress that came down to her ankle and was slit up the front well past her knees. It had a high collar, was cut to show off her arms and plunged beguilingly almost to her waist in the back. Her hair was down and her morale up as she surveyed the end result in the mirror.

She'd just slipped on her four-inch heels when she heard the doorbell. It took her longer than she was happy about to get to the door. But it was worth it once she opened it.

Patrick look one look at her and whatever he'd been about to say apparently vanished.

She grinned at the silent compliment. "Your mouth is hanging open, Cavanaugh."

He could feel the itch starting again. The one that had her name all over it. Walking in, he did a complete three-sixty around her. "You clean up good."

"There's that silver tongue again." She could feel herself beaming and told herself she was behaving like an idiot. "Thanks."

Walking in, he looked around. "Hey, it doesn't look like a toy factory exploded in here anymore."

Picking up her coat, she started to slip it on. "That's because I took all the toys in after work last night."

Patrick moved behind her, helping her with her coat when one of the sleeves got stuck. She looked up at him in surprise.

"How did you get started with that, collecting toys?" he clarified.

She'd been doing it for three years now. First up in San Francisco, then here. "I needed something to help balance out what I saw going on in the streets." She picked up her small clutch purse and headed for the front door. "There's a lot of reaffirmation to be found in the eyes of a child hugging a toy that they never expected to have even in their wildest dreams." She paused to lock the door. "It reminds me that there are more good guys than bad in this world."

He surprised her by taking her arm. "I wouldn't have thought you needed reminding."

"Even Pollyanna needs her batteries recharged once in a while."

"Pollyanna?"

He'd parked in the last spot available in guest parking. As they walked, the wind played with the ends of her hair, whipping them around. "Disney movie about a chirpy kid who only saw the good in everything."

Patrick opened the passenger side for her. "And you didn't star in it?"

"The part went to Hayley Mills." She didn't bother adding that it had been made before she was born.

"Who?"

She laughed and shook her head as she got in. "Never mind."

Patrick rounded the hood and got in on his side. "Just how much trivia is lodged in that brain of yours?"

Hiking her dress up in order to get comfortable, she noticed that Patrick made an effort not to look at the bit of thigh she'd accidentally flashed. It made her smile inside. "You really don't want to know."

The trouble was, Patrick thought as he started the car, he did.

Chapter 17

There were cars parked all up and down both sides of the cul-de-sac as well as two blocks in either direction. It was obvious to anyone who drove by that a party was in progress somewhere close by.

The site for the party wasn't difficult to pinpoint. Every light was on in the house in the middle of the block.

The sounds of muffled laughter emanated through the closed windows and door, beckoning them as they approached. A glance toward one of the windows on either side of the wreath-decorated door showed that the front room, and very probably the whole house, was filled to capacity and then some with celebrating people.

"Are you sure there's room for two more?" Maggi asked dubiously as Patrick knocked on the door.

The front door opened just then. The dark-haired

man in the doorway must have heard her. "Always room for more," he assured.

The man was tall and thin, and flecks of gray shot through his thick mane. So this was what Cavanaugh might look like in another two decades, Maggi thought. The man wore a light blue sweater that brought out his intense blue eyes. He was quick to take her hand, enveloping it in a strong, warm handshake.

"Andrew Cavanaugh," he introduced himself. "And you must be Maggi McKenna."

"Must be," she murmured as she eyed Patrick with no small surprise. "You mentioned me?"

Patrick shook his head. If anything, he was a shade more surprised than she at his uncle's greeting. "Not a word."

Andrew laughed, always tickled when he could still flex his detecting muscles. "Hey, just because I don't clock in every day at the station house anymore doesn't mean I don't still have my ways of finding things out."

As he spoke, he moved behind Maggi and began to help her with her coat. When the coat slipped off, he raised his eyes to his nephew's face and smiled his approval.

Andrew folded the coat over his arm and confided, "You have the honor of being the first woman Patrick's ever brought with him to a family function."

Tinged in long-suffering annoyance, Patrick's exhale was fairly audible.

"I think Uncle Brian's looking for you." He pointed to another man in the distance.

"We're going to have a nice long talk, you and me," Andrew promised Maggi before he slipped away with her coat.

The din around them was warm and comforting.

She'd always wished she was part of a large family and when she'd fantasized what holidays would be like, they'd been exactly like this.

"I like him."

Patrick lifted one shoulder in a half shrug. "Yeah, he's a great guy. Talks too much sometimes."

She gazed up at him, smiling. A collection of feelings danced through her. She let them dance. For now. "Not like some people."

He wasn't about to get drawn into any kind of discussion about his so-called shortcomings. He'd brought her here for one reason. To talk himself out of what he was starting to feel. He wanted to find lasting fault with her. So far, his uncle wasn't helping.

"Want something to drink?"

"Sounds good to me." As he turned to walk to the kitchen, she was quick to follow in his wake.

The kitchen proved to be currently the only room in the house that didn't look as if it was about to burst at the seams. She watched Patrick rummage through the refrigerator with no hesitation. He seemed more relaxed here than she'd ever seen him.

"You look at home here."

"I am." Taking out a fresh tray of ice cubes, he deposited them into the depleted bowl on the table, then refilled the tray with water before putting it back into the freezer. "I liked staying here better than in my own house. There was laughter here." Realizing he was exposing too much, he abruptly stopped talking. Instead, he nodded at the array of bottles on the table beside the bowl of ice cubes. "What'll you have?"

"White wine'll be fine."

He poured a glass for her, then selected red wine for himself.

Maggi smiled as she brought the wine to her lips. "What, no beer?"

"Beer's for everyday." He studied her as he spoke, wondering if this had ultimately been a mistake, bringing her here. "Wine's for special occasions."

"And whiskey's for drowning your sorrows." The statement came out of nowhere and she really had no idea why she said it. Or why he suddenly looked so annoyed, so distant.

"I don't drink whiskey."

She'd obviously stumbled into a sensitive area. "Sorry."

"No, I'm the one who's sorry," he said ruefully. There'd been no call for his harsh tone. She was just talking. No way could she have known what his life had been like, growing up with a functioning alcoholic for a father. "Didn't mean to snap at you. My father drank whiskey." A sense of self-preservation had him avoiding her eyes as he spoke. If he saw pity there, he didn't know if he could trust his reaction. "It was his oblivion of choice, which would have been fine if it had obliterated him. But a lot of times, getting drunk would just set him off. Some men get silly when they drink. Some get mean."

It wasn't hard to read between the lines. "And your father was the latter."

"Yeah." Even after all this time, it was a difficult thing for him to admit.

He didn't have to draw her a map. The subject was painful for him. Maggi abandoned it.

"So, was your uncle right?" He looked at her, puzzled. "Am I your first?"

He thought about the other night. She couldn't be talking about that. "What?"

"Am I the first one you ever brought to a family gathering?" she enunciated slowly.

He made an impatient face. "I don't keep track of those kind of things."

Yes you do, but you don't want to admit it. The warm feeling that slid over her was partially blocked by the specter of guilt that cast a shadow over everything in her life. None of this could go forward, she reminded herself. Because it was rooted in lies. Her lies.

Maggi jumped subjects again. She looked toward the threshold. Several people entered the kitchen. Someone had made a joke in the next room and a volley of laughter was heard. "Lot of people here. They're not all relatives, are they?"

He knew that to Uncle Andrew, sometimes it felt that way. "Hardly." Taking her arm to move her out of the way as more people came in search of libation, he ushered her into the living room. "There are eleven Cavanaugh cousins, counting my sister and me, and of course there's Uncle Andrew and Uncle Brian. The rest are assorted friends, mostly from the police force, but there're a few judges and people from the D.A.'s office. My cousin Janelle is an assistant D.A."

She tried to recall if she'd ever heard the name Janelle Cavanaugh. "Is she the only one who isn't on the police force?"

"Just her and Patience. Patience is a vet."

"Really? I love animals." Maggi looked around at the sea of people in the living room and the section of the family room she was privy to. She tried to find a woman who looked like a female version of Patrick. "Is she here?"

His brows drew together. "Yeah, she's here."

God, but he sounded guarded. What did he think she

was going to do, pump the woman for childhood stories about him?

"Do I get to meet her, or are you going to shove me into a box if she comes close?"

He made no effort to locate his sibling for her. Instead, he downed the rest of his drink, then set the glass on a nearby table. "What do you want to meet my sister for?"

"Because I'm your partner." Maybe fair exchange was the way to get him to relax. "I'll introduce you to my father if you drop by tomorrow."

"I don't know—"

The moment she'd said it, she knew she wanted him to come. No matter what the end result of all this was going to be, she wanted him to spend Christmas with her. "Tit for tat, Cavanaugh. I came to your family gathering, you can come to mine. Only difference is there'll be a lot more elbow room." Sold on the idea, Maggi was not about to take no for an answer. "Three o'clock. Bring your sister. I'm making a turkey and you can help us have fewer leftovers."

He didn't feel like standing in the middle of his uncle's house arguing with her. Things could be worked out later, when there was less than half the town within earshot.

"Okay, maybe. If she's not busy," he qualified.

"If she is, you can come by yourself. Unless you've made other plans." She looked up at him.

His uncle always made Christmas dinner, but he knew Uncle Andrew would understand if he went to Maggi's for Christmas. "No, no other plans."

"Patrick? Patrick, is that you?" Maggi turned around to see a petite young woman with Patrick's mouth approaching them. She had flame-red hair and her green eyes were wide with surprise. "I didn't recognize you with a woman standing next to you." Her eyes making a quick assessment, she smiled broadly as she put out her hand to Maggi. "Hi, I'm this big lug's younger, more attractive sister, Patience."

"I'm Maggi McKenna, his—"

"Partner," Patience completed in surprise. Her grin widened into one of glee. "Yes, I know." Her eyes shifted to her brother. "She doesn't look like a pain in the butt, Patrick," she observed innocently.

Patrick blew out a breath. The verdict was in. Coming here had *not* been a good idea. "Patience never learned to think before she spoke," he growled as he glared at his sister.

"That's okay, I like spontaneous," Maggi told the younger woman. She felt herself hitting it off with Patience instantly. "I get to find out a lot more that way."

"So, how do you like working with my brother?" Patience shifted so that her body blocked Patrick's. "You can be honest. I had to grow up with him."

Maggi crossed the minefield cautiously. "It's interesting."

Patience glanced over her shoulder at her brother. She nodded her approval. "Tactful, too. I think this one's a keeper, big brother." She turned back to Maggi. "Most of his partners start talking to their guns by the second week. Transfers usually come by the second month."

"Can't budge her with a crowbar," Patrick muttered as he picked up another wineglass. It was hours before he had to drive home. Right now he was thinking that he'd done smarter things in his life. Bringing Maggi here was a mistake.

Patience leaned into Maggi. "You hang in there,

girl,'' she cheered the other woman on. ''He's got a rough surface, but once you scratch it, there's a pussycat underneath.''

Maggi laughed. ''I was thinking more along the lines of a mountain lion.''

''Oh?'' Patience raised an interested eyebrow in Maggi's direction. She looked from the woman to her brother and then smiled impishly. ''Excuse me, I think I need some more wine.''

''Less,'' Patrick informed her tersely as she started to walk away. ''You need less wine.''

Patience shook her head. ''He never stops trying to boss me around. I'm twenty-six years old, Patrick,'' she told him fondly, then brushed a kiss across his cheek, ''and can stand on my own two feet.''

''Too much wine and you'll wind up not standing at all,'' he called after his sister's retreating form.

When he looked back at Maggi, she had that cat-got-into-the-cream look on her face.

''I'm glad you brought me. I'm finding out a lot about you.'' When he scowled at her, she just kept on talking. ''For instance, I never would have thought you were the protective type.''

Definitely a bad idea. Next time he had an impulse, he was going to sit on it until it passed. ''I didn't bring you here so that you could spin theories about me.''

She cocked her head. ''Why did you bring me here?''

He struggled against a very strong desire that could not be acted upon here. Fortunately. ''Does everything have to have a reason with you?''

Maggi's expression was the very personification of innocence. ''I thought you liked logic.''

He reached for the glass in her hand. "Let me go refill your glass."

Maggi looked down at her glass. "It's not empty yet."

But Patrick made his claim. He needed a couple of minutes to himself. Away from her. "No rule that it has to be." With that, he walked off.

Maggi sighed, staying where she was.

"Never saw him this skittish before. He must really like you."

The deep male voice was right behind her. Maggi turned around and found herself gazing up into Andrew's eyes. She shook her head. He read far too much into this. "I think I just rub him the wrong way."

"Then he wouldn't have brought you here, would he?"

"I'm afraid I really don't know quite what your nephew is capable of." She shrugged half-helplessly.

For now, Andrew decided to leave the subject alone. It was enough that Patrick had brought her. If it was meant to be, the rest would work itself out. Maybe with a little help from him, but not yet. All in all, she was a lovely young woman, just the kind he'd envisioned for his nephew. Her being in law enforcement didn't hurt, either.

Andrew regarded her thoughtfully. "McKenna, I used to know a McKenna. Matthew McKenna. Great cop."

Pleasure lit up within her. It always did when she heard something nice about her father. "Thank you, I'll tell him you said that. He's my father."

Andrew laughed, pleased. "Small world. Tell him hello for me. Better still, bring him around sometime." He gestured about the teeming area. "Always room."

She didn't want to get ahead of herself.

What ahead? Once reports are filed and he finds out what you've been up to, you're never going to see him again. He'll make sure of it.

She smiled politely. "Thank you, I really appreciate the invitation, but I think that depends on how Patrick feels."

He understood her reticence. Patrick was not always the easiest man to get along with. "He's a good kid. Turned out all right seeing as how he was always butting his head against a wall."

Her interest piqued, she looked at the older man. "Excuse me?"

Andrew couched it as well as he could. "My brother Mike had trouble with the ground rules when it came to raising kids. He never realized that you needed to praise 'em as well as correct them." He nodded at a late arrival who called out to him. "Nothing Patrick did was ever good enough. A lot of kids turn out bad with that kind of background."

"But he had you." Her observation caught him by surprise, but as he started to demur, Maggi said, "Anyone can see how he feels about you. Personally, I think you worked miracles with him." She kept an eye on the kitchen doorway, waiting for Patrick to return. She didn't want him to hear her talking to his uncle about him. "When I first met him, I wouldn't have guessed that he had any family ties at all."

"He runs deeper than most people know," Andrew told her.

Just then, she saw Patrick working his way toward them. He held a drink in each hand. He'd not only topped off her glass, but gotten a new one of his own as well. "I think I see my drink coming."

One of the things Andrew attributed his longevity to was his keen sense of survival. "I'd better slip away before he thinks we're conspiring against him." He smiled at her. "Nice talking to you."

By the time she said, "Same here," Andrew had already disappeared into the crowd.

But not soon enough for Patrick to miss his presence. He handed Maggi her glass. "What were you and Uncle Andrew talking about?"

She surprised herself with how easily she could slip into a lie.

"My dad." Maggi consoled herself with the fact that she hadn't told him a complete lie. Andrew *had* mentioned her father. "The two of them worked together a time or two."

Patrick groaned.

She didn't think what she'd said merited that kind of response. "What's wrong?"

"Cousins, six o'clock. A whole flock of them."

Before she knew it, Patrick took her hand and ushered her toward the patio door and the yard that lay beyond. But their path of escape was cut off. Too many bodies in the way to reach the exit in time.

His cousins descended on him before he ever had a chance.

Left with no choice, Patrick surrendered. He introduced her to his uncle Andrew's daughters, Callie, Teri and Rayne and braced himself.

The next five hours slipped by faster than she thought possible. And then she was saying good-night, promising to return some other day as Patrick all but hurried her into his car.

She didn't stop smiling all the way to her house, but

she had to admit, when they arrived there, she half expected Patrick to stop his car only long enough for her to get out. When he cut off the engine and walked her to her door, she knew she believed in the miracle of Christmas.

Maggi took out her key. "I had a wonderful time, Cavanaugh. Thanks for inviting me."

"You already said that," he reminded her. "In the car."

The man did not take thanks graciously, she thought. "Maybe it bears repeating."

There was a leaf in her hair. She'd brushed against a tree branch getting into his car. Patrick removed it, his fingers touching her hair. Needs rose a little higher. "And maybe you're just nervous."

Breathe, Mag, breathe. "What would I have to be nervous about?"

He nodded at the door behind her. He noticed she wasn't opening it. "Maybe you're afraid I'll ask myself in."

"And maybe I'm afraid you won't," she countered.

Somehow his hands found themselves around her waist. Even through the coat, she felt small. "Anybody ever tell you you're pushy?"

"I get that all the time." She took a breath. *Mistake number five hundred and twelve.* "So, would you like to come in?"

Yes, his brain responded. Which was exactly why he tried to refuse. "It's late. I'd better not."

He was wavering, she could see it. He was as uncertain about all this as she was. Two people in a boat made out of paper, approaching the rapids. She turned her face up to his. "Whatever you say."

He started to leave, he really did. His foot was poised

to pivot away from her and take the first step that would
lead him from the apartment door to his car.

But somehow, he couldn't push off. Not when the
moonlight was glistening along her lips. Not when
every fiber of his being wanted him to kiss her.

"How come you don't have any mistletoe?"

She blinked. Had she heard him right? "What?"

"In your doorway. You have the door gift-wrapped
with a wreath smack in the middle, but you don't have
any mistletoe."

"I thought it might be overkill." She raised herself
up ever so slightly, bringing her mouth even closer.
Tantalizing him. "But if you'd like, you could pretend
there's a mistletoe hanging right there." She pointed
overhead.

He never took his eyes off her. "Works for me."

The next moment, he'd enveloped her in an embrace
that shut out the world and opened the door to a far
more intimate, dangerous place.

Chapter 18

As he assaulted her senses with openmouthed kisses, Patrick took the key from her. Though it felt as if his hands never left her body, somehow he managed to open her front door.

The instant he did, he moved them inside, away from prying eyes. She heard the door shut, felt the warm flare of intimacy taking hold.

The whole room was spinning as if she'd consumed more than her share of alcohol instead of the very little that she had. Maggi drew her head back, dragging in the air she so badly needed.

Something was happening here, she thought. Something very special. She didn't want to name it.

Maggi draped her arms around his neck. "Smooth," she commented, as her eyes indicated the door.

He turned on the light. He wanted to see her, all of her.

The soft nap of the velvet aroused him as it moved against his palms.

"Necessary." Where was the zipper on this thing? He couldn't find one. "You don't want to be arrested on Christmas Eve for indecent exposure."

Unable to hold back, Maggi rained kisses on his face, his throat. The eagerness built. Her heart started to hammer faster again. "Am I going to be indecently exposed?"

"Just as fast as I can figure out how to get this dress off you," he breathed.

Maggi took a step back. She smiled up into his eyes as she reached behind her neck and undid three tiny hooks that held her gown close to her. The two ends parted, sighing as they slid from her shoulders.

Patrick felt his body tighten like a string being drawn across the bridge of a violin. He tugged on the fabric still hugging her waist. The top of her dress sagged the rest of the way down to her hips. He placed his hands over them, bringing Maggi closer to him as his mouth covered hers.

The velvet moved from her hips and sank to the floor. When he finally looked at her an eon later, she stood before him wearing only her heels and a small gold locket around her neck.

Perfect.

Swallowing did nothing to alleviate the dryness in his mouth.

"Nothing indecent about this," he murmured.

The look in his eyes made her feel beautiful. And so eager she could barely stand it. Her hands flew as she unbuttoned, unzipped and pulled, bringing him to the same stage of undress as her within several hard heartbeats.

The rest became a blur of pleasuring, of reexploring and reclaiming. It was both familiar and new. And very, very special.

Trembling, she cleaved her body to his. Soft against hard. Desire spiked through her like an erratic pulse. She was certain he was going to take her right there, before the darkened Christmas tree. Heat traveling through her at lightning speed, she reached for him.

He chose that moment to sweep her from the floor and pick her up in his arms. His voice was low, raspy. "Your bedroom."

She wasn't even sure if she'd heard him. There was this rushing noise in her ears again and all she wanted was to make love with him right here, right now.

"What?"

"Your bedroom, woman," he growled. He didn't want to take her a second time on the floor, as if he was some kind of animal that couldn't contain himself. The least he could do was offer her the nicety of a bed. "Where is it?"

"Where I left it." For just a beat, her mind went blank. "Back there." She pointed vaguely to the rear, then framed his face with her hands as she kissed him hard, excitement racing through her at speeds so great Maggi didn't think she would ever catch her breath again.

As she felt him cross the threshold, she remembered the state in which she'd left the room. There were clothes all over the bed and draped on the chairs.

"It's messy," she warned.

"It's about to get messier."

Without looking, he used his elbow to clear away a space as he laid her down. The next second, he was there beside her, his body twining with hers.

She had no time to protest. Patrick's mouth was over hers, his hands sweeping along her body, making it hum songs she never thought it knew.

Clothes tumbled to the floor as she and Patrick twisted and turned, finding new places along each other's bodies, finding new highs.

She wanted this to go on forever. No tomorrows, no yesterdays; they were both framed in lies. All she wanted was now. Forever now.

Now was pure.

She tightened around him when he entered her, lifting her hips from the bed, losing herself entirely in the act. Praying that he would remember this moment when the rest happened.

"You keep looking at your watch, Mag-pie. You still have something in the oven?"

Preoccupied, Maggie had entered the kitchen to get a bottle of cider from the refrigerator. A few feet away was a long dining room table, formally set. Twelve close friends, both her father's and hers, milled around, catching up and waiting for dinner to be served.

But Patrick wasn't among them.

He's not coming. What did you expect? Flowers? Christmas presents? Snap out of it, Mag. You're a modern woman, not some Victorian wuss.

Her hormones were all over the board today. She felt like crying, like laughing. Like running to the window to watch for him. Like throwing up because she was so nervous.

All morning, she'd been completely out of synch. She chalked it up to rushing around so much. But she'd wanted everything to be perfect.

As if it mattered. The people out there didn't care. They were her friends.

And he was...

He was a definite unknown in all this.

Patrick had left her apartment shortly before two, despite the fact that she'd harbored the secret hope he would spend the night. But that would have meant waking up next to her on Christmas morning. Too much commitment on his part, she supposed.

Apparently so was showing up for Christmas dinner.

She turned around, sparkling cider bottle in hand. She wasn't about to lie to her father, even if she couldn't tell him the full story.

"No, Dad, I thought maybe my partner and his sister would show up." She closed the door. "I invited them over."

Matthew quietly studied his daughter as she spoke. "So you're getting along with him, this new partner of yours?"

She thought of last night. Of the way Cavanaugh had made her body sing. "Yes, Dad, I'm getting along with him."

Matthew's eyes never left his daughter's face. Something in her voice gave him pause. "But it's complicated, isn't it?"

She sighed, shaking her head, an amused smile on her lips. "Once in a while I wish you were a little less intuitive."

The microwave oven bell went off. Since he was closer, he opened the door and looked in. The rolls were ready. "I have to be. You never tell me anything. When you were a girl, you had all those girlie secrets of yours and I wasn't allowed in. Now that you're on the force, it's even worse."

She brushed a kiss across his cheek impulsively. She was more grateful for his existence in her life than she could ever put into words. "You know I can't talk about a case."

"I thought we were talking about your partner—" Matthew's eyebrows drew together. The light came on. "He's your case? You're working with Mike Cavanaugh's kid, aren't you?"

"You know I am."

She looked at her watch again. Cavanaugh was more than half an hour late. Something told her he wasn't going to show up no matter how long she held dinner. Maybe last night had scared him off. God knows the teeth-jarring intensity of making love with him scared the hell out of her. Even so, she had to resist the temptation to call him and demand to know why he was standing her up. If she did that, he'd have an inkling that having him over for dinner meant something more to her than another place setting at the table. The less she gave away, the better.

A little late for that, wouldn't you say, Mag?

She bet the bastard hadn't even told his sister she'd invited them.

Suddenly she squared her shoulders. She had guests who were waiting and a turkey to carve. "C'mon, Dad, it's time to eat. I'm not about to keep everyone else waiting for one rude man."

But as she began to walk out of the kitchen, Matthew drew her aside for one last father-daughter moment. "Men are funny, Mag-pie. Sometimes, when they stumble onto a good thing, instead of embracing it, they run."

Maggi raised her chin. "You don't need to make excuses for him."

"No—" he squeezed her hand "—but maybe you do."

"If you're bucking for Father of the Year, you've already got the award. Now get out there and start getting our guests seated—" she set the bottle of cider down on the sideboard "—while I go and bring in the turkey. Remember, Captain Reynolds sits as far away from me as possible. His teeth blind me when he smiles."

"Not a problem." He stopped only long enough to kiss the top of her head. "Attagirl, Maggi. You do me proud. But then, you always did."

She thought she'd gotten proper control over her emotions. That idea went out the window the second she saw him walking into the squad room. She had to struggle with the very strong urge to throw something heavy at him.

Bastard.

She took a deep breath. What the hell was the matter with her? She felt like some kind of Ping-Pong ball being lobbed back and forth over the net in a championship tournament.

It wasn't easy, but she managed to compose herself by the time he reached her desk. "Did you have a nice Christmas?"

He'd dreaded this ever since he'd gotten up this morning. Yesterday, he'd behaved like the kind of man he'd always despised. He'd acted like a coward. Instead of coming over to her house, or at least calling with some kind of half-assed excuse, he'd ignored the situation entirely in hopes it would go away.

Like it could.

"It was okay." Patrick felt as if he stared down at

a bomb he didn't know how to defuse. Because he didn't. Women were a complete unknown to him. Being close to Patience hadn't educated him in the slightest. But then, Patience had never stirred these kinds of emotions within him.

"I went to my uncle's," he began, then stopped abruptly, frustrated. He couldn't remember the last time he'd tried to render an excuse. "Look, I know I should have called—"

"There was so much noise, I probably wouldn't have heard anyway." She shrugged carelessly. "Hey, no big deal. I thought it might be nice, that's all. But you don't owe me an explanation." *Yes, you do, and you're doing a damn poor job of it.* "I told you once there're no strings and I meant it."

"Look, I'm sorry, okay?" He lowered his voice, not wanting anyone else to hear. "It's just that something's going on here, between us," he clarified when she looked at him in surprise, "something I can't begin to figure out."

Ditto. "Not everything can be reduced to a black-and-white equation you can plot out with graph paper, Cavanaugh. Some things just *are,*" she emphasized. And then, because she wasn't up to dealing with her own feelings, she changed the subject to something they could both work with. "I've been doing a little more thinking about this thing concerning your ex-partner." There was still no word about the man who had supposedly shot him, and she had an uneasy feeling there wouldn't be. Dugan was still missing. "The bullet they dug out of his body, they logged that in as evidence, didn't they?"

"Sure. But they already know it belonged to Dugan's gun." Relieved to put the awkward situation on hold for the time being, he gratefully sank his teeth into the tidbit she offered up. "Why, what are you getting at?"

Maybe something, maybe nothing, she thought. "I'm just fishing. Follow me for a second," she urged. "Maybe the bullet didn't really come from Dugan's gun. Maybe someone else shot Ramirez and Dugan was 'persuaded' to take the fall for someone else. Someone higher up."

If that was true, Patrick thought, the very foundations of the department would come crumbling down. "Who?"

"That part I don't know yet." She smiled ruefully at him. "I guess being around you has gotten me slightly paranoid."

"Paranoid is better than oblivious." He sat down in the chair beside her desk, glad to be working. Glad not to let his thoughts drift too far into uncharted waters. Facing down an unknown enemy was a lot easier than dealing with unknown emotions. "I've tried talking to some of the other people who were there that day, as well as his old partner, Foster, and either no one else knows anything—"

She ended the sentence for him. "Or they're not saying anything."

"Exactly."

The day was slow. Maybe because of the season, Death had called a holiday and there were no new homicides on the board. It gave most of the detectives who hadn't taken the day off to be with their families time to play catch-up with their paperwork. No one would notice if they were missing for a while.

Maggi leaned forward. "What do you say we get on down to the evidence room and see what we can find?"

He'd been toying with the same idea, but he wanted to go alone. And after dark. "The sergeant there isn't just going to let us waltz in there."

Maggi rose from the desk. "You let me handle Sergeant Warren."

He followed her out of the squad room. "You know him?"

The man had been at her table yesterday. "According to my father, he was the man who held the camera when my parents gave me my first bath."

Patrick shook his head as they entered the stairwell that led down to the basement and the evidence room. "You're just one surprise after another, aren't you?"

"Keeps life interesting."

That was one way to put it, Patrick thought.

Sergeant Philip Warren was a corpulent man with a booming laugh, very little hair and six months to go before retirement. When he saw Maggi and her partner walking toward him, he set aside the copy of *Fish and Stream* and greeted them heartily. Visitors were scarce down in the bowels of the evidence room and Sergeant Warren liked to talk.

He winked broadly at Maggi. "Hey, long time no see. What's it been? Twenty, twenty-one hours?" he joked. "Great meal, Maggi, thanks again for having me over."

She smiled warmly. "Just a simple turkey dinner, Sergeant. This is my partner, Patrick Cavanaugh. He would have been there yesterday—" she couldn't help giving him one zinger "—but he was detained."

"You don't know what you missed out on," the sergeant confided. "It tasted like heaven." He patted his all-too-large belly fondly. "Gets me hungry just thinking about it."

Patrick had a feeling that the man grew hungry thinking about almost anything.

"So—" Getting himself as comfortable as possible, the sergeant looked from one to the other. "What can I do for you?"

"Has it been slow here, Phil?" she asked.

Patrick stared at her, surprised she was being so direct. When she'd said she knew the sergeant, he'd expected her to execute some kind of diversion to distract the man while he slipped into the evidence room and got the bullet in question.

"Having trouble keeping my eyes open, Maggi. It's always like this around the holidays. People even forget I'm down here."

"You know what you need?" she told him. "A quick run to the vending machine on the first floor. Get some energy food. Saw some of those chocolate marshmallow bars you're so partial to."

Warren seemed to understand immediately. His eyes shifted toward the man next to her and then back again. Maggi nodded, silently answering his question. Patrick was to be trusted. "Sounds like a good idea, but I don't have anyone to cover for me."

"That's okay, I can hang around for a bit, make sure anyone who might come along signs in first."

Warren was already coming around the desk. "You always were a good girl, Maggi." Standing close to her, he dropped his voice even though it was just the three of them here. "Ten minutes, Mag, can't give you more than that."

"More than enough," she assured him. "I'll be standing right here when you get back. And Phil?"

"Yeah?"

"Thanks."

The man nodded, making his way down the long hallway that led to the elevator bank at the end of the corridor. Maggi waited until she couldn't hear his foot-falls any longer. She turned toward Patrick.

"Okay. Go."

He pushed open the door that led to the dark, ill-lit room. "One surprise after another," he murmured again.

Maggi stood guard, hoping no one would come. Hoping that Patrick would be able to find the proper area. She'd only been inside the evidence room once. It was comprised of rows and rows of gray metal shelves with carefully tagged evidence.

Human nature being what it was, it was easy to mis-file things. Chances would have doubled of finding the evidence involved in Ramirez's shooting if she'd gone in with Cavanaugh, but she couldn't very well leave the desk unmanned. If a superior officer just happened to come by, the sergeant's job and subsequent pension would be on the line. That was no way to pay Warren back for going out on a limb.

She held her breath until Patrick came out of the room again. His expression was grim, but any questions she wanted to ask had to be put on hold. She heard the sergeant walking down the hall. He'd returned as prom-ised, ten minutes to the second.

Warren laid his stash of six candy bars on the desk. "You were right. They had the marshmallow bars. Want one?"

"Thanks, I'll pass. I'm still working off my share of the chocolate cheesecake."

"You look just fine," the sergeant told her. "Doesn't she, Cavanaugh?"

"Just fine," Patrick echoed.

"I'll see you later," Maggi told the sergeant as he busily peeled back the wrapper on his snack. Warren nodded in response.

"Well?" she asked Patrick eagerly the second they put some distance between themselves and the evidence room.

"It's not there."

Her eyes widened. They weren't talking about an incident that had happened several years ago. This was recent. If the evidence was missing, it was on purpose. "The bullet? What do you mean it's not there? Are you sure you were in the right area?"

"Of course I'm sure." She could hear the frustration in his voice. He held open the stairwell door for her. "It's not there. Neither is Dugan's service revolver. They're both missing."

Her heels hit the metal stairs, echoing as she made her way to the first floor. "Or were taken."

He set his mouth firmly. "It's beginning to look like a conspiracy, isn't it?"

She sighed. "Hate that word, but yes, it does. Considering the kinds of deposits Ramirez made, this could be very, very big." She stopped at the top of the stairs and turned to look at him. "Are you sure he never said anything to you?"

He felt a flare of temper and banked it down. "I don't lie, Mary Margaret. I've got my faults, but that's not one of them."

No, she thought, *it's one of mine.*

"I know," she said quietly. She began to yank the

door open only to have him put his hand over the knob and do it for her.

"You're looking a little green around the gills. You okay?"

"Fine, terrific," she lied as her stomach suddenly lurched. This had to be what feeling seasick was like, she thought. Miserable. "Nothing a little antacid won't cure." She didn't want to think about her stomach. If she kept busy, this strange, queasy feeling would go away again the way it had yesterday. "Let's get started on making up a list of people in the department Ramirez had contact with."

That took them far beyond the realm of friends and the list that he had written up himself. "That could take forever."

She looked at him. "Got any better ideas?"

"Not at the moment." He blew out a breath. "Okay, let's get to it."

Chapter 19

The silence within the small, pale blue tiled bathroom was almost deafening.

Maggi stood staring at the slender stick in her hand. She wasn't sure just how much time had gone by. The darkened color at one end told her the same thing that the three other indicators now rudely housed inside her bathroom wastebasket had.

She was pregnant.

As if life wasn't already complicated enough.

Biting off several choice words about fate's rotten sense of humor, she threw the stick into the basket with the rest of the pregnancy testing paraphernalia.

Damn it, anyway.

She'd been throwing up for a week now, every morning like clockwork. The minute her eyes were open, her stomach insisted on crawling up into her throat. Once purged, she'd start to feel better and her nervousness would begin to fade. She'd gotten the kits just to put her own mind at ease, to convince herself that she was only experiencing some new kind of flu and nothing more.

Maggi took a deep breath as she struggled to pull herself together.

A baby. Cavanaugh's baby.

Ain't that a kick in the head?

Now she had two secrets to keep from him. She didn't want him to know she was carrying his baby, not when the situation was so dicey. There was no real indication that Patrick had any stronger feelings for her than those that lasted the duration of their lovemaking. If she told him about the baby and then he asked her to marry him, she'd never know if he had any feelings at all because, in her mind, the proposal would strictly be motivated because of the baby. And if she told him and he backed away from her, well, that would hurt too much to bear.

Silence was the best option. The only option.

Maggi looked at herself in the mirror. *Great little dilemma you've gotten yourself into, Mag.*

She had absolutely no idea what she was going to do beyond the next moment. She needed to get dressed and go on with her life for as long as she could.

Like a cadet reporting for duty, Maggi squared her shoulders. She had a report to file and a partner to back, although the latter, she suspected, would not be for very much longer.

Maggi ignored the pang she felt in her heart.

Hearing the almost furtive knock on his doorjamb, the tall, distinguished man sitting behind the desk looked up. The moment he did, every nerve ending in his body went on the alert.

His voice was deceptively calm, gracious. His ability to seem warm and outgoing had gotten him to where he was. And would eventually see him to where he wanted to be.

"What's up?"

Officer Foster licked his almost nonexistent lower lip. "We've got a problem."

The man's eyebrows moved together a fraction of an inch. "Close the door."

Foster quickly shut it behind him. He glanced at the chair in front of the desk but made no move to take it. He knew better than to sit without being invited. Or to talk out of turn even though the words were hovering in his mouth, vying for release.

The man at the desk closed the file he was looking over. "All right, what's wrong?"

The words flew out in a rush. "He's still nosing around, asking questions, talking to some of the guys. Taylor saw him and his partner coming out of the stairwell." Foster swallowed nervously. "They might have been down in the evidence room."

The man laughed shortly. "And they might have been groping each other in a dark, private place."

Unsure if the remark was meant to be humorous, Foster attempted a grin. A smile spasmodically came and went. "Wouldn't mind doing that myself with her, but not him. Cavanaugh's not like that. He doesn't mix business with pleasure. Hell, we're not even sure he has any pleasures."

There was no humor evident in the other man's dark eyes. "Has he talked to you?"

"Yeah, right at the start. I told him Ramirez was a square deal when we were working together." Foster added quickly, eager to show that he could keep his wits about him, "but I'm not sure he believed me."

The gaze was flat, the scrutiny deep. Unable to endure it, Foster shifted uneasily from one foot to the other.

"You've got the face of a damn angel," his superior retorted. "Why wouldn't he believe you?"

"That's why I came to you." Foster looked nervously over his shoulder, afraid the door would open at any moment and someone would overhear. "Because he says he wants to talk to me again when I've got a little time."

"Make the time," the man instructed quietly. His eyes pinned his subordinate. "And you know what to do."

Foster ran his fingertips over his sweaty palms. He'd been afraid of this. "I don't know if I can."

The other man didn't bother masking his disgust. Men like Foster were necessary drones, expendable pawns, and nothing more.

"Think of it as laying the foundations for your retirement plan." He shifted, leaning over his desk, holding Foster prisoner in his gaze. "You can either spend your golden years on some warm, inviting beach, or in a maximum security prison, courtesy of the state. The choice is yours. That is, if you actually make it to trial," he added significantly.

Foster knew what that meant. That he would meet a fate similar to Ramirez's, whose only misfortune was in being in the wrong place at the wrong time and whose conscience had finally gotten the better of him. Or like Dugan, whose body hadn't been found yet and probably would never be.

"The choice is yours," the man repeated softly, curdling the blood in Foster's veins.

Foster nodded, knowing what he had to do. Not liking it at all. He hadn't signed on for this. Garnering protection money from wealthy store owners who could well afford it in exchange for favors and protection was one thing. The cold-blooded elimination of problems, which was what he was being told to do, was a completely different matter.

But it all boiled down to self-defense. If he didn't do this, didn't defend himself against what might happen if Cavanaugh stumbled across the truth, he would die. That was guaranteed. And he knew he wasn't ready for that.

"Okay," Foster said, his mouth so dry he felt like choking, "I'll do it."

"Good man. Let me know how it goes. And Foster," he said just as the smaller man was about to leave.

"Yes?"

"Don't screw up."

"No, sir," Foster promised. He hurried out of the room, knowing he had to leave before he threw up.

Patrick's hands were clenched into fists at his sides as he walked down the long corridor.

He'd done nothing wrong, absolutely nothing wrong.

That still didn't ameliorate the uneasy feeling that insisted on dancing through him. He'd been summoned to appear before John Halliday, the head of IA.

Now.

A summons usually meant that he was either under investigation or required to give testimony about someone who was. Anticipation introduced a foul taste into his mouth. Either scenario was not one he remotely welcomed.

Although Internal Affairs was a necessary evil, like everyone else, Patrick thought of the people who worked for IA as belonging to the rat squad. They were people whose sole function was to ferret out the bad in everyone. A few well-placed chosen words could turn almost anything into a suspicious act.

And now those words would concern him.

Maybe this was about Ramirez, he thought. Could be someone higher up had gotten wind of the same thing he had about his late partner and was now doing some digging into the man's dealings. Which probably meant that he was also a suspect. Just as he figured Foster might be mixed up in all this. Only difference being that he assumed someone was innocent until he found evidence to the contrary. IA worked in the reverse. You were guilty until proved innocent.

It was a little like the KGB, Patrick thought as he stopped before Halliday's door. He paused before knocking. Damn, but he hated this. Any way he sliced it, he was about to walk into an unpleasant experience.

He hadn't even told Maggi where he was going. The less involved she was in this, the better.

There he went again, he upbraided himself, wanting to protect her. He was going to have to do something about that.

And while he was at it, he was going to have to do something about the way all his days seemed to wind up at her apartment. In her bed. And he was going to have to do something about the way he could think of nothing else but taking her into his arms and making love with her.

Patrick shook his head. He felt as if his own will had

been stolen and someone else's had wantonly been substituted. He didn't know whether to laugh and enjoy it while it lasted or run for the hills. Because he wanted it to last forever.

He still hadn't spent an entire night with her and there was still a part of himself he was holding back. But his hold was slipping. Eventually, he knew he'd lose his grip on it altogether. And give all of himself to her.

Patrick knocked and waited.

A deep voice on the other side of the door instructed a genial "Come in."

Braced and ready for anything, Patrick turned the knob and walked in.

And discovered that he wasn't really braced at all. Or ready for anything. Especially not for what he saw. Not for Maggi sitting there in the room.

"Leave her out of this," he snapped, forgoing any attempt at a perfunctory greeting. "Whatever you think you have on me, she has nothing to do with any of it. She hasn't even been my partner for very long."

"No, just long enough," Halliday responded. "Take a seat, Detective."

Patrick drew himself up even straighter, giving redwoods a run for their money. "I prefer to stand."

Halliday's eyes narrowed. "That wasn't a request. Sit, Detective Cavanaugh," he ordered. "You're making me nervous."

Reining in the very strong desire to grab Maggi's hand and just walk out of the office, Patrick sat down on the other chair. He kept his gaze fixed on the man who'd called him in. He hated the fact that Maggi was being dragged into this because of him.

Steepling his fingers, Halliday leaned back in his chair as he kept his eyes on his subject.

"I've heard some very good things about you, Cavanaugh. And some bad. It's up to me to figure out which are true, which aren't. I can't do that kind of thing without help." He paused significantly, letting the words sink in.

Patrick's eyes shifted to Maggi, trying to read her expression. She looked uneasy. What had gone down here? What had Halliday made her do? He would swear on his life that she wouldn't lie, wouldn't implicate him in anything just to save her own career.

So what was she doing here?

"What am I being accused of?" Patrick demanded abruptly.

In contrast, Halliday's voice was calm, soothing. "All in due time, Detective."

He wasn't about to wait while Halliday played games to amuse himself. "I've got a right to know *now*."

Halliday merely smiled. "Most people sitting in that chair would be asking for legal counsel and to have their representative called in by now."

"I don't need a representative. I haven't done anything wrong," he growled through clenched teeth.

"You're not pure as the driven snow, Cavanaugh." The smile on Halliday's lips was unreadable. "I know you've bent your share of rules." He glanced down at the neatly typed report on his desk, the one signed by Mary Margaret McKenna. "But there's no evidence to prove that you're guilty of what you were initially accused of."

Patrick was losing patience fast. With little to no provocation, he'd leap over the desk and shake the answers out of Halliday.

"What?" Patrick demanded. "Just what the hell am I accused of? And by who?"

"It was an anonymous call, stating that you were responsible for Ramirez's death. And that you were up to your neck in dirty tricks. Scamming, bribery, collecting protection money from the locals. The man called you a dirty cop on the take and said that when Ramirez found out and was going to blow the whistle on you, you forced Dugan to kill him and make it look like an accident."

Patrick clutched at the armrests, all but breaking them off. "That's a lie."

Halliday moved his chair slightly to face Maggi. "That's what Detective McKenna tells me."

So that was it, they were grilling Maggi, trying to make her turn against him. Talk about misjudging characters. "Leave her out of this."

"I'm afraid I can't do that," Halliday informed him, his voice mild. "I was the one who sent her into this. To investigate you," he added when Cavanaugh continued to stare at him darkly. He indicated the report on his desk. "She's cleared you."

But Patrick's brain had stopped processing information, halted by Halliday's first remark. "You did what?"

"Bottom line is that you're cleared, Cavanaugh. You could run for president and withstand media microscrutiny based on the report McKenna turned in to me."

Patrick's eyes pinned Maggi to the wall. "You're with him?"

The accusation pierced her like two arrows.

"She's part of IA," Halliday told him. "Undercover, actually. Having her here while I talk to you flies in the face of protocol, but it was at her own insistence."

He glanced at Maggi. Halliday deemed himself to be a fair judge of people. "I imagine she was hoping to smooth things out."

Patrick rose to his feet, his expression stony. Ignoring Maggi, he addressed Halliday. "Am I free to go now?"

Halliday flipped Patrick's file closed. "Yes." But as Patrick began to leave, he added, "And Cavanaugh, leave the internal investigation to us. We'll be looking into Ramirez's connections and ties," he told him pointedly, "not you."

"Whatever you say," Patrick replied curtly.

Turning on his heel, he walked out of the room.

In the space of ten minutes, Patrick's entire universe had been turned completely upside down. The woman who had somehow managed to slip into his world through the cracks and become closer to him than he'd ever allowed anyone else to get, had been part of the rat squad all along, sent in to spy on him.

Spy on him. The words echoed inside his brain, mocking him.

Damn, so much for trusting his own instincts. He was worse than some wet-behind-the-ears recruit, he thought in utter self-disgust.

The clicking sound of heels hurrying along the vinyl flooring registered on the perimeter of his mind.

"Patrick, wait."

Patrick just kept walking down the hall as if he hadn't heard her. Maggi stepped up her pace until she managed to overtake him just shy of the elevator. She moved in front of him, preventing him access to the buttons.

"I said wait."

With both hands on her shoulders, he moved her

roughly aside, then punched the Down button. He'd never felt so explosive, so angry.

"Your report's filed, Mary Margaret," he spit. "You don't have to hang around me anymore."

The best thing was to walk away, to let him cool off. But the look of contempt in his eyes sliced her open from end to end. She had to make him understand.

"Patrick, please—" she caught hold of his arm "—let me explain."

He shrugged her off, curbing the impulse to shake her, to demand why she'd made him feel so much when all she was doing was spying on him. He knew it was unreasonable, but so were his emotions.

"Explain what?" he asked coldly. "There's nothing to explain. You were sent in to spy on me. You spied, it's over."

The last two words slammed into her. Never mind that she'd known they were coming, that she'd been trying to prepare herself for them all along. She didn't want it to be over. Not like this.

"Patrick, I had a job to do—"

"And you did it." His tone cut her off at the knees. "Very commendable." He turned from the elevator. The anger in his eyes took her breath away. "Tell me, did you get time and a half for sleeping with me? Or was that just a new part of the job description?"

He couldn't have hurt her more if he'd spent months orchestrating his words. She felt the sting of tears and pushed them back. "Don't be like that—"

"Oh? And how would you like me to be?"

Incensed, he grabbed Maggi by the arm and pulled her into an alcove, aiming for some semblance of privacy in this goldfish bowl he'd found himself in.

"You lied to me," he accused. "You burrowed your

hooks into me and pumped me for information any way you could.'' And then he told her the real source of his pain. The real source of the betrayal he felt. ''I opened myself up to you the way I never had to anyone else before.'' Disgusted, he thrust her away from him, shaking his head as he mocked himself. ''Damn it, I bought the whole puppet show, didn't I? The decorations, the Christmas tree, the toy drive—nice touch, by the way,'' he said sarcastically. ''Did you find out that my mother, sister and I had to stay at a St. Agnes Shelter one year, was that what motivated you?'' When he thought about how he'd felt, standing there in her living room, listening to her…his stomach just turned.

''No, I *do* collect toys for kids. All of that was real, *is* real,'' she insisted. ''I didn't pretend to be anything I wasn't.'' She didn't want him to think that had been to manipulate him. Most of all, whether or not they were ever together again, she didn't want him to hate her.

Sheer contempt for her and her kind blazed in his eyes. ''Except that what you were was part of the rat squad.''

He knew better. He knew how the system worked. It was in place so that they could police themselves and keep them all clean, keep the public from doing the job for them.

''I couldn't tell you that. It was my job to clear you.''

Did she think he was some kind of mental incompetent? They all knew how IA operated. ''It was your job to find dirt that would stick.''

''But I didn't.''

''Damn straight you didn't, because there isn't any.''

She felt herself getting angry in self-defense. ''Evidence can always be manipulated, Cavanaugh, you know that.''

''So if I didn't perform satisfactorily, you would have turned me in?''

Maggi threw her hands up in frustration. ''That's not what I'm saying. Patrick, be reasonable.''

''I am being reasonable.'' He glanced at his watch and then strode back to the elevator. When she attempted to block him, he growled, ''Now get the hell out of my way.''

Something was up. She could tell by the look on his face. ''Where are you going?''

The elevator doors opened again. The car hadn't gone anywhere in the interim. Much like them, Patrick thought, anger eating away at him. ''That's no longer any business of yours, is it?''

A sense of panic began to set in. What was he going to do? ''I'm still your partner.''

He got into the elevator and pressed the Close button. The look in his eyes forbade her to follow him in.

''Wrong. Again.''

The elevator doors shut, underscoring the sinking feeling in the pit of her stomach.

Chapter 20

"Foster, you in here?"

Patrick's voice echoed back to him from within the confines of the empty warehouse he'd just entered. Filled with rusting metal rows that extended upward of two stories, the building had once held a profusion of boxed toys. Now it stood abandoned, as barren as the bankrupt toy store chain that had once required its contents.

He strained his eyes to see. Ramirez's old partner had called to tell him that he had some information for him but that Foster would only meet him here. The man feared reprisals. It was here or nowhere. Patrick had had no choice but to agree.

A movement on the left caught his attention. Foster, slight for his uniform, stepped out of the shadows. His sandy-colored hair looked darker in the poor light coming through barred windows with years of dirt and grime on them.

"Yeah, I'm here." Foster beckoned him away from the entrance. "Come on in."

Patrick left the door behind him standing open. He scanned the area as he approached. There was no sound except for Foster's breathing. Was the other man nervous? Did he feel threatened?

Was this just another wild-goose chase? Questions crowded Patrick's mind.

"Don't you think this is a little dramatic?" he asked. "A coffeehouse or diner would have been better." Foster's body was a symphony of motion. He *was* nervous, Patrick thought.

"I told you, I didn't want anyone overhearing us."

Patrick drew the only conclusion he could. "So there is something you want to tell me. Why didn't you say something when I questioned you the last time?"

"Couldn't." Foster became steadily more agitated as he talked. "Things've changed. But you can't say this came from me."

They were both aware of how the system worked. Guarantees couldn't be made. "I'll protect you for as long as I can, Foster, but I can't make any promises, you know that."

Foster struggled with what he knew he had to do. With what he didn't want to do. "Then maybe there's nothing to say."

No way was he going to let Foster out of here without the other man telling him what he knew. "Yes, there is. You wouldn't have gone in for this cheap movie effect if there wasn't."

For a second, the cornered-rabbit expression was gone. Foster looked around the dust-laden building. Nostalgia came over his thin features.

"My dad used to be the foreman here. Brought me around to play when I was a kid."

Patrick curbed his impatience. The man was stalling. Why? "In a warehouse?"

"He was a single dad and this was cheaper than having someone look after me after school. This place used to be where Melbourne Toys kept their inventory." Foster pointed toward shelves in the rear of the building. "That's where they kept the boxes with the action figures. I'd wait until no one was looking then work open the side of a box. A toy here, a toy there, nobody noticed."

The nostalgia gave way to a shrug. "Maybe it started here, I dunno. Thinking that it was all right to take something as long as nobody noticed. As long as you took from someone rich instead of the average guy in the street." Foster looked at Patrick, a defensive tone entering his voice. He was no longer talking about toys and petty theft. "We never took anything from the mom-and-pop places, only the ones who could afford it."

Was it just the two men, or did this involve more people? He had a hunch, he knew. But he needed more than just a hunch. Patrick tried to siphon the information from the other man carefully. "By took, you mean what?"

Foster sneered. "Don't play dumb, Cavanaugh. Money. What else would I be talking about? The owners paid us, we took care of them. Any tickets, any violations, they didn't get written up."

Patrick didn't have to be a genius to know how the operation worked. "And if they didn't pay, the violations were written up and fined even if they didn't exist."

"Something like that."

Time to push. "How many of you were there?" Fear entered Foster's eyes. "Ramirez's account was pretty healthy," Patrick said.

"Enough." As he spoke, Foster began to move around, to pace. "Eddie wasn't part of it, not the way you think. He stumbled onto what was going on and got paid to keep his mouth shut. When he didn't want to keep it that way any longer, things happened." Foster shrugged helplessly. "I'm sorry. He was a good guy."

Patrick could almost believe Foster regretted what had happened. But it was too late for regrets. "Who had him killed? How far up does this go?"

Foster shook his head. "Sorry, privileged information. On both counts."

"You're going to have to come clean." He wasn't going to allow the man to get away, not after this. One bad cop gave them all a bad name.

Foster's eyes became steely. "No, the only thing I have to do is this."

Patrick mentally cursed himself. His anger at McKenna's deceit had clouded his judgment, dulled that sixth sense of his that always warned him when something was about to go wrong. Or maybe it had just gotten impaired after totally going haywire because of Maggi.

It was the only explanation for why he didn't see it coming. Why he didn't see that he was walking into a trap.

Patrick found himself looking down the business end of the gun in Foster's hand.

Foster thought he could read what was going on in Cavanaugh's mind. "No, it's not regulation issue. It belongs to a dead man. Nobody's going to be able to trace this.'' His eyes narrowed slightly, but his voice wavered as he said, ''Or find you.''

A shot rang out. Foster screamed and the weapon he'd been aiming at Patrick went flying from his hands. Patrick made a dive for it. Only when he had the gun in his hands did he turn around to see the small figure running in through the warehouse entrance.

Maggi. Goddamn it, it was Maggi. Was she out of her mind?

''What the hell are you doing here?'' he demanded roughly.

Maggi's eyes were on the fallen patrolman, watching for the one false move that would trip them up. ''Tying up loose ends, saving you, take your pick.'' It was damn hard to sound flippant, what with her heart in her mouth and all.

Instinct had made her follow Patrick when he'd left the police station even while she'd counseled herself to give him some space. She knew she didn't like being crowded when she had to work something out for herself. But patience wasn't her long suit in this case.

Maggi was eternally grateful that just this once she hadn't listened to her head, but gone with her instincts and her heart. If she hadn't, Patrick could well be dead by now.

''How about dying alongside of him?''

The question came from the row of dust-encrusted shelves just behind them.

Captain Amos Reynolds stepped out, a gun in his hand. Contempt flared in his eyes as he glanced in Foster's direction. The latter looked as surprised as Maggi felt to see the senior officer.

This was bad, Maggi thought, very bad.

"Get up, you idiot. I knew you'd botch this," Reynolds said to the other man.

Foster began to take a step forward, but the look in Reynolds's eyes froze him in place. "I'm sorry, I'm sorry, she got the drop on me."

Anger and disgust creased the captain's handsome face. "Do you have any idea how pathetic that sounds?" He moved the barrel of his weapon to point at Foster. The other man jumped uneasily. "Three bodies are just as easy to get rid of as two." Smoothly Reynolds swung his hand back to aim at Patrick. "Drop your weapons, you two."

Patrick's hand only tightened on his. "You can't kill both of us."

Reynolds's gaze was unrelenting. "I can and I will unless you do exactly as I say. I'm not about to let you mess up something that's been going on for ten years. Everyone was protected, no one got hurt."

As if that made it right, Patrick thought. "Tell that to Ramirez," he spit.

Reynolds appeared unfazed. "That was unfortunate. It was only meant to be a warning, just a wound. But he moved." Reynolds looked in Maggi's direction. "It worked with your father."

Maggi's mouth dropped open. "My father?" Anger colored her cheeks. Reynolds wasn't fit to mention her father's name.

"Don't look so indignant." The soothing tone of Reynolds's voice only served to agitate her further. "He doesn't know anything. But he was starting to ask uncomfortable questions. Getting him off the force was the best way to deal with it." His smile was cold. "You don't worry about inconsistencies you've stumbled across when you're busy trying to cope with regaining the use of your leg.''

All pretense at civility terminated. His eyes darkened. ''Now I'm not going to ask you again. Drop your weapons.'' He took aim at Maggi. ''Or she goes first.''

Patrick had no other choice.

If he dropped his weapon, they'd be gunned down where they stood. He knew it.

It was going to be a matter of split-second timing. Shoving Maggi out of the way, he took dead aim and fired. Reynolds went down, spasmodically getting off one shot before he fell face forward to the floor. Dead.

Patrick whirled around and trained his weapon on Foster.

''Don't even think it,'' he warned. He kept his gun aimed at Foster as he warily approached the fallen captain. ''Get his weapon, McKenna.'' When she made no answer, adrenaline kicked up another notch. He glanced in her direction. ''McKenna?''

''Give me a second,'' she breathed, trying to gather herself up from her knees. Her shoulder felt as if it was on fire. Touching it, she looked down at her hand, which was covered in blood. Blood also oozed from her right shoulder, soaking its way into everything.

''Oh, my God, Maggi, you're hit.''

Her teeth clamped down on her lower lip as she struggled to her feet. ''Can't put nothing over on you, can I?'' She sucked in air. Every breath hurt.

Guilt snapped its jaws around him. He should have pulled her down. Instead of sparing her, he'd pushed her right into Reynolds's line of fire.

''Is it bad?''

Trust Cavanaugh to understate something. It was almost funny. ''Other than feeling like someone just set me on fire, no," she answered between clenched teeth. And then she stopped. "Listen." The sound of sirens in the distance pushed their way through the silence. "Better late than never, huh?"

She'd almost forgotten about that. On a hunch, she'd called for backup the moment she saw Foster. A man who didn't have anything to hide didn't go around meeting people in abandoned warehouses, didn't take these kinds of precautions.

It was getting hard to stay focused. "Don't let him get the drop on you again," she warned Patrick.

It was the last thing she said before the darkness claimed her.

Maggi had opened her eyes, but he didn't think she saw him. She looked so pale as she lay there on the gurney, so white she almost faded into the sheet.

He was afraid to say her name, afraid to call out to her and not have her respond. So as he sat beside her in the ambulance, he held on to her hand as tightly as he could. He willed her to hang on, silently forbidding her to slip away.

He'd never felt terrified before, not even when he'd been a small boy and his father had gone on a rampage, smashing things around the house, threatening to kill them all. Then his thoughts had been centered around protecting his mother and sister. But now there was nothing he could do to protect Maggi.

Nothing he could do to make her whole.

It was out of his hands and he hated the feeling of helplessness. Hated the fact that he was sitting here, maybe impotently watching her life slip away.

He wanted to yell, to rail.

He could do nothing.

Patrick bent very close to her ear, so that only she could hear him.

"I'm not going to let you go, you hear me? I forbid you to die. God damn it, Maggi, you can't do this to me. I love you."

Her face remained still and pale, her color a contrast to the blood spread out on her shirt.

Patrick closed his eyes and tried to remember how to pray.

Patience came flying down the long corridor. The moment she saw him, she threw her arms around her brother, embracing him. Patrick had called her less than twenty minutes ago. She'd broken speed limits to get here, using her cell phone to call the people who needed to be called as she drove to the hospital.

"How is she?" she asked breathlessly.

He shook his head. "I don't know. They won't tell me anything." He sighed, feeling like a man who was just about ready to leap out of his own skin. "She's in surgery."

There'd been no time for details when he'd called her. Only that Maggi had been shot and that he was in the hospital with her. "What happened?"

He'd been asking himself that same question over and over again in the past half hour.

"I thought she was clear. I shoved her out of the way. Reynolds was going to kill her." Stopping, Patrick dragged in air. It didn't help to calm him. Nothing would help until he knew Maggi was all right again. "Instead, I pushed her right into the line of fire."

Patience tried to lead him over to the chairs lined along the hallway. He didn't budge, remaining against the wall as if he was holding it up. Or maybe it was holding him up.

"She's going to be all right, Patrick. This is the best hospital in the county."

"Yeah, right," he said numbly.

But people died in good hospitals, didn't they? Oh God, what if…?

He couldn't bring himself to finish the sentence, even in his own mind.

They heard the sound of footsteps approaching quickly. The next moment, Matthew McKenna came racing down the hallway, his face as ashen as Maggi's had been when they had wheeled her into surgery.

He'd never met Maggi's father, but Patrick only had to take one look at the man's face before he knew. Straightening, he met the other man halfway.

"Are you Maggi's father?" There were suppressed tears in the man's eyes as he nodded. "I'm Patrick Cavanaugh, Maggi's partner. I'm the one who called you." Belatedly, he remembered he wasn't alone. "This is my sister, Patience."

"They told me at the front desk that she was in surgery. Do we know anything yet?" Patrick shook his head. Matthew tried to get control over his fears. "What happened?"

"She saved my life," Patrick replied simply. There was no doubt in his mind that if she hadn't shot the gun out of Foster's hand, he would have been dead right now.

Taking a breath, he pulled himself together and filled in his sister and Maggi's father as best he could about what had happened in the warehouse, ending with Foster's arrest and Maggi being taken into surgery. Reynolds had gone to the morgue in a body bag.

Matthew listened to it all in solemn silence. When Patrick finished, he nodded.

"I had a feeling all along that something wasn't right, but I had no way of proving it and I didn't want to let Maggi in on my suspicions. I knew she'd try to do something like this. Stubborn as all get-out, that girl. Thinks she's Joan of Arc the way she carries on about doing the right thing. I was afraid she'd take this into her own hands," Matthew McKenna said.

He didn't know, Patrick realized as he looked at Maggi's father. Matthew McKenna had no idea that his daughter worked for IA. She'd kept it from him.

"She's headstrong that way," Patrick agreed, not adding that it was also part of her job. Her being part of IA wasn't his secret to tell.

They heard several voices coming from around the bend. The next moment, Patrick saw his uncles Andrew and Brian heading toward them. He looked at Patience.

"I called them after you called me." She looked at Maggi's father. "Patrick told me that you know my uncles. I thought maybe you might need some company right now."

Matthew felt as if he'd aged ten years since he'd received the call from Patrick. He was grateful for Patience's thoughtfulness. He couldn't be distracted, but being around old comrades helped keep some of the demons at bay.

"Thank you."

Patience nodded. She glanced at her brother. If only there was someone she could call for him.

Patrick stood apart from the others, although it wasn't easy. The corridor had become crammed with people who knew Maggi, family friends and veterans of the force who had watched her grow up from a golden haired toddler into the woman she was, as well as people she worked with now. Carving out a space for himself was difficult, especially when everyone was trying to bolster each other.

He didn't care about other people's stories of miraculous recoveries or statistics that tipped the scales in her favor. None of that mattered. The only thing that mattered was what was going on behind the closed doors of the ground-floor operating room.

He felt as though he were standing in a time warp, holding his breath, vacillating between anger and fear.

When the blue-gowned internal surgeon finally made his way among them and asked, "Who's here for Maggi McKenna?" everyone replied in the affirmative and crowded around the physician.

Matthew pushed his way into the center. "I'm Maggi's father."

"How is she?" Patrick demanded, cutting the man off. He'd been the one the surgeon had briefed as quickly as he could about Maggi's situation. The surgeon wouldn't have even done that except that Patrick had rushed alongside of him as Maggi was being hurried into the operating room.

The surgeon looked close to exhaustion.

"She's one hell of a lucky girl. Half an inch closer and the wound would have been fatal." He seemed as relieved as the people crowded around him. "But we got the bullet out and she's going to be just fine, although she needs a lot of rest."

Patrick knew how receptive Maggi would be to that. The instant she started getting better, she would want to be back in active duty. "Don't worry, I'll sit on her if I have to."

"I wouldn't advise that if I were you." The surgeon smiled weakly, removing the surgical mask from around his neck. "At least not on her stomach."

There was something in the other man's voice that made Patrick wary. "Her stomach?"

"I'm sorry, little joke to ease the tension on my part. That's just my way of saying that the baby's fine, too."

"Baby?" Patrick echoed incredulously. For the second time that day, he felt as if he'd been punched straight in the gut. Taking the man's arm, he drew him over to the side. "She's pregnant?"

"Yes. Just barely." The surgeon's eyes searched Patrick's face. He must have made the assumption that Patrick was his patient's husband. "I'm sorry, did I just spoil the surprise?"

Feeling shaken and hardly aware of what he was doing, Patrick clapped the surgeon on the shoulder. "No, you did just fine, Doc. Just fine."

He left his hand there a moment longer before withdrawing it. Balance became a matter of intense concentration. Patrick felt as if someone had just taken away the ground from beneath his feet.

Chapter 21

Maggi's surgeon finally allowed Matthew and Patrick in to see her once she was out of recovery and safely in her room.

"But only for a few minutes," he cautioned before opening the door for them. "She's conscious but she's still very weak."

Matthew nodded solemnly as he passed the physician. The moment he saw his daughter, clear colored tubes running through her arms, his heart constricted. Positioning himself on one side of her, he took Maggi's hand in his, lightly kissed her forehead and said, "You're getting off the force."

Maggi smiled at her father. Her eyes flickered over Patrick. He was here. She hadn't imagined it. And he was all right. He and her baby were all right. That was all that mattered.

"Hi, Dad." Her voice sounded raspy and distant to

her own ear. "Didn't the doctor tell you not to get me upset?"

His grip tightened slightly around her hand. "I'm older. I'm not supposed to be upset first." Tears sprang to his eyes as he thought of what could have been. "Oh Mag-pie..." Unable to finish without cracking, his voice trailed off.

All the emotions she'd felt when she'd first gone to see him in the hospital returned. She wished she could have spared him this. "I know, Dad. I was standing on the other side of the railing not that long ago, remember?"

He nodded. "I like better being the one to get shot. You don't worry as much." He bent over and kissed her cheek. This wasn't over, but right now, she needed her rest. He glanced toward Patrick. The young man was restless. It was easy to see he wanted some time alone with her. "We'll talk later," Matthew promised.

"Won't do any good," she warned. A smattering of the sparkle had returned to her eyes and Matthew took heart in that.

"I'll be right outside if you need me." Feeling a rock had been lifted from his heart, Matthew slipped out and left Patrick alone with his daughter.

The words erupted out of Patrick the second the door was closed. "What the hell were you thinking, flying in like some goddamned superhero?"

"Probably the same thing you were when you went in." She was weak and it was costing her to talk. But things had to get said. "Y'know, a person shouldn't be afraid or be too proud to accept help, especially when there are guns pointed at him."

"You could have been killed," Patrick said.

"So could you," she countered though with far less energy than she would have wanted to. "And if you had been, it would have been my fault. I couldn't have that on my conscience."

"Why would it be your fault?"

She took a deep breath, fighting against the desire to close her eyes and drift off. "Because you weren't thinking straight after you walked out of Halliday's office. Anyone could see that."

Patrick struggled against the urge to shake her. To grab her and hold her close to him, never letting her go. Instead, he forced himself to remain where he was and just look at her. "Can you blame me?"

"Yeah, I can. You know how the job works."

"And you were only doing your job, right?" He didn't want to be having this same argument again. It led nowhere. And besides, she was right. "Sorry. It's behind us now and yes, I do know how the job works." He hadn't realized until this moment just how shaky he felt, as if his insides were one huge mass of undulating Jell-O. "And better someone fair and impartial like you than someone on the take and under Reynolds's thumb."

She took in a deep breath, trying to tack her words onto it. "Does it stop with Reynolds?"

To take his mind off her surgery, Patrick reported the matter to Brian, who, as chief of detectives, promised to take it from there.

"Too soon to tell, but it's a lot dirtier than we thought."

Bits and pieces of thoughts floated through her head. She thought of Alicia and her children. "What about Ramirez's wife?"

"I think I can keep her clean." Unless something drastic came to light to change the picture, the woman was safe. He paused. He didn't want to talk about the case or other people. Not when there was something so much bigger before them. "Doctor said you were going to be fine."

She smiled weakly. She'd never had a doubt. Not about herself. She supposed that was vain in a way, but her own mortality had never occurred to her. "I'm tough, like my dad."

"Baby's going to be fine, too." Each word had been measured out. He looked at her intently. "Is it mine?"

Her heart felt as if it had been pricked. Did he doubt her? The other deceptions didn't matter. This he should have known. "Do you have to ask?"

"Why didn't you tell me?"

She didn't look away. "Again, do you have to ask?" Maggi tried to read his expression and couldn't. A sinking feeling took hold, trespassing on the physical pain. If Patrick was happy about the situation, she would have known it, felt it. He obviously wanted nothing to do with her baby or her.

"I'm not going to ask you for anything except maybe input on the baby's name when the time comes." The scowl didn't leave his face. Her spirits sank a little lower. "You don't even have to do that if you don't want to."

He felt like the last man standing after a day-long blitzkrieg. So many emotions bounced around inside of him he couldn't begin to sort them out or even make heads or tails out of the mess. He was unaccustomed to having any emotions at all, much less a conflicting squadron. It had been one hell of a day. The woman he loved wasn't who he'd thought she was. On top of that, she had almost died saving his life. And then to discover that she was carrying his baby, well, it was just too much for him to handle. At least, right away.

"Baby's name is up to you," he told her, his voice distant, detached. "Seeing as how you've been calling all the shots so far."

"Not all the shots." She pulled her courage together, knowing she would never get another chance to be so nakedly honest, and knowing she had everything to lose. But she had to say it, had to tell him, no matter what the consequences. "I didn't plan on falling in love with you. I didn't even plan on liking you."

Love. He tried to absorb the word but couldn't, not when he felt so numbed.

"Yeah, well, plans don't always work out, do they?" He needed distance, time and distance, to be fair to her. To be fair to himself. He nodded toward the door. "The hall's full of people who want to see you. I've probably gone over my time limit." His voice was flat. "I'll see you later."

With that, he walked out of the room.

Maggi forced her tears back.

Patrick didn't remember walking out of the hospital. Didn't remember driving around in his car or where he and the next two hours eventually went.

His thoughts were all tied up in knots, much the way his gut was whenever he began to think of what might have happened to Maggi in the warehouse and how the scenario in the operating room might have turned out.

He could have lost her.

And lost himself.

Like a homing pigeon relying completely on programming and instinct, Patrick found himself returning to the precinct. Parking, he yanked up the hand brake. All the frustration he'd endured these past few hours came to a head, threatening to explode within him. Explode out of him.

Getting out of his car, he walked into the building and made his way up the stairwell until he reached the floor that housed IA.

Without sparing her a glance, he strode past Halliday's secretary.

About to go home, the woman looked up, taken completely by surprise. Belatedly she realized where he was going. "Wait, you can't go in there."

"Shoot me," Patrick snapped, leaving the woman utterly speechless.

John Halliday was on the phone when the door to his office was abruptly thrown open. The man in the doorway looked as if he was loaded for bear.

"Speak of the devil," Halliday murmured into the receiver. "He just walked in. I'll talk to you later." Hanging up, he rose from his chair. "Cavanaugh, I didn't expect to see you here."

Patrick curbed the urge to shout at the man, to let loose with a string of expletives. That would hardly release the fury he was experiencing. Instead, he measured out his words as evenly as he could.

"Maybe if I'd been here to begin with, you could have saved everyone a hell of a lot of time and effort." He stood toe-to-toe with the man, their eyes level. "You should have asked me directly. I would have cooperated with any investigation."

Halliday surprised him by laughing. "You don't exactly have the best reputation for working and playing well with others, Detective. Instead of answering questions, we figured you'd storm off, forewarned. We weren't sure if you really were in on it, the way the informant claimed, or how deep all of this went. Having someone on the inside was the best way to go. You know, sometimes things have to be done according to someone else's rules, not yours.

"By the way, you might be interested to know that the informant turned out to be Foster. He confessed half an hour ago. He's ready to flip on everyone, as long as we can guarantee that he'll stay alive."

But Halliday could see that Cavanaugh's reputation was the last thing on the man's mind. Halliday indicated the telephone. "That was her on the phone— McKenna—filing her last report. Woman's amazing. Flat on her back and she's still thinking about the job. I'm going to hate to lose her."

Patrick became alert. "Lose her?"

Halliday nodded. "She asked for a transfer. Said she didn't like dealing in lies anymore, even for a good cause."

Patrick told himself he didn't care. He knew he was lying. "Where does she want a transfer to?"

"She said she'd get back to me about that. Had to think about what to do with the rest of her life." Halliday looked at him pointedly. "You might like to help her with that."

"Me?"

Halliday snorted. "Give me a little credit here, Cavanaugh. All that emotion exploding out of you like lava from Mount Saint Helens isn't just because you think your honor's been impugned. I'm not saying anything else here, except that I don't think, off the record, that McKenna's the kind of woman any man in his right mind should allow to get away—provided she was interested in him in the first place.''

Halliday took his coat from the rack and slipped it on.

''Now, if there's nothing else, I'd like to go home to my wife and tell her I love her. I can't remember the last time I said that to her and she deserves to hear it. G'night, Cavanaugh.''

Patrick walked out in front of him.

He drove home. To try to be alone with his thoughts. To try to pick up pieces of the life he'd had until McKenna had walked into it, messing everything up.

The first thing he saw when he let himself into his condo and turned on the light was the Christmas tree in the center of the living room.

The one that she had brought him.

It sagged like a little old man, its branches weighed down by the decorations she'd insisted he'd take. He'd been so wrapped up in his work, he'd forgotten to get rid of it.

Pine needles were scattered on the carpet like pale green dandruff. He hadn't remembered to water it, either. Nothing but a pain in the neck, that's what it was.

He remembered opening the door and seeing Maggi peering around it.

He touched a branch and was surprised to find that it wasn't as brittle as he'd thought it would be.

Having Maggi in his life meant always being surprised. If she wasn't in it anymore...

Turning on his heel, Patrick shut off the light and went back out.

* * *

Daylight tried to push its way through the white curtains her father had drawn shut before he'd left for the night.

Maggi stirred.

The slight motion brought an army of pain marching through her with huge combat boots. She felt worse today than yesterday.

Except for her heart.

That was as bad as ever. She expected it would be for a very long time to come.

Resisting the temptation of falling back into blessed oblivion, Maggi forced herself to open her eyes.

She wasn't alone in the room.

Startled, Maggi automatically reached for the weapon that wasn't there and cried out in pain from the effort before she could bite it back.

Patrick immediately stumbled out of the chair where he'd spent the night, remnants of sleep fleeing from his eyes.

"You want me to call the nurse? The doctor? What?"

Her head felt as if it were filled with cotton. Was this just another dream? She'd had several already, tiny vignettes in which Patrick had the dominant role. Sometimes he told her he loved her, sometimes he cursed her out. She was too exhausted, too emotionally drained to endure another go-around.

"Are you a dream?"

Her voice was strong. He could feel relief slipping through him. "Most people refer to me as a nightmare."

He saw her reach toward him and he took her hand in his as he sank back down in the chair he'd dragged over to her bedside.

Maggi swallowed. Someone had filleted her throat while she was asleep. Every word seemed to be scraping along raw skin.

"What are you doing here?"

"Getting a really bad backache."

He'd been in her room since one in the morning, having slipped in past security. The one nurse who had come in to check on Maggi's condition had been persuaded to allow him to stay. He figured she felt sorry for him. He was hoping Maggi would, too.

"Why are you here? Did you forget to get something else off your chest?" Maggi was too leery to allow herself to be happy that he'd come back. Not after the way he'd reacted to hearing about the baby.

"Yeah, I did. The cobwebs."

Maybe this was a dream. She could have sworn he was talking about cobwebs. "Excuse me?"

"The cobwebs from around my heart," he explained. He was doing his best to be romantic, but in his mouth, the words came out all wrong. "I've never used it very much except clinically. You know, for pumping blood through my veins and all. I never knew I could use it to feel with." He gave up the effort, knowing he'd made a mess of it. "Until you started putting me through hell."

Her mouth curved slightly. "You're not very good at this, are you?"

Still holding her hand, afraid to let it go, he blew out a breath. "The worst."

Still unsure where this was going, Maggi felt sorry for him. He looked as uncomfortable as a nudist about to deliver a speech at a fashion show. "Then maybe you should cut to the chase, Cavanaugh. What is it you're trying to say?"

Talking wasn't his thing; it never had been. "That I've said some things I didn't mean to."

"You're going to have to be more specific than that."

Restless, he dragged a hand through his hair. She should understand, not make him say it. "I didn't mean to be a jerk."

Her smile widened. He felt as if the sun had come out. "Go on, you're getting better."

He told her what was in this new organ that he had discovered. "When I saw you on that stretcher…when I thought you weren't going to make it…I didn't want to make it, either, Mary Margaret."

"You weren't shot."

"Didn't matter." As far as he was concerned, taking a bullet would have been a hell of a lot easier.

Something came back to her. She stared at him as the fog around her brain dissipated, allowing her to pull the fragments together. "Did you say something to me during the ambulance ride? I thought I heard you say 'I love you' but I figured I was out of my head."

He looked at her, his expression grim. "You weren't out of your head. I said it."

"And?"

"I meant it."

"Just then?" she prodded, watching his expression. Feeling hope bubbling up inside. "It was a pretty dramatic moment. People say things they don't mean in situations like that.''

"Yeah, they do.'' He paused, then added, "But I don't.''

"Then you love me.''

"Yeah.'' He almost sounded as if he meant it be-grudgingly.

"Say it, damn it.''

He sighed, resigned to his fate. "I love you, Mary Margaret.''

Maggi rolled her eyes. Why had he used her name? "Oh, please don't spoil it.''

Patrick allowed himself a smile. "Sorry, that's how I think of you. That's what the priest is going to say when he marries us, isn't it? Do you Mary Margaret McKenna take—''

"Hold it.'' Maggi grabbed his hand, pulling his attention back to her. "Did I miss something here? How did we get from the ambulance to the church?''

He looked at her, knowing he was never going to feel about anyone the way he felt about her. Surprised that he did feel like this about anyone. "In big, giant steps, Mary Margaret, in big giant steps.''

She hated being tethered like this. She wanted to get up, to throw her arms around him. With no other option, she played out the moment. "You realize you didn't even ask me. A girl likes to be asked.''

He looked at her solemnly. "I didn't want to take a chance on you saying no.''

How could he even think that? "Do you honestly think I would?''

"You're a constant surprise to me, Mary Margaret, a constant surprise.''

"This isn't a surprise," she told him. "This is a sure thing." And then she grinned. "You can bet the farm this time."

"How about I just bet the rest of my life?"

"Works for me," she told him.

Shifting from the chair to the corner of her bed, Patrick took her into his arms, carefully avoiding the IVs she was still attached to.

"Yeah, me, too," Patrick agreed just before he kissed her.

* * * * *

If you liked INTERNAL AFFAIR,
you'll love Marie Ferrarella's next
CAVANAUGH JUSTICE *romance,*
DANGEROUS GAMES,
coming to you from Intimate Moments in
February 2004.
Don't miss it!

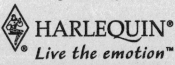

LEGACIES . LIES . LOVE .

This brand-new *Forrester Square* story
promises passion, glamour
and riveting secrets!

Coming in January…

WORD OF HONOR

by
bestselling Harlequin Intrigue® author

DANI SINCLAIR

Hannah Richards is shocked to discover that
the son she gave up at birth is now living with
his natural father, Jack McKay. Ten years ago
Jack had not exactly been father material—
now he was raising their son.
Was a family reunion in their future?

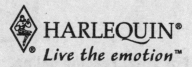

HARLEQUIN®
Live the emotion™